THEIRS TO COVET

A MFM ENEMIES-TO-LOVERS ROMANCE

TARA CRESCENT

Text copyright © 2020 Tara Crescent
All Rights Reserved

No part of this book may be reproduced in any form or by any electronic or mechanical means including information storage and retrieval systems, without permission in writing from the author. The only exception is by a reviewer, who may quote short excerpts in a review.

This book is a work of fiction. Names, characters, places, and incidents either are products of the author's imagination or are used fictitiously. Any resemblance to actual persons, living or dead, events, or locales is entirely coincidental.

Cover Design: Angela Haddon Book Cover Design https://angelahaddon.com/

Editing by Molly Whitman at Novel Mechanic, www.novelmechanic.com

v20240731

CONTENT NOTE

Part of this story's plot deals with fertility treatments. If this is a difficult topic for you, please skip this book.

1

SOPHIA

I've gone out on a lot of first dates. Sometimes, the guy I'm with turns out to be a decent human being, and we agree to go out again. But more often than not, the opposite happens.

Three minutes into dinner, I've realized that tonight's date is going to be a complete bust.

So far, Matthew Barnes has:

1. Insisted we go out for dinner instead of grabbing a coffee like I suggested.
2. Picked the restaurant without soliciting my opinion.

Both things have me a little on edge. I don't like high-handed men. But as I sit down, I caution myself to keep an open mind. Maybe Matthew's not good at this. Maybe he's just nervous.

Then the waitress shows up, and Matthew *proceeds to order for me.*

"I'll have the seafood platter," he says. "Don't stint on the lobster. And Sophia will have the steak. Medium-rare."

Umm, what?

He turns to me. "It's very good here," he says smugly. "You'll love it. You're not on a diet, are you? Tell me you're not the sort of girl that only eats salad."

My mouth falls open. This is wrong on so many levels that I'm at a complete loss for words, and by the time I remember to speak, the waitress is gone. Short of running after her, I'm stuck eating a steak that I neither want nor can afford.

Also, not to be petty about it, but I like my steak well-done. Sorry if that offends the red meat purists out there, but medium-rare is only a step up from raw, and ugh.

As far as I can tell, Matthew is roughly the same age as me. How does one live in today's society and think it's acceptable to order for someone *on a first date?*

Disqualified.

I met Matthew at the grocery store, and we struck up a conversation in the cereal aisle. He looked helpless. "I can't find the Grape Nuts," he said. "I've walked up and down this aisle three times. Am I losing my mind?"

He looked charmingly frazzled. I laughed and found them for him. We commiserated at the sheer number of brands of cereal available for sale. Then he asked me out. "Don't worry," he added. "The cereal is for my niece. I'm single."

Most of the guys I go out with I've met online. I've never been asked out in the grocery store—is that even a thing? I was confused and flattered in equal measure. I wouldn't have said yes, but the last three online dates were complete busts, and I thought I'd try something different.

So much for that.

Our meals arrive. I don't want to be the person who sends my food back, so I grit my teeth and nibble at the undercooked steak. Matthew doesn't notice and spends the next twenty minutes talking about himself. I learn about his construction business. How clever he is because he can write off his new truck as a business expense. I'm treated to a step-by-step replay of his last golf round. "I could have turned pro," he brags. "But I focused on my business, and it's paid off. Big-time."

Yes, I get it, Matthew. You are very rich. Yay for you.

At the half-hour mark, he finally asks me about myself. "What do you do, Sophia?"

"I'm the Director of Outreach at the Highfield Community Health Center," I reply. "Do you know it? We offer low-cost healthcare to people that don't have insurance and have to pay out-of-pocket for services."

"Community healthcare?" Matthew's face turns red. "I bet my tax dollars pay for it. Everyone wants a handout nowadays. Why don't they just get a job?"

I count to ten in my head. I've heard a variation of this argument more times than I can count, and I have a lot of practice keeping my cool. "Many jobs don't offer healthcare," I reply calmly. "A lot of corporations keep people part-time so they don't have to put them on their benefits plan."

"What kind of jobs?"

"Fast food," I respond. "Retail. Waitstaff. Our waitress tonight is unlikely to have healthcare." The electricians and plumbers that work for Matthew's company probably don't have benefits either. He's already mentioned that he classifies them as independent contractors. But in the interests of diplomacy, I don't point that out.

"If our waitress wanted a better job, she should have gone to college."

There are several things I could say about that. I could point out that student debt is at an all-time high. I could tell him that having a college degree is no guarantee of finding a decent job. I could talk about jobs that require advanced degrees but pay like crap. Social workers. School teachers.

But none of that will get through because Matthew is convinced about his rightness, and it's not my job to teach him empathy. It's not like I'm going to see him again. I'm thirty-five, and I want a child. My biological clock makes me ruthless. I don't want Matthew Barnes to be the father of my child—perish the thought—which means I can cut him loose.

"Let's change the subject," I suggest mildly. "Did your niece like the cereal you got her?"

Twenty minutes into the meal, I can't take it anymore. I excuse myself to go to the washroom and call my brother Andre. "I need to get out of here," I tell him. "Can you call me in ten minutes with an emergency?"

He laughs into the phone. "Grocery store guy not working out?"

"You have no idea."

"I thought you found him charming."

"First impressions can be misleading." So misleading. "Actually, on second thought, don't wait ten minutes. Call me in five."

"That bad? No worries, Soph. I've got you."

True to his word, Andre calls me five minutes later. "My brother," I say to Matthew. "Sorry, I have to take this." I pick up the call. "Hey, Andre. What's up?"

"Soph," he says, his voice loud enough to be heard through the receiver. "We have an emergency here. Your cat is projectile vomiting all over the house. She hisses at me when I get close to her. Where are you? You have to get back home."

I struggle not to laugh. Andre is absolutely brilliant. He sounds at the end of his tether. If I really had a cat, I would be panicking.

I'm not as good an actor as he is. "Oh no," I exclaim, a little too loudly. What would a concerned pet owner say next? "Poor Foofoo. Call the vet. Her phone number is on the refrigerator door. Tell her I'll be bringing Foofoo in."

Matthew can hear the conversation, of course; Andre hadn't kept his voice down. He makes a face. "You have a cat?"

"I have three," I lie shamelessly, getting to my feet and digging in my purse for money. The damn steak was sixty bucks, and I've barely eaten a quarter of it. I should get a box—Andre might want it. "There's Foofoo, Mimi, and Sir Farts-A-Lot." Matthew's expression indicates that he thinks I'm a crazy cat lady, and I lean into the stereotype. "Foofoo has a sensitive stomach, the poor dear. She does like steak, though. Maybe I'll take the rest to her."

"You're taking your cat a T-bone?"

His expression is priceless. *I love it.* "Nothing's too good for my little monster," I tell him, putting four twenty-dollar bills on the table. I pick up my plate and look around for our waitress. "I'm so sorry. I have to go."

ANDRE IS in the backyard when I get home. I kick off my heels and join him there. "How bad was it?" he asks with a grin.

"I thought it was bad when he ordered for me, but then he said that everyone wants a handout these days, and that was worse."

"Sounds like a winner." My brother drinks some of his beer. "What did you get?"

"A steak. I barely ate any of it. The leftovers are in the refrigerator. Help yourself."

"Thanks, Soph. You hungry? You want me to cook you something?"

Andre is a chef. He's usually at work on a Friday night, but he's been at home for the last couple of days getting over a stomach bug. He rarely cooks at home, so if he's offering to make me something, he must be chomping at the bit to get back to his kitchen.

"Nah, I'll just make myself a sandwich." I steal his bottle of beer and take a swig. "Four awful dates in a row."

"It happens. What's the big deal?"

I give him an annoyed glance. It's dark in the backyard, and my glare bounces off Andre. "Really? We're doing this again? I'm thirty-five. I want to have a baby. I'm already considered someone of advanced maternal age. I don't have time to waste."

My brother shakes his head. "You know, for a supposedly smart person, you're being pretty dumb. Getting pregnant isn't the only way to have a child, *as you should know.*"

"I'm not going to adopt. Papa and Dad didn't have the easiest time of it." That's putting it mildly. They couldn't legally adopt us because they were a gay couple. As for my birth mother. . . The kindest thing I can say about her is that she was troubled. She would show up outside our house, drunk and loud and belligerent, demanding that my fathers give her money. I spent a large part of my childhood terrified that she'd take me away from my home.

"So what?" Andre's teeth flash in the dark. "They didn't let it stop them."

Andre is ten years younger than me. He wasn't around

for the worst of it. I think I've healed okay from the trauma, but I'm absolutely determined not to go the adoption route. I'm not being rational, I know, but when I have a child—if I have a child—nobody will ever be able to threaten me the way Denise had threatened my fathers.

I've tensed up. He reads the set of my shoulders and lets it go. "Okay, fine. No adoption. What about artificial stuff?"

"Are you talking about a sperm donor?"

"Yes," he says. "Your timeline is tight, right? You're thirty-five. You'll have to meet someone and get pregnant almost immediately if you want to have a baby before you're forty." I look up in surprise, and Andre says, "I do listen when you talk."

"I know you do. It's just. . ." I don't know why I've never thought of going the donor route. "I don't know. It's expensive, for one. And I'll be a single parent."

"Your baby will have two grandfathers, three uncles, and an aunt who will dote on her."

I can't help smiling at the enthusiasm in his voice. "You think I'll have a girl?" Andre makes it sound like it's real, this baby, not a dream that gets more out of reach with each passing day.

"Either is good," Andre says diplomatically. "If it's a boy, I'll teach him to play basketball, and if it's a girl—"

"Let's not stereotype my unborn child. You'll teach her to play basketball, too."

He rolls his eyes. "Yes, Soph."

There's something to his idea. Before starting every date, I tell myself to have low expectations, but my brain doesn't always cooperate. If a guy has a great dating profile, I get hopeful. When it turns out that he's not forty-five like his profile says, but sixty, I get angry. I started the 'Find a Partner ASAP' project a year ago, and ever since then, my emotions have been on a non-stop roller coaster ride. If I went the donor insemination route, I could stop the endless parade of first dates. I could just *breathe*.

"Thanks, Andre." I get to my feet. "I better turn in. Busy day tomorrow."

"You're working on Saturday? Again?"

"You sound like Papa," I tease. "It's the fundraiser tomorrow, you idiot. Why do you remember my dating stories and not my work ones?"

"Siri, find me a polite way to tell Sophia her work stories are boring."

I smother my laughter and punch his arm. "I can't believe you've forgotten how stressed I was a couple of weeks ago. Our landlord wanted to sell the building, remember? And then, out of the blue, Xavier Leforte called and offered to help. I told him we needed two million dollars to buy our building outright, and he didn't even blink."

"Xavier Leforte, the sex club guy?"

I raise an eyebrow. "How do you know about Club M?" I ask severely. I don't want my baby brother mixed up with that crowd. Not after what happened to me.

Ten years later, my palms still sweat when I think of the aftermath of my first and only threesome. I'd been working at a hospital in Pennsylvania in those days. A small team of us—Riley, Nia, George, Jaime, Beckham, and me—had been in an early-career, rotational development program. Somehow, the hospital administrator, Florence Caldwell found out about Damien and me. My heart still races when I remember the way Mrs. Caldwell's lips thinned. "A reprehensible error in judgment," she'd said.

And then she'd fired me.

"I could ask you the same question," Andre replies. "But

I won't because I don't want to think about my big sister having sex."

"Is that why you're pushing the IVF route?" I quip. "I'm heading in. Night, bro."

I grab his empty bottle, toss it in the recycle bin, and head upstairs to bed, forsaking the sandwich in favor of sleep. My dreams that night are tangled. Damien Cardenas makes an appearance, as does Julian Kincaid. They're the men I slept with at Xavier Leforte's sex club. I've tried not to think about them for years, but there they are again, popping up in my subconscious.

But I also dream about a baby girl. I'm holding her in my arms and smiling down at this tiny miracle, and we're surrounded by my beaming family.

When I wake up, my decision is made. No more bad first dates. No more untrustworthy guys. Donor sperm it is.

2

JULIAN

My sister Hannah calls me out of the blue. "I have some news," she says. "I'm getting married."

I haven't heard from her in more than eight months. The last time we talked was in December, right after the reading of my father's will. She hadn't been chatty then. Considering the circumstances, I can't say I blame her. My father left the entirety of his estate to me: the crumbling mansion that was our childhood home, his dwindling investment portfolio, the moth-eaten furniture, and the gloomy portraits. Hannah got nothing. In a final, cruel twist, he'd insisted she attend the reading of the will in person so she could learn, in real-time, that he had cut her out of his will.

Fuck that. My parents treated her like garbage all through our childhood. I never understood why, but I wasn't about to perpetuate it. I got Kincaid Castle appraised. The appraiser gave me two figures. One was for the amount the house was worth in its current dilapidated condition, and the other was for the amount it would be worth if I fixed it up. I had a lifetime of injustice to make up for, so I sold my condo in New York and wrote her a check for the larger amount. I moved back to my childhood home in Highfield in January with the intention of fixing it up, selling it, and getting the hell out of here.

It's now September. The house is still a disaster.

"Congratulations," I say now. "Who's the lucky guy?"

"His name is Samir, and I'm the lucky one. You want to meet him?"

"I'd love to."

"How about this weekend? We'll drive down."

WE MEET at a bar close to my home. It's good to see Hannah. Really good. "Thanks for the money," she says, giving me a hug. "You didn't have to."

"Of course, I did." I shake hands with Samir. "Good to meet you."

I buy the first round, and the three of us get chatting. "I like him," I tell Hannah when Samir gets up to buy the second. "Not that my opinion should matter, given everything." I search my sister's face. "He makes you happy?"

Her eyes light up. "He does, yes. Every single day."

"And everything else? How are things with you?"

She lifts her shoulders in a shrug. "I'm getting there," she says. "Samir encouraged me to see a therapist."

I should do that too. "Is it helping?"

"Yeah, I think so. Dr. Welch has been great." She looks at me. "She wants me to talk about my feelings."

Samir is still talking to the bartender. He's obviously giving us space. To do what? Have an emotionally intense conversation about our parents? Ugh. I pull a pencil out of my pocket and start doodling on the napkin. It's a bad habit I have. When things get messy and complicated, I retreat into my comics. I bury myself in work and pretend the outside world doesn't exist. "That's good."

"She thinks I bottle my emotions. She said that I needed to get better at advocating for myself. It would help me resolve some of my issues." She smiles wryly at my sketch. "You draw when things get difficult. I avoid my problems by running away."

"Avoiding your problems is a bad thing?" I quip. "That's my default answer to everything."

"Yeah, Julian, I know." She holds my gaze. "I've been angry with you for a very long time. You were the golden child. You could do no wrong. I found it hard not to resent you."

When Hannah turned seventeen, my parents told her that there was no money for her college education. My sister looked at them, then looked at the brand-new car they'd gifted me when I turned twenty-one and decided she was done. There was a huge blowout. Hannah told them she wouldn't let herself be treated like garbage any longer, and she moved out. She never saw them again.

I take a deep breath. My first instinct is to run. My second is to be defensive. I want to blurt out that I didn't create the damn situation. I was a kid too. I didn't know how to handle things any better than Hannah did. But that's not right. As hard as my parents' favoritism was for me, it was so much worse for her. And I'm her big brother. I should have watched out for her better. "I'm sorry. I really am. It was so hard for you, and I wish I'd done more to protect you from it. If there's anything I can do to make amends..."

"There is one thing."

I tilt my head to the side. "I'm being set up, aren't I?"

There's a glimmer of mischief in her eyes that takes me back in time. When we were kids, we stayed with my grandparents for one summer. One beautiful, perfect summer where we were siblings, not forced adversaries.

"A little bit," she admits. "One thing that my therapist has been helping me with is making peace with my childhood. Samir and I talked about it. I want to get married at the house."

I don't think I heard her correctly. "At Kincaid Castle? Seriously?"

"I want to replace bad memories with good ones. Can I?"

I think about the house and the state that it's in. After my mother died, my father let the property fall apart. He didn't have the money, but I also think he lost the ability to care.

The place needs a *lot* of work. I put my leg through the floorboards today and nearly broke my neck. There are pails all over the attic where the roof is leaking. There's no furniture to speak of, the carpets have holes, and the wallpaper is faded and torn. Spider webs festoon the corners. There might be a mold issue that I'm trying very hard not to think about.

Ever since I moved in, I've been in deadline mode. I've had no time to fix the place up. Even the thought of it is overwhelming.

I guess I can't avoid it any longer. "Of course." I ruthlessly squelch the thought of how much work is involved in getting the house wedding-ready. Hannah hasn't asked me for help in years. I haven't been there for her. This time, I won't let her down. "When are you getting married?"

"Christmas."

"This year?" I manage to keep the panic out of my voice. That's four months away. *Fuck.*

She notices my reaction. "Is that going to be a problem?"

Yes. It's going to be *impossible.* "No. Christmas is great." If

Hannah is trying to replace bad memories with good ones, then the timing makes perfect sense. Our parents treated us differently, and the inequity was never starker than at Christmas. I'd be surrounded by toys, and Hannah would get shockingly little in comparison. "Christmas is perfect."

One way or the other, I will make this happen.

"Will you give me away?"

Her softly-spoken question drags me from the problems of the house. "Really?" I stare at her in shock. "You want me to do that? After everything?"

She nods wordlessly.

I force the words out past the lump in my throat. "I would be honored, Hannah." No matter how much money it's going to cost, Kincaid Castle will be ready. My baby sister's wedding will be perfect.

BACK HOME, my heart sinks as I walk from one dust-filled room to the other. This place is a wreck. I have four months to fix it, and I don't know where to start.

I pick up my phone and call Damien. "Hey," I say without preamble. "What's the name of your contractor? The one who worked on your cottage?"

"Isaac Foster," my best friend replies. "Are you finally doing something about that dump? Why now?"

"I'll tell you tonight." A community health center opened up in Highfield last year, and Xavier Leforte is hosting a fundraiser for it. He'd explained why, but I was working when I got his email, and I don't remember any of the details.

I hang up on Damien and dial Isaac Foster. I get his voicemail. Biting back my frustration, I leave my name and number and beg him to call me back.

Shockingly, he does. "The mansion on Hill Street? The one with the green shutters? I thought it was condemned. I had no idea someone was living there."

"Yeah. Me. I need a contractor to fix it up by Christmas. Can you do it?"

"No can do," he replies instantly. "I'm sorry. I wish I could, but I'm booked solid. Everyone wants to renovate this year, and I have more work than I know what to do with."

Fuck. "Do you know anyone who might do the job?"

"Hmm. Try Greg Liu."

Greg Liu doesn't have any availability either. "Next year, yes," he says. "This year, impossible. Sorry."

I spend three hours on the phone and Internet trying to find someone, anyone, who will do the work. I leave dozens of messages all over, but I get nowhere.

I am totally screwed.

My phone beeps, reminding me it's time to get ready. I head into the bathroom I've been using and turn on the shower. About fifty percent of the time, I get hot water. Today's not one of those days. I hastily shower in icy cold water and get dressed, muttering curses at my father, and then I head out.

Damien is already at Summit when I arrive. He takes one look at my face and hands me a drink. "Tell me about it," he says, sounding half-amused and half-sympathetic.

I fill him in, and he whistles between his teeth. "Yikes," he says. "That's quite a challenge."

"That's the understatement of the year." I gulp down the whiskey he's handed me, and it burns a path of pure fire down my throat. "What the fuck am I going to do?"

"You could start by treating the Oban with more respect," he replies with a pained expression on his face. "It's a twenty-one-year Scotch, for fuck's sake. You don't gulp it down. You sip."

"Damien. Focus."

"Fine. If it were up to me, I'd blow the whole place up and start over. What does Hannah think?"

"What do you mean?"

"Well, she has to know what kind of condition the house is in, right?" He takes in my expression and gives me an exasperated look. "You didn't tell her. Why not?"

"I didn't want her to feel guilty about the money." The situation is not optimal, but my need to do right by my sister outweighs the inconvenience of living in Kincaid Castle. At least the hot water tank has stopped working now, when it's still warm outside. I'll feel very differently about my cold shower in January. "It's not her problem to deal with. It's mine."

I must look mutinous because he sighs. "Okay, fine. Can she have the wedding outside?"

"In December?"

"Right, the weather. What about the greenhouse? It's large enough, isn't it? Unless Hannah will have more than two hundred people at her wedding."

"She said a hundred and fifty."

Damien quirks an eyebrow. "Hannah knows a hundred and fifty people?"

"Samir has a large family." A waiter passes by with a tray of champagne, and I grab one. Maybe I can gulp this down without getting grief about treating the bloody Scotch with respect. Although, given Xavier's taste in champagne, I'm sure I'm drinking a ludicrously expensive brand. "The greenhouse isn't in great shape, but it might be fixable in four months." I think about the current plumbing situation and the state of the downstairs bathrooms. "Maybe. I can probably do some of the work myself."

"You can?"

"I used to work for a contractor, remember?"

"That was over ten years ago," he points out. "And don't you have to work on the *Medusa* storyboard?"

"Shockingly, I'm ahead of schedule there. I can make it work if I have to. And I have to, Damien. I owe Hannah this. Anyway, enough about me. What's been going on with you?" I survey my friend. "You look terrible."

"Fuck you," he replies without heat. He takes a sip of his Scotch with an appreciative expression on his face. "I'm jetlagged. I was in Shanghai two days ago. Tokyo before that. Siberia last week. I don't know if I'm awake or asleep."

"Stop whining. They're all in the same general area of the world."

Damien flips me off. "Thank you, Julian," he says. "I wasn't looking for a geography lesson as much as I was looking for sympathy."

The Cardenas Group is a conglomerate headquartered in Peru. Mining mostly, but they've got their fingers in a lot of other industries. Damien is the Chief Operating Officer. It seems exhausting and thankless. "You have competent managers. You don't have to do everything yourself."

His face tightens fractionally. "It's not that simple, and you know it." He takes another sip of his Scotch, which restores his mood. "Come on, we better go in. Xavier gets huffy if we blow off his fundraisers."

We enter the ballroom. I look around, and my gaze lands on a blonde woman talking to Xavier Leforte. She's wearing a glittery black dress, and when she looks up and sees me, her face goes pale.

Sophia.

The memories crash into me. Ten years ago. Same castle. The opening night of Club M, the private club in the basement. Sophia wanted a threesome with Damien and me. Or was it Damien's idea? Mine? I don't remember. Time has blurred some details, but it hasn't erased one thing.

It had been the hottest night of my life.

She says something to Xavier and hurries away.

Xavier walks over with a frown. "I didn't know you knew Sophia."

Damien is looking as dazed as I feel. "We've met, yes," he manages.

"Really?" Xavier's eyes narrow. "That's not what Sophia said. She said the three of you slept together, and then, the morning after, Damien got her fired."

What?

3

DAMIEN

"What?" I blink in confusion. Why would I get her fired? That doesn't make any sense. My head is spinning with a mixture of jet lag and shock. Seeing Sophia here after all these years has me reeling. "No. Of course not."

"She seemed pretty certain," Xavier says.

I glare at him. "What the fuck, man? How long have you known me? I. Did. Not. Get. Sophia. Fired."

That's not how things had gone down.

Ten years ago. Here, in this very castle. It was the opening night of Club M. After what happened with Stephan and Lina, I walked away from kink. Vanilla and nothing else, I'd sworn to myself. The only reason I showed up was to support Xavier.

And, to my shock, Sophia had been there.

She wasn't a stranger; I knew her from work. Sophia worked at a hospital in rural Pennsylvania. At the time, I was working at a management consultancy firm, and we'd been hired to improve their profitability. It wasn't a complicated project. The hospital was a miserable place, and after a couple of weeks there, it was obvious why. Most of the problems stemmed from the administrator, Mrs. Caldwell. She micromanaged everyone. She belittled them and questioned their abilities on a daily basis, and as a result, the employees hated their jobs.

Sophia was the bright spot. She was interested in me. I was interested in her too, but I wasn't going to do anything about it. We flirted. To me, flirting was second nature, something I did as easily as breathing. But that was it. I didn't want to take it further because it didn't seem right. The only thing I had time for was a purely sexual encounter, and I didn't think Sophia was that kind of girl.

Or so I believed until she followed me to Xavier's club.

We'd had a threesome that night, Sophia, Julian, and me.

And when I called her a day later, she sent my call to voicemail and didn't respond to my texts. Three weeks later, her phone was disconnected.

She blew me off. I could have tried harder to contact her, but I wasn't oblivious. As much as I wanted to see her again, I could take a hint. It was clear what happened. She regretted the escapade and wanted nothing to do with us.

Xavier is still looking at me. "This is a misunderstanding," I say through clenched teeth. "I will sort it out."

"Okay," he replies. "I trust you to take care of it. Now, Jodi's trying to catch my eye, which means it's time for us to take our seats for dinner." He smiles easily. "She's extremely competent and only a little terrifying. Have a good evening, you two."

SUMMIT'S executive chef has outdone herself. The food is delicious, but I barely pay attention to what's in front of me. I brood throughout dinner. I make polite conversation with the people at my table, but my attention is on Sophia.

Toward the end of the meal, Xavier strides to the front of the room and makes a speech. He praises the work the Highfield Community Health Center has done in the short time they've been open, encourages us to bid generously, and then turns it over to Sophia.

She gives a passionate speech about the importance of accessible health care. I'm interested in what she's saying, but I can't focus. My thoughts wander. I find myself angry with Sophia. If she truly believed I got her fired, she should have confronted me. She had my number; she could have called and yelled at me. Demanded an explanation. I left her countless messages—she could have responded to any of them. Instead, she'd jumped to the worst possible conclusion.

Which *stings*.

When I met Sophia, I'd been struggling. I'd walked away from kink. I'd been at Lina's funeral; I'd seen the damage BDSM could inflict. I denied my needs, convinced that my sexual preferences were incompatible with a sane, safe lifestyle.

Sophia had changed that. She looked like the kind of girl you'd bring home to meet your mother. When she showed up at Club M, I thought the sex club would scare her off. I thought she'd be scandalized.

Instead, she was intrigued. She looked around with bright eyes. Julian and I had flirted with her shamelessly, and she'd flirted back. We hinted at a threesome, and her eyes had dilated with desire. There had been some kind of show going on at the center stage, something with music, naked bodies, and stylized humping. It was designed to arouse, but I didn't need it. Sophia's interest, her willingness to experience new things, were aphrodisiac enough.

I thought I'd moved on from Lina and Stephan's deaths, but the true healing came that night. My friends had been reckless, but Sophia wasn't. She was level-headed and responsible, and she was also kink-curious. I thought I had to pick between one or the other, but that night, I realized I could have both. I thought I had won the lottery.

That night had been the start of my road back.

I walk up to her after dinner. "Xavier said you think I got you fired," I blurt out. *Smooth. Way to ease into it. Nice job, Damien.* "I didn't."

She gives me a long look. "Whatever," she responds dismissively. "It was a long time ago. As you can see, I've landed on my feet."

It's blatantly obvious she doesn't believe me. It's also just as obvious that even though she pretends otherwise, being fired ten years ago still upsets her.

That gives me pause. Makes me a little less defensive. "Sophia," I say softly. "I didn't. I would never."

Her expression hardens. "The fact remains that I got fired because Mrs. Caldwell found out I slept with you," she snaps. "As she pointed out when she let me go, that violated the employee code."

"That makes no sense. I wasn't even an employee of the hospital."

"And you think that being in the right would have protected me? You think that HR would have taken my side over Mrs. Caldwell?" She tries to shoulder past me. "Will you excuse me? I have an auction to run."

If I were a nicer guy, I'd step out of the way. "Who told Mrs. Caldwell we slept together? I certainly didn't."

"I don't know," she says. "It doesn't matter. That experience taught me an important lesson, Damien. I'm grateful for that."

Don't ask, *don't ask*. Never ask a question you don't already know the answer to. "What did you learn?"

"I learned to stay away from people like you," she snaps. "You're the heir-apparent to a multi-billion-dollar company. You float around in a world of privilege. You have no idea what the world is like for the little people. It probably didn't even strike you to be discreet."

What the hell? We were in Xavier's private sex club. How much more discreet could we have been? "Oh, come on," I protest. "That's a very unfair depiction. You don't know me."

"I know your type. I'll prove it to you. You have an assistant, don't you?"

I blink at the sudden change in topic. "Yes."

"How long has she been working for you?"

"It's a he. Luis has been with me for eight years."

"Is he married?"

"You don't think I know? Yes, he's married to a lovely woman. Martina is from Argentina and is a chef at a steakhouse in Lima. They have two children. Twin girls." I strain my memory for their names. Emma and Maria? Ella and Olivia? Oh, crap.

She sees the look on my face and goes in for the kill. "When's his birthday?"

I open my mouth and shut it. "Some people are good at remembering dates, and some people aren't," I finally mutter defensively. Damn it, could she be right? Luis keeps my world running, and I appear to have forgotten the names of his daughters. I don't like what that says about me.

Sophia doesn't miss my reaction. "I rest my case."

I make a mental note to check in on Luis and transfer my attention back to the woman in front of me. Damn, she's beautiful. "Fine. You've made your point. I admit I may need to pay more attention to the people around me. But I'm also not the asshole you've decided I am."

"If you say so."

For fuck's sake. I'm not getting through to her, and it's driving me nuts. I should just let it go, but I can't.

And then an idea strikes me. A bold, *insane* idea. "This community health center is important to you, right?" Her passion had shone through in her speech. "And its funding is precarious. As you said, I'm *very* privileged. I'll make you a deal."

Her expression turns wary.

"You think I'm an asshole? Okay. For the next month, you teach me to be a good, empathetic person. In return, I'll donate a million dollars to your organization."

Shock fills her eyes. "You're nuts."

"I've heard that before."

"This is an absurd idea. Empathy can't be taught."

"Really? You don't think people can change? You don't believe they can improve?"

She hesitates, torn. "I didn't say that."

"So, I can be taught." I tilt my head to the side. "Are you up to the challenge?"

Call me a jerk, but I have her. She cares deeply about the Highfield Community Health Center and its mission. Tonight's fundraiser will solve their rent woes, but they still need money for equipment, salaries, and so much more. A million dollars is not the kind of money she can walk away from.

"You want me to teach you empathy, and in return, you'll donate a million dollars to the health center." Her jaw tightens. "Let's make one thing crystal clear. I'm not sleeping with you."

"Come on, Sophia. Do you believe I think so little of you? I'm not asking you to."

She straightens her shoulders. "Fine," she bites out. Her eyes flash with barely concealed rage. "It's only four weeks. It probably won't kill me. I'll do it." Then she pastes a smile on her face and pushes past me. "Mrs. Howard, it's so good to see you." Now that she's not talking to me, the ice has melted. Her voice is warm as she clasps the older woman's hands. "Thank you so much for your support."

Someone thrusts a glass into my hands. "I saw you talking to Sophia," Julian says. "You look like you need a drink. What did you do, Damien?"

"Why do you think I did something?"

"Because I know you. You're generally sensible, but every so often, you do something profoundly stupid."

He's not wrong. "I'm taking a month off work," I reply. "I paid Sophia to give me empathy lessons."

Julian blinks. "Let's take this from the top. You're taking a month off. You, Damien Cardenas, Chief Operating Officer of the Cardenas Group, are taking a full month off. What happened? Are you dying?"

He's closer to the truth than he thinks. "I had a medical scare," I finally admit. "Don't worry; it's nothing. My family doctor arranged a battery of tests, and everything came back clear. But he told me to slow down, and so, here I am."

Julian's expression makes it clear that we're not done with this conversation. But there are people around us, and now's not the time to get into details. "How is your family taking it?"

"They don't know."

"What? Why haven't you told them?"

"Because." I spread my hands. "It's only been three years since my father died. My mother will worry herself sick. She will insist that I see a thousand specialists. Tomas will blame himself. Victoria and Cristiano will feel guilty that they don't do more in the business. It's a lot easier to keep it quiet. I told my mother and stepfather I needed a change of scene. I've promised to check emails and call into meetings as much as I can. Which reminds me, I have a meeting in four hours. I should switch to water."

Julian glances at his watch. "Four hours from now, it'll be two in the morning."

"Yes, I'm calling Melbourne."

"How is this taking time off?"

I lift my shoulders in a shrug. It is what it is. Julian knows my family situation. My mother won't delegate to anyone that isn't family. My stepfather Tomas doesn't know what he's doing, Vicky has two young children and refuses to travel, and Cristiano and his partner Magnus are trying to get married and have a baby. I pick up the slack, something I've been doing all my life. "This is the best I can do."

"Okay," he says. "Tell me about the empathy lessons."

I recap my conversation with Sophia. "I didn't get her fired," I finish in frustration. "Why won't she believe me?"

"I don't know," he replies. There's something in his tone that makes me take a closer look at his face. How does Julian feel about all of this? Is he reeling from seeing Sophia again, the way I am? Does her presence here bring back memories of that perfect night? I don't know; I don't ask. That fire has been stomped out. It's not like we're going to rekindle it.

"I don't know how anyone found out," I continue. "I didn't mention Sophia to anyone. At least, I don't think I did. But maybe I'm wrong. It was ten years ago." I sip the Oban Julian brought me. "Maybe my privilege blinds me to other people's concerns. Maybe she's right, and I do need empathy lessons."

Julian raises an eyebrow. "I don't buy it," he says. "There's a much simpler explanation."

Jet lag has made me stupid because I have no idea what he's talking about. "Which is?"

"Maybe you really like Sophia. Maybe you're looking for a second chance with her."

I drain the rest of my drink—Australia meeting be damned. "Fuck off, Julian."

4

SOPHIA

I rage and fume all weekend. Silently, mostly. Andre is back at work, which is to be expected. Simon, my other brother, is a contractor and usually doesn't work on the weekends. But he's running behind on a job, which means he's nowhere to be seen either.

How dare Damien do this? How dare he hold my love for the community health center over me? And what's his agenda? I implied that he was doing this to sleep with me, but let's be real. I don't actually believe that's his motivation. I'm not conceited enough to think that sex with me is worth a million dollars. Even if you have as much money as Damien Cardenas has.

So what's his plan? What's the game? I don't think he wants to be a better person. I'm not stupid enough to think that one conversation with me is enough to change his obliviousness.

On Sunday evening, we do our weekly family dinner: my fathers and my oldest brother Ben live in California, Andre, Simon, and I live in Highfield, and my sister Aurora lives with her husband Juan Pablo and daughter Dawn in Santa

Fe. Thankfully, technology is a marvelous thing. The time difference between the East and West Coast complicates things. Simon, Andre, and I eat a little later than normal, and my fathers and Ben eat at five, which is earlier than they're used to. We make it work. Family dinner is a tradition in our household, one we're determined to preserve. The last time someone missed Sunday dinner was when Aurora was in labor with Dawn.

Simon sets the table while Andre and I fiddle with our iPads. Once everyone's online, we begin the meal. The first five or ten minutes is always a discussion about our meals, and this time is no exception. "What are you eating?" I ask, looking at Aurora's image on the screen. "Is that cereal? You're eating cereal for dinner? You?"

Aurora is very big into healthy eating.

"Yeah, yeah, I know," she sighs. "JP and I didn't have enough energy to cook today. Dawn was up all night screaming her head off. We took turns soothing her."

"Ouch," I say sympathetically.

"What's wrong with my granddaughter?" Dad demands. Ben, who's with them in person, smothers a grin. Dawn is the first grandchild, and Lenny Thorsen is very much a doting grandfather.

"A stomach bug. Thankfully, the worst seems to have passed. She's sleeping now."

"Where's JP?" Papa asks. When I was a kid, Hank Carver Johnson was the one who insisted on family dinner. His expression is so familiar that it makes my heart ache. It's the same expression he had when he insisted I put down the book I was reading, take off my headphones, and come downstairs for family dinner. *Because we are a family, Sophia, and it's important for us to eat together.*

"He's helping his dad build a deck," Aurora says. "He

was supposed to be back already, but he's running late. What are you guys eating? What'd you make, Dad? Andre?"

"Please," Simon snorts. "As if Andre cooks at home. I made pasta. There was a recipe on the TikTok—"

"Oh, the one with cherry tomatoes and feta?" Aurora looms closer to peer at her screen. "Is it any good?"

"It's fantastic."

Once the food conversation is over, we take turns talking about what's been going on with us. I hesitate when it's my turn. All weekend long, angry thoughts of Damien have warred with memories of that magical night. I usually tell my family everything, but I kept my threesome hidden. Not because I thought they would have disapproved—my family is pretty open-minded—but because of the subsequent firing. Mrs. Caldwell had been *horrible*. She implied I was a slut, but even worse, she made it seem like it was because of my family. "Raised by two men," she'd spit out. "It goes to show, doesn't it?"

My fathers gave me a stable home. They smothered me with love. I will never do anything to hurt their feelings. So I hid the fact that I got fired. It took me three months to find another job. Three terrifying months. Ben loaned me some money for rent, but he didn't have much either. It was rough going for a while.

It's probably unfair that I'm blaming Damien. The real villain in the picture is Mrs. Caldwell. But that summer, as I became increasingly desperate to find work, it was Damien I resented. I wouldn't have been in this situation if he'd kept his mouth shut.

And Julian? My feelings for him are more complicated. I can't articulate why I resent Julian, but I do. When he didn't come over during the fundraiser to say hi, it felt like our night together hadn't even mattered. Or maybe he's forgotten all about it. Maybe he's forgotten me.

"Sophia?" Ben prompts. "What's going on with you?"

I talk to my family about important things. Damien and Julian are not important, but my decision to go the IVF route is. "I went on another terrible date."

Ben, Aurora, and Simon laugh. Dad grins, and even Papa cracks a smile. "What?" I ask defensively.

"How long did the date last?" Aurora asks Andre. "Did you time it like you were supposed to, or did you forget?"

"Wait, what?"

Andre avoids my outraged gaze. "She called me at seven-thirty-one. She left home at six-thirty. Let's say it took her twenty minutes to get to the restaurant, which would make it—"

"Forty-one minutes," Ben announces. He glances down at his phone. "Aurora, you're this week's winner."

My mouth falls open. "Hang on," I say slowly. "Are you assholes betting on my dates?"

Both my fathers give me rebuking looks for the swearing. I let it bounce off me. "Seriously?" I demand.

"Of course we are," Ben replies calmly. "I thought I'd win this week for sure. Sure, you always think there's something wrong with the guys, but this time, you agreed to have dinner with him. I figured you'd make it through the main course. Sixty minutes, that was my number."

I always think there's something wrong with the guys? Does Ben think I'm being too picky? Too critical? *What the hell?*

"Nah, he ordered for her," Andre says. "A medium-rare steak. It was pretty good, actually. I had it for breakfast the next day."

The little traitor. I can't believe he was *timing* my date.

"I'm glad you enjoyed it," I tell him bitterly. "You owe me sixty bucks."

Andre opens his mouth to say something. So does Aurora. Ben leans back to watch the chaos unfold. We love each other—very much—but our fights as kids were legendary. Papa looks like he remembers and clears his throat. "That's quite enough," he says firmly. "Ben, stop betting on your sister's dates. Aurora, send Soph half your winnings. Sophia, no charging Andre for the steak."

"You heard him," Dad says mildly. "Hank has spoken."

Aurora nods meekly. Ben looks a little mutinous, but he grunts, "Fine. Who's next? Simon?"

"I'm not done," I interject. "Andre and I were talking after my date, and he made me see I've been going about this the wrong way. I've made a decision." I suck in a breath. "I'm going to look into sperm donors."

I brace myself for their reactions. Brace for one of them to tell me that it's extremely difficult to be a single mother, and am I sure? But of course, that doesn't happen. We might squabble like a barnful of cats, but when it matters, we're *always* there for each other. "That makes sense," Dad says. "You were in such a hurry to find someone that it made me nervous. People think that a bad partner is better than no partner, but they're wrong."

"I have an appointment on Wednesday."

"Good for you, Sophia," Papa says. "Simon, how's work going?"

"Busier than ever," my brother replies. "It's a good time to be a contractor. Ben, you don't want to move here, do you? I could use a hand."

. . .

I'M SITTING in the backyard after dinner, enjoying the warm September night, when Aurora texts me.

Hey, I'm sorry about the bet. I didn't mean to be an asshole.

No worries. You might be an asshole, but I love you anyway. I sent Dawn something, by the way. It should be there tomorrow.

More Duplo? You spoil her.

I'm not the only one; we all do.

JP has two sisters. Dawn sees them all the time. If I have to resort to shameless bribery to be her favorite aunt, I will.

You're going to have to work harder. Heidi is getting a puppy.

Oh, that is not fair. *That bitch,* I write with fake indignation. JP's sister Heidi is the sweetest person ever, but come on? A puppy? The contest is over.

Aurora sends me a laughing emoji.

So, you're really doing the sperm donation? I'm glad. You're going to be a great mom.

You think?

I KNOW. Will you stay in Highfield? After the baby is born, I mean.

I haven't thought about it. For the first year after I moved to the East Coast, I felt acutely homesick. Things are different now. Highfield feels like home. We finally finished renovating our house. Okay, Simon did most of the work while Andre and I hovered around pretending to help, but still.

My friends are here. My job is here, and I like it. I really enjoy working with Patricia Adams, the Director of the Highfield Community Health Center. My health insurance won't cover the cost of fertility treatments, but I can access six months of maternity leave, which is really generous.

I might not be able to afford it. It might not work. Too soon, you know?

True. Hey, I'm sorry again. Whatever reason you have for not trusting men, I know you, and I'm sure they're justified.

I trust men, I type automatically. Then I stop myself and delete the words.

My siblings aren't wrong. I used to trust everyone. I used to take people at face value. Not anymore, and I don't have to look too deep in my heart to know when that changed.

I don't want to rehash the past. I haven't thought about Mrs. Caldwell in years, but seeing Damien and Julian at the fundraiser brought back those feelings. My composure is unraveling. All weekend, I've been on edge and off-balance, and I don't like it.

Time to get back on track. I have goals. I want to have a baby, and I need to raise more money for the health center.

Damien Cardenas and Julian Kincaid are part of my past. Their reappearance in my life is a blip that I will get through.

5

DAMIEN

As expected, I didn't really need to attend my two a.m. meeting. The Australian division of the Cardenas Group is switching payroll software providers, and the team in charge of vendor selection is presenting their findings. Payroll is important; I get that. We employ a lot of people, people who depend on their salaries to pay their bills and feed their families. But Jack Rutherford, the president of that division, is on this call. He's closer to this issue and more than capable of making this decision.

This is a complete waste of time.

I sip a cup of extra-strong coffee and listen to the presentation. There's a discussion about the various options, and the committee selects two companies to shortlist. Looks like we're done. Good.

I lean forward. "Jack, if you have a minute, could you give me a call?"

My phone rings almost immediately. "Is something wrong?" he asks.

Rutherford worked extensively with my father. Not as much with me. I've only talked to the man a handful of times. I haven't needed to. The Australian subsidiary takes care of itself.

"Help me understand something." I drain the dregs of my coffee with a grimace. My pulse is racing, and my throat feels dry. Too much caffeine and not enough sleep. "It seems like your team had everything under control. Why did I need to be involved?"

He sounds confused when he replies. "It's company policy."

"What is?"

"Major purchases require a sign-off from the head office," he says. "It was a rule your father put into place."

I wipe my hand over my face. Even with customization, the payroll software costs less than a million dollars. The Australian division makes many times that amount every year. This is not a major purchase.

"Why didn't you invite someone from the corporate IT team, then? Ramesh? Shana?"

"That wasn't how your father liked it," Jack replies. "He liked it to be a member of the family."

Oh, for fuck's sake. My parents built the Cardenas Group up from nothing into the conglomerate that it is today. However, it's still run like a family company. Sometimes, that's a good thing. Other times, like now, it's insane.

And I can guess why I got roped into this meeting. Jack, trying to follow the rules, would have invited my mother or Tomas. Their shared assistant, Gisele, guards their time with ferocious zeal, so she would have declined the meeting and forwarded the request to Luis instead.

Vicky doesn't take meetings at two in the morning. Neither does Cristiano. Which leaves me.

It's always me.

This level of micromanagement is crazy. Insane. Our top

people are going to get poached away from us if we second-guess their every decision. Jack has run the Australian division for the last eight years. He delivers double-digit revenue growth every single year. And in the mining sector, which makes his achievement even more impressive. Employee retention is significantly better than the industry average. Morale is excellent.

Rutherford is ferociously competent. Why are we treating him this way? We should shower him with rewards, not putting these ridiculous constraints on him.

"I'll talk to my mother and Tomas about that ridiculous rule," I say. "But Jack, in the meantime, here's what we're going to do. You can keep inviting me to the meetings, but I'm going to decline them all. If there's anything you think I need to attend, let Luis know, and he'll make sure I'm there."

When I'm done with the meeting, I call Melanie Succar, who works on my strategy team, and tell her what Jack Rutherford told me. "We need to streamline things," I tell her. "There's a bunch of rules that make no sense for a company our size. Can you investigate and come up with a list of recommendations? I'm looking for both short-term and long-term stuff."

"I'm on it," she promises.

I finally crawl into bed at four in the morning. Of course, sleep doesn't come. My body doesn't know what time zone it's in, but that's not the only reason.

I'm also thinking about Sophia.

I haven't allowed myself to think about that night for so many years. What would be the point? But now, seeing her again, it all comes back to life. The feel of her skin. The sound of her laughter. The gleam in her eyes. She had been a powerfully addictive drug in my blood, and I hadn't wanted to let her go.

I don't get why she blew us off. I don't understand why she thinks I got her fired. I really don't. Why would I? It was a good night. The sex was off-the-charts fantastic, but it was more than that. *We had a connection.* I could have sworn we all felt it.

It hadn't felt like a one-night stand for either Julian or me. We both wanted to see her again. We might not have been ready for marriage and children—we were in our mid-twenties, and that kind of commitment felt like a long way off—but we knew she was important. We knew we didn't want to let her go.

Yes, we hooked up in a sex club, and there was some spanking and bondage. But there was also kissing and cuddling. We fell asleep together, all three of us. We liked her, and we didn't hide it. We didn't play it cool.

At least, that's what I thought.

It's bewildering to me.

The years have been kind to Sophia. She's just as beautiful as she used to be. No, more. The girl with the shining eyes has become a self-assured, controlled woman, and I'm a moth to her flame. Lord help me, but I want to get her on a bed and thrust into her. I want to hear her moans again. I want to watch that control unravel.

Maybe you're looking for a second chance with her.

Damn it, I hate when Julian is right.

I don't even know what motivated me to suggest that deal. It was an impulse. She was at the point of walking away, and I would never see her again. I was desperate to prevent that.

Still, it's a good cause. We give money to plenty of nonprofits, and the Highfield Community Health Center is a worthy recipient. I even own a home in Highfield. I bought this lake house a couple of years ago, much to the confusion of my family. "But it's in the middle of nowhere," Vicky said when I told her what I'd done. "New York, I understand. Boston is historic. Washington is a necessary evil. But this?"

My family won't be surprised that I've given a million dollars to a community health organization. *If they even find out about it.* If I want to keep the questions to a minimum, I can just donate that money out of my personal funds, not the company's.

I end up getting two hours of sleep, maybe three. Thanks to jet lag, I wake up at seven, make myself a cup of coffee, and walk out to the lake. It's a beautiful day. The surface is flat, a sleek glass mirror that reflects the cloudless blue sky.

If I don't look at my phone or pay attention to the seventy-four urgent emails in my inbox, I can pretend it's everything the doctor ordered.

Ignoring my phone is easier said than done. I get through my first cup without looking at it. Then I give in to the impulse and regret it immediately.

I have six meetings on my schedule tomorrow.

Six.

I told my family I needed a break. I asked them to keep the meetings to a minimum. I've been in Highfield less than twenty-four hours, and already, the demands have started.

I call Luis first thing Monday morning. "My calendar is packed," I complain in Spanish. "Six meetings today, Luis. What the hell?"

Luis sounds just as exasperated as I feel. "Señor Cardenas, I have told people you are unavailable. I have declined all non-essential meetings. I am trying. But your mother insisted that you sit in on the Pardini meeting, the Acra takeover prep, and the Minsk contract negotiations."

My mother insisted.

I have to get a handle on this.

The Cardenas Group is a multinational conglomerate. We operate in seventy-three countries. Last year, we earned two-point-three billion dollars in revenue. But we started out as a family company, and it shows. Like many family businesses that have grown bigger than the founders expected, we don't have any structures and processes in place.

My father worked himself to death. My mother remarried, but she can't seem to change her old patterns. She installed Tomas, her new husband, as the CEO because outsiders can't be relied on. Only family can be trusted.

Tomas, who used to head up the Accounting department at Cardenas and was on the brink of retirement when my father died, is woefully unqualified for the CEO job. He's miserable. Vicky, who's juggling a demanding job and two young children, is at her wit's end. Cristiano is moving to New York, getting married to his partner, and trying to have a baby. He doesn't have time for pointless meetings, either. A year ago, Magnus almost left him. Ever since then, my brother has pulled back from the firm. "I won't let work wreck my life," he said flatly. "I won't let it come between Magnus and me again."

We've all tried to change the situation, but my mother, the controlling shareholder, won't hear of it. She insists we preserve the status quo. Any attempts to modernize or delegate are met with, "That isn't how your father would have done it."

Nobody gets more stuff dumped on their plate than me. I am the oldest son. My mother doesn't have as many expectations of Victoria. Partly because Vicky is a woman—internalized misogyny is a hell of a drug—and partly because my sister has a family. I've thought about getting married and knocking somebody up for the same measure of space, but it probably wouldn't work. In Maria Cardenas' world, women take care of children, while men work at the family firm.

Any sort of change would involve a very hard conversation with my mother. I might have to threaten to quit. I might have to do more than threaten. But that would devastate her, and I can't do that. Not yet. My father died only three years ago. She needs time.

So I'm trapped. We're all trapped.

"Señor?"

Two weeks ago, I thought I had a heart attack. My doctor told me if I didn't make the appropriate lifestyle changes, I would follow my father into an early grave.

I don't want that.

"Who's attending the Pardini meeting on our end?"

"Anita Formoso."

"Okay, good. Anita can handle it. I trust her judgment. I won't make the Acra call either, which is a preliminary discussion between our lawyers and theirs. They can hammer out the contract details without me there. Have Rafal send me a summary of the discussions. Same with the Minsk negotiations and the rest of these meetings."

"Got it."

I'm preparing to hang up when I remember yesterday's conversation with Sophia. "Luis, when's your birthday?"

"October thirteenth," he responds, sounding confused. "Why?"

Because according to Sophia, I don't pay attention to the people around me. Because I lack empathy. "When it rolls around, schedule yourself the day off," I tell him.

"Señor Cardenas, are you okay? Are you ill?"

"No, no, I'm fine." I cross my fingers and continue. "And

Emma and Olivia?" I really hope I've got their names right. "Everything's good at their new school?"

Luis sounds puzzled. "Yes. They're enjoying it very much. They have been there for a year now, you know."

"Oh." Has it really been a year? I feel foolish now. Luis probably thinks I'm losing it. "Okay, great. Talk to you later."

AT NINE, I call Sophia at work. A woman picks up the phone. "Highfield Community Health Center," she says. "Can I help you?"

"Could I speak to Sophia Thorsen, please?" I might not remember the name of Luis' children, but remembering Sophia's last name is not a problem. I don't know what that says about me.

"Just a minute."

Sophia picks up a moment later. "Sophia Thorsen," she says cheerfully. "Hello?"

"It's Damien Cardenas."

"Damien." Enthusiasm drains from her voice in an instant. "What a pleasure."

Yeah, that sounds believable. The Health Center is hard up for money, and I'm not above using that to get what I want. "I thought we might continue the conversation we started on Saturday night."

"The conversation where you promised to donate a million dollars to the Highfield Community Health Center in return for empathy lessons? I thought about what you said, and the only explanation I came up with was that you were drunk."

"I wasn't. Are you free for lunch? I'd like to discuss the donation I'm planning to make to the Highfield Clinic."

"It's the Highfield Community Health Center," she bites

out. "And unfortunately, yes. I happen to be free for lunch. Where would you like to meet?"

"I'll pick you up. Noon? Great. See you then." I hang up before she can protest.

I have no illusions about lunch. Sophia would prefer to have nothing to do with me. She's going to be hostile, snipe at me, and make sarcastic jokes at my expense. And I'm looking forward to it, more than I've looked forward to anything in recent memory. I don't know what that says about the state of my life, but there it is.

My mother's number flashes on my phone.

I reluctantly answer.

"Are you sick, Damien?" she demands.

What does she know? Dr. Zambrano wouldn't have said anything to her, as that would violate his ethics. What has she heard, and who from?

"What are you talking about?"

"Luis told Gisele that you were acting strangely. And you canceled all your meetings today? What is going on?"

Ah, okay. "Nothing is going on, Mama."

"Then why did you have Luis cancel all your meetings?"

I try to keep the exasperation out of my voice and fail. "Because I slept two hours last night. I can barely keep my eyes open."

Relief fills her voice. "That's it? You had me worried there. Take a day off, of course. Take two, if you need. Victoria will cover for you."

"She doesn't have to, Mama. We have good people working for us. They will handle it."

"Or the meetings can be postponed," she says, completely ignoring my interjection. "If we have to, that's what we'll do."

"Do not postpone the meetings. Anita and Rafal are more than capable of dealing with this."

My words finally get through. "The Pardini meeting, okay. Acra, fine. But the Minsk negotiations are important, Damien. I'll have your sister do it." Her voice softens. "Get some rest, mijo. I'll talk to you tomorrow."

Twenty minutes later, I get a text from Vicky.

I have to attend the Minsk meetings? Damien, what the hell? Tonight was date night. Miguel and I haven't gone out for three months.

I take a deep breath and type out a reply.

Go on your date night. I'll handle it.

Nothing changes. Nothing ever does. Thank fuck for lunch with Sophia.

6

SOPHIA

Unfortunately, yes. I happen to be free for lunch.

I've never been this rude to a prospective donor in my life. It's shocking, really. And it's good that my boss Patricia didn't overhear me because she would have been justified in firing me on the spot.

Damien brings out the worst in me. That wasn't the case ten years ago. When I met him at the hospital, I really liked him. More than that. I had a humongous crush on him. I would seek out every opportunity to talk to him. I knew what time he came in, and I would strategically arrange to be in the office kitchen at the same time so we could bump into each other over coffee. I figured out his favorite lunch places, and I started frequenting them myself. Thinking back on twenty-five-year-old me, it's frankly a little embarrassing.

In hindsight, it's obvious that I'd been a little in love with Damien Cardenas, even before the threesome.

It was the first time I felt this way about a guy. I lost my virginity in high school, and I slept with a couple of guys in college. But none of them made me feel the way Damien did. When we talked, his dark brown eyes would focus on me. His entire attention would be on what I was saying. I was addicted. I couldn't get enough of him.

Then, one night, on some mad impulse, I followed him to Club M and realized Damien was not just the hyper-competent consultant who worked at the hospital. There was a lot more to him than he let on. He had a hidden side. A dark one.

That thought should have scared me, but it didn't. It excited me. If Damien was a pool, I was ready to jump into the deep end.

And then he introduced me to his friend Julian Kincaid.

Julian made me laugh. He had a dry, sly sense of humor. Have you ever met someone for the first time and felt like you've known them all your life? That was the way I felt about Julian.

I decided fairly early on that I wanted both of them. So, I flirted outrageously. I let my fingers graze Julian's when he handed me a drink. We did one round of tequila shots, and I licked the salt off Damien's hand.

They flirted back. The double entendres got increasingly outrageous. There was a group of very acrobatic naked people on the stage, and the droll commentary Julian kept up over their performance had me giggling. And then Damien's dark eyes rested on me. For the first time that evening, he asked me what I was doing there. "I didn't expect to see you here, Sophia," he said, his voice a low, seductive murmur. "I didn't realize you knew Xavier."

I didn't know how to play games in those days. I just blurted out the truth. "I followed you here. I told the security guard that I was with you."

He picked up my hand and brought it to his lips. He kissed my palm and then sucked a finger into his mouth.

Desire exploded inside me. "Did you find what you were looking for?" he asked, his eyes never leaving my face.

"Yes," I responded in a whisper. "I found the two of you."

Damien hesitated for a split second. Julian didn't. "According to Xavier, there are private rooms in the basement," he said, taking charge. "Evidently, there's more to Club M than orgies on the main floor." His gaze slid over me like a caress. "Want to check it out?"

"Private rooms." I wet my lip with my tongue. Their eyes followed the movement, their expressions hungry. "For sex?"

"Sex, yes," Damien replied. "But also bondage and domination. Have you been tied up before, Sophia?"

I hate Damien. He got me fired. But that moment. . . I remember everything about it with crystal clarity. I have masturbated to that memory for ten years. Even now, it has the power to make me wet.

Damien Cardenas asked me if I'd been tied up, and a thrill shot through my body. It was as if he was speaking to every secret desire in my soul. I came alive at that moment. I had an intense desire to experience what they offered. I craved it. I *needed* it.

"No. But I'd like to be."

It didn't even strike me to ask whether this was a safe thing to do. Whether this was sensible. Because it was Damien, and he wouldn't hurt me. I'd only just met Julian, but I *knew* I could trust him. Don't ask me how. It was a bone-deep certainty.

So much for my instincts. I thought I was safe, but I was wrong. Somehow, word got out that we'd slept together. It wasn't me; I didn't tell a soul. I hugged that night close to me, my own cherished memory.

If I hadn't been careless, then they were. And I got fired.

Enough, Sophia. I shake my head and drag my attention

back to work. It's a good thing what I'm doing doesn't need concentration because my focus is shot. I handwrite thank-you notes to everyone who participated in Saturday's fundraiser on autopilot. I stuff brochures and our wish lists into envelopes.

Ten minutes before noon, I head to the washroom and stare at my reflection in the mirror. It's all very well to pretend that I don't care what Damien thinks of me, but the uncomfortable truth is that I do. I brush my hair and tie it back in a severe ponytail. I refresh my lipstick and add a fresh coat of mascara.

Donna, who answers the phone, comes in while I'm doing my makeup. She takes in my reflection, and her eyes widen. "Whoa, hot date?" she asks. "Is it the guy I put through to you this morning?"

"It's not a date," I say severely. Donna is both an incurable romantic and an unrepentant gossip; the last thing I need is the entire office talking about my personal life. "I'm having lunch with a potential donor."

"You're wearing cherry red lipstick for a potential donor?" She tilts her head to the side. "Tell me more."

Yeah, okay. That's quite enough of that. "Who's answering the phone while you're in here?" That's admittedly a mean thing to say to a pregnant woman, but her questioning has hit a nerve, and I'm ready to fight.

She heaves a sigh. "Sheesh, fine. It's a donor. No more questions." She gives me a sly smile. "I'm going to make sure I'm sitting at the front desk exactly at noon. Your mystery donor had the sexiest voice. I want to see what he looks like."

Lovely.

. . .

It would be far more convenient if Damien had a potbelly and a wart on his nose. Unfortunately, when he shows up, he looks like sex on a stick.

I've seen Damien in a suit, and I've seen him naked. Today, he's neither. He's wearing dark jeans and a white linen shirt rolled up to the elbows. Sunglasses hide his eyes. He used to be clean-shaven when I knew him, but sometime in the last ten years, he's grown a beard, a neatly trimmed one. It suits him.

Donna's eyes are very round. *Great.* We're going to be talking about Damien Cardenas for the next week, at minimum.

"There you are," I say brightly, making a vain effort at rushing him out before Donna gets more water-cooler material. "Let's go."

His eyes flicker to the receptionist, who is staring at him avidly. His lips twitch. He knows that I'm trying to get him out of there, and he's deciding if he's going to cooperate.

"I'd love a tour of the facility, Sophia."

Jackass. I *hate* him. "Let's do that later. I'm starving."

"Of course." He waits until we get outside, looks around to make sure there's no one in earshot, and then murmurs, "After all, I do know what a healthy appetite you have."

My body remembers that voice. My insides tighten. My heartbeat speeds up. I stop dead in my tracks. "No," I say flatly. "If this is going to be a lunch filled with sexual innuendo, I'm not playing. We are going to discuss work. Nothing else."

He glances my way and realizes I'm dead serious. Contrition fills his face. "Fair enough," he says. "I'm sorry. It won't happen again."

He sounds sincere. Why am I not buying it? Oh, wait. It's

because it's Damien Cardenas who can, if he sets his mind to it, charm the pants off anyone. Including me.

We walk to the parking lot. "I can drive myself," I tell him. "Where are we going? I'll follow you in my car."

"Oh, for fuck's sake." He throws me a deeply exasperated look. "Are we going to fight about every single thing? Get in the SUV, Sophia."

He is a donor, I tell myself, not for the first time. *He might give your organization a lot of money. Be nice.*

The SUV in question is a brand-new Range Rover. A large, muscled beast of a vehicle. I open the passenger door before Damien has a chance to get it for me and hoist myself into the seat. "Is this yours?"

"Yes."

I have to bite my tongue to keep from making a joke about the size of his penis. It takes superhuman effort. If I say something about compensating for his equipment, Damien will remind me that I've seen his cock. He might ask if I need a refresher to remind me. There will be banter. I might enjoy the battle of wits, but it would not be professional. Not at all.

"Where do you live?" I ask instead.

He pulls out of the parking lot. "If I'm being grumpy, I would tell you that I live in airport lounges. I maintain a residence in Hong Kong and one in Toronto, and of course, there's the lake house in Highfield. But I divide my time largely between New York City and Lima. Why?"

Simon bought a new truck last year for his contracting business. He'd agonized over his decision, spending weeks wondering if he could take on the additional cost. Meanwhile, Damien Cardenas *maintains residences in Hong Kong and Toronto, and of course, there's the lake house in Highfield.* It must be nice to be rich. "Is the SUV a rental?"

"A rental?" He looks puzzled by my line of questioning. "No, it belongs to me. Renting is too much of a hassle."

I open my mouth to say something about how out of touch he is. Then I shut it. *He has offered to give your organization a million dollars, Sophia. That money will go a very long way. Remember your resolution to be nice?*

"Why do you own a lake house in Highfield?"

"That's a simple question with a complicated answer," he replies. "But first, Italian or Mexican for lunch?"

"Highfield doesn't have a Mexican restaurant. Just the taco place out on the highway."

"Taco Gus. Julian told me the food there was good."

"But Taco Gus is…" My voice trails away. Taco Gus is a dive. I love the place, but I can't see Damien fitting in. "It's not fancy," I warn him.

"I don't care. Do you?"

"Tacos sound amazing."

"Perfect." He loads up the route on the nav system. His phone buzzes three times while he does that. Text messages flash on the console screen, but he ignores them. "To answer your question," he says, "It all started with Xavier's castle."

He turns right. His phone buzzes again. It's distracting as hell. I don't know how he ignores it. If it were my phone, I'd have thrown it out of the window by now.

"It was built in the early 1900s by a shipping magnate," he continues. "He made his money in Detroit and Pittsburgh, and he built the castle when he retired. Xavier's family bought it in the eighties. It was pretty run down by then. Nobody had lived there for more than thirty years."

Xavier Leforte must have spent a lot of money on renovations. His castle is pristine. Beautiful and inviting, it's a luxury resort now, one that just happens to house a sex club in the basement. When Patricia celebrated her fiftieth birthday, the party was at Summit. (At the restaurant, obviously. Not at the sex club.)

"Xavier and I went to college together. We would come here a lot. He was fascinated by abandoned buildings. Still is. We would drive out from Boston, and he would wander through the empty castle. I've always liked Highfield, so when the lake house came on the market a couple of years ago, I bought it."

"Just like that."

I thought I did a good job at keeping my voice neutral, but whatever else he is, Damien isn't a fool. "Yes, Sophia," he bites out. "I bought the lake house on impulse. I bought the Range Rover on impulse too, and most of the time it sits around in my driveway, unused. Feel free to tell me how irresponsible I am."

I wince. I'm being judgmental, and he has every right to call me on it. "I'm sorry."

"Okay." He gives me a sunny, dazzling smile. "I bought the lake house the year after my father died. None of us saw it coming. One day he was alive and well; the next day, he'd been felled by a massive heart attack." He sighs. "College was a simpler time. I think I wanted to recapture some of that feeling."

Oh. I didn't expect him to tell me that. It appears that I'm forgiven. *Just like that.* I'd forgotten how easy-going Damien was. He didn't hold onto grudges; he never stayed angry. You always knew where you stood with him.

"I'm sorry," I say softly.

His phone pings again. He looks stressed. I can't see his expression—the sunglasses hide his eyes—but every time he gets a message, his shoulders tense. I looked up the Cardenas Group this morning. Damien's father died three years ago. His mother is the primary shareholder. She remarried, and her new husband is the CEO, but it's rumored that Damien's the one who really runs the company.

Is he happy? He doesn't look it.

We arrive at Taco Gus, order our tacos—Damien orders in Spanish, of course, filling me with envy—and take a seat on the patio. Damien gets a beer, and I stick to water. While we're waiting for our food to arrive, I get to the point. "Are you serious about the donation? Or is this some bizarre game you're playing?"

His eyes rest on me, a warm caramel pool I could drown in. "Is that what you think?" He pulls out his wallet, extracts a folded piece of paper from it, and hands it to me.

It's a check made out to the Highfield Community Health Center for a million dollars. He even got the name right.

I stare at it, my fingers trembling. Intense relief flows through me. Three weeks ago, the community health center had been facing eviction. I thought we would have to shut down. I was convinced I was going to be unemployed again. There aren't a lot of outreach and fundraising jobs in this part of the country. I thought I'd be forced to move.

Then Xavier Leforte held a fundraiser for us, ending our eviction woes. And now Damien's given me a check for a million dollars.

Something of what I'm feeling must be visible on my face. Damien's expression changes. His voice goes soft. "Sophia, hey. Are you okay?"

No. I'm really not. I think I'm going to cry. And I really don't want to be that vulnerable in front of Damien Cardenas.

I take a deep breath and stuff my emotions back down my throat. "Thank you for your generous gift. Please allow me to express my gratitude on behalf of the Highfield Community Health Center. We appreciate—"

He holds up his hand. "We had a deal, remember? You're going to teach me how to be a better person."

"Damien, I have no idea how to do that. I'm not a teacher. I'm not a philosopher. Binge-watching *The Good Place* isn't going to magically make me Chidi Anagonye."

"Good," he says. "Because I don't want to listen to lectures about Aristotle. I don't learn well in the classroom." He gives me a wicked smile. "I'm more hands-on."

Okay, momentary wobble over. "Remember the discussion that we had about double entendres? That was less than an hour ago. You said—"

"That it wouldn't happen again." He makes a face. "It's a bad habit. I'm sorry. *Again.*"

He wrote my organization a million-dollar check. The least I can do in exchange is humor him about this stupid class. "I will figure out a curriculum."

"Of course. Since I only have a month, we should meet three times a week. I'm looking for a total transformation."

I fight the urge to upend the bowl of salsa on his head. Three times a week. Then his words sink in, and I realize that something's been nagging at me. "You're here for a month. Why? What brings you to Highfield anyway?"

He lifts his shoulders in a shrug. "I'm taking a break. It was either sailing around the world or sitting on my ass by the lake. I chose the lazier option."

"A month-long break?" Technically, I get three weeks of vacation. Except I've never taken it. We're a small organization. It's just not feasible for me to disappear for an extended period.

"What can I say? It's a family company. I'm one of the idle rich."

I roll my eyes. Damien worked sixteen-hour days as a management consultant. Unless his personality has undergone a very drastic shift, he's lying. "I very much doubt that. Your phone has not stopped ringing."

He glances down at the offending instrument, which picks that moment to vibrate again. "Yes, it's very annoying. Please excuse me for a minute." He picks it up, gets to his feet, and vaults over the fence separating the patio from the parking lot. He tosses the phone into his SUV and returns to his seat. "As much as I'd like to fling it dramatically into the lake, Luis will just ship me another."

"You're avoiding my question, Damien."

"I'm not the only one avoiding questions," he retorts. Frustration fills his face. "What gives, Sophia? What the hell happened? I thought we had something that night. Why didn't you call me? Why didn't you tell me you got fired?" He glares at me. "And then you changed your phone number to avoid me? What the hell—"

Seriously? I stare at him, my own temper fraying at the edges. "Damien," I cut in. "I have no idea how to tell you this, but the world does not revolve around you. I got fired. I couldn't make rent. I was desperately searching for another job. Sex with you was the last thing on my mind."

Liar, my conscience whispers.

"And I didn't change my phone number to avoid you," I continue angrily. "It got disconnected because I had no money to pay my bills."

He goes very still. "Oh."

He doesn't say much for the rest of our meal. He doesn't needle me. He holds off on the innuendos. We talk instead about the health center. He asks me what our plans are, and

I wax eloquent about our five-year roadmap. I tell him how his gift will be used. He listens seriously and asks intelligent, perceptive questions.

I should be relieved. I should be delighted. I tell myself it doesn't bother me that he's not flirting with me anymore.

But I'm lying.

7

JULIAN

I walk through Kincaid Castle again when I get home from the fundraiser and take a cold, hard look at the task I have in front of me. It's daunting. The place is in terrible shape. At dinner, I started wondering if I was overstating how bad the mess was. If anything, I was understating things. It's a disaster.

I've been living here for almost nine months. All that time, I've avoided dealing with my house in favor of work. There's always something else to do. But I can't avoid it any longer, not unless I want to let down my sister. *Yet again.*

Damien suggested the greenhouse. Instead of drowning in despair at the magnitude of the problem in front of me, I head there and turn on a light switch. Shockingly, it works. Sort of. Weak flickering light illuminates the space in front of me.

Once upon a time, this was my favorite part of the house. It was always warm, even in the dead of winter. Tropical plants filled the area. Glass panes let in sunlight, and the air was scented with the fragrance of hundreds of flowers. Potted orange trees grew here when the ground outside was covered in snow, and golden koi darted in a pond dotted with lotus blossoms.

Hannah and I would come down here to feed the fish when we were young. I even had a pet turtle, Harry. To me and Hannah, the greenhouse, or the conservatory, as my parents liked to call it, was a place of refuge. My mother occasionally tended to the plants, but my father never bothered. Here, it was just the two of us.

I can't romanticize the past. Hannah's memories of this place are undoubtedly very different from mine.

But it wasn't just Hannah who was unhappy. Even as a child, I could see the disparity in how we were treated. Children have an innate sense of fair play. I knew it was wrong, and it bothered me, and I didn't know how to change things.

My turtle is long-dead. The pots are cracked and broken, and the plants are withered husks. The glass panes are filthy and caked with dirt. Some of them are cracked, and some have shattered, letting in air from the outside. The glass roof is wrecked. The floor is covered with a moth-eaten carpet and littered with debris.

I don't have to be a therapist to understand why I haven't done a damn thing to fix Kincaid Castle. Restoring it to its former grandeur seems wrong somehow. As if I'm putting a glossy veneer over our childhood.

If it were up to me, I'd let the place fall apart. But Hannah wants to get married here, which means I need to push past my emotions and do this for my sister.

I look around at the mess. This is going to take a lot of time. I need to keep searching for a contractor, but I can't rely on finding one. My initial search hasn't yielded any results, and I can't afford to wait much longer. I need to get started.

I kneel down and roll the faded carpet aside. There's

terracotta tile underneath, the tile I remember from my childhood. Under-floor heating kept the tiles warm, even on the coldest days of the year. I remember my father saying something about it in one of our rare phone conversations. He put down the carpet because the heating had stopped working.

I pull out my phone and start to make a list of all the things I'll have to do. The under-floor heating needs to be fixed, as does the plumbing since Hannah's wedding guests will need hot water in the bathrooms. I need to replace the broken panes of glass. The roof needs attention, as does the pond. And, if I manage to get all of that done, I'll need to buy plants to fill the space.

One thing at a time. The tile floor is the first thing to tackle. I need to go to a hardware store as soon as I wake up tomorrow.

I WORK on the greenhouse all of Sunday and most of Monday morning. I make very slow progress. It takes me all of that time to just clean the place up. I make five trips to the dump.

And I try not to think about Sophia. About the night we spent together. About what might have been, if only we hadn't lost touch.

But it's *impossible* to scrub her from my thoughts. Seeing her at the fundraiser has torn the veil and yanked the memories back to the forefront. When I met Sophia, *Kingdom Night*, one of my comics, had just become a runaway bestseller. Meander Games paid me a six-figure advance to storyboard their upcoming video game. My career was taking off.

There were many wins that year. Even so, that night with

her was the best night of my life. That night, real-life was on pause, and the air was alive with magic.

Then everything went to shit. My mother received her cancer diagnosis. I told her to call Hannah. "She would want to know," I said. "She would want to help." Of course, my parents wouldn't hear of it. There had been arguments. So many appointments with so many doctors. Oncologists. Specialists. Chemo. My father broke his leg, and he couldn't put any weight on it for three months. Caring for both of them fell to me.

I tried to hold onto Sophia. I desperately wanted to see her again. But when I called her, she wouldn't answer the phone. She wouldn't return my texts. I got the message. She wasn't interested in staying in touch, and even though I didn't understand why, I needed to respect her decision. So I let her go.

I should have gone up and said hello to her at the fundraiser. I don't know why I didn't. Maybe it was the sense that if I did, she would upend my life again.

Or maybe I didn't talk to her for the same reason I've avoided Hannah. I like to steer clear of hard conversations and difficult, inconvenient emotions.

SHAUN ZHAO, my agent, calls me Monday afternoon. "Are you sitting down?" he asks, his voice vibrating with excitement. "Because I have news."

I've managed to vacuum up most of the dirt, but the floor's certainly not in any condition to sit on. There's not a chair in sight either. Not that it matters; Shaun's question had been rhetorical.

"What's going on?"

"Levine Entertainment has bought the film rights to

Revenant."

Revenant is a comic I made four years ago. It's set in a magic-friendly, post-apocalyptic world and is my biggest hit to date. It was made into a wildly popular game, and I've attended conventions where women cosplay as my protagonist Lola. People write fanfic about her, shipping her with Cavuto, the assassin who's hired to kill her.

Hollywood has expressed interest in the comic before, but nothing's come of it. Until now.

"That's great." I do my best to sound thrilled, but honestly, it doesn't seem like a big deal. Studios have bought options for my comics before, but things never move to the next stage. Still, selling the option should yield a nice sum of money, which I could use to renovate the house.

"No, Julian, you don't understand. This isn't great. It's *stupendous*. Levine has secured funding for a six-episode series. They want you to co-write the screenplay. They've sent me a preliminary contract. They plan to begin filming early next year. This isn't just an option. *Revenant* is getting made, my friend."

I shake my head in disbelief. Shaun was right; I should have been sitting down. "No way."

"This is the big one. Can you be in LA for the pitch meeting on Friday?"

My head is still spinning. "Fly to California? It can't be done remotely?"

"The producer wants to meet with you personally."

I run my hand over my face. Holy shit. This is real. I've had comics made into games, but this is a show. This is *big*. "Yeah, yeah. Sure thing. Send me the details—I'll be there."

I hang up, then I realize where I am. The greenhouse. I thought I had nothing going on for the next four months. I thought I had all that time to do the renovations. But if *Revenant* is getting made into a show...

It doesn't matter. I refuse to let Hannah down. I'm just going to have to make it work.

DAMIEN SHOWS up unannounced with a box of pizza shortly after seven. "I sent you a text," he says. "You didn't respond." He looks around at the now bare room. "I see why."

"Yeah, sorry. My phone is upstairs." I survey the space through his eyes. "When you suggested holding the wedding here, I didn't really think it would work. But now that I've cleared out the junk, it's actually bigger than I thought."

We take the pizza into the kitchen. I open the refrigerator, hand Damien a beer, and take one for myself. "What's going on with you? Tell me what your doctor said."

He waves off my concern. "It's not a big deal."

"Don't give me that, Damien. I'm not a fool. You haven't taken a day of vacation since your father died."

"I thought I had a heart attack. I didn't. Still, Dr. Zambrano recommended time off. I'm following his advice."

"How many meetings did you attend today?"

"Just two. I didn't come here to talk about that. I had lunch with Sophia today."

I go still. A flash of jealousy surges through me, almost immediately followed by remorse. Am I going to sulk if Damien pursues Sophia? No way. I refuse to be that guy. Damien can go out with whomever he wants.

Damien takes a look at my face. "It wasn't a date, you idiot. We discussed the community health center."

I tell myself that the emotion I'm feeling isn't relief. "I'd forgotten about your insane plan. How did that go?"

"As expected." He looks at me. "We tried to call her, do you remember? And then her phone was out of service?"

"Yeah?"

"Her phone was disconnected because she didn't have enough money to pay the bill." His expression is troubled. "I had my team investigate. After she got fired ten years ago, Sophia spent a month living out of her car."

Shock slaps me. I put down the slice of pizza I was eating. She was homeless? While I lived in my comfortable, heated New York apartment, Sophia lived out of her car. Yes, I had problems. But I had shelter. I had a place to live, a roof over my head.

"I thought she was avoiding us because she regretted the threesome," he continues. "Instead, I find out she was struggling. At the fundraiser, Sophia said I had no idea what life is like for the little people." His expression is bleak. "She's right."

I'm not paying attention to him. I'm still reeling. Sophia mattered to me. That night meant something, but you'd never know that from the way I acted. Yes, I didn't know that she got fired, and I certainly didn't know she was forced to live in her car, but that's no excuse. What does it say about me that I didn't bother to find out?

Nothing good.

Damien sticks around after dinner and helps with the greenhouse. We start to pull up the tiles, which is a lot harder than it sounds. We make it through less than a tenth of the area when he has to leave. "I have to attend yet another conference call," he says wearily. I open my mouth to say something, and he holds up his hand to forestall me. "I'm working on it."

He lets his family walk all over him. Then again, who am I to point out his flaws when I have so many of my own?

I wake up on Tuesday morning, determined to make serious progress on the greenhouse before flying to Los Angeles. But the problem with working with your hands is that it doesn't always still your mind. I could sink into the drawing if I were working on a comic. I could think about what my characters were saying and doing and tune out the world.

But it's not the same with the greenhouse. Over and over, my mind returns to Sophia.

I drive to the hardware store to pick up some supplies. On the way back, I pass the community health center. On impulse, I pull into the parking lot.

A heavily pregnant young woman is seated at the front desk. She stares at me for a long moment. "Can I help you?"

I glance down at myself and realize that I'm covered in tile dust. *Crap.* I should have showered. Changed. Run a comb through my hair. Too late for any of that.

"Is Sophia around?"

"Yes," she replies. She gives me another once-over. "Let me get her."

Sophia comes out a few minutes later. She's wearing a navy-blue dress that skims her knees. Her legs are bare, and she's wearing brown sandals on her feet, with toes painted a pretty shade of pink.

She looks like she's ready for a garden party, and I'm covered in dust from head to toe.

Then she notices me, and her eyes widen. "Julian?"

8

SOPHIA

I'm working on more thank-you notes when Donna comes into my office and tells me there's a construction worker to see me.

"A construction worker?" I repeat, puzzled. "Are you sure?"

"Yeah," she says, nodding her head emphatically. "Absolutely. He's covered in dust. He's really hot, though, so that's okay." She gives me a curious look. "I didn't know that you were in the middle of renovations again. And isn't your brother a contractor? Is he too busy to do the work himself?"

"I'm not renovating anything," I reply. "We're done with the house." Donna met Simon at last year's office holiday party, so that can't be who it is. I get to my feet to investigate.

Waiting in the lobby is literally the last person I expect to see. Julian Kincaid.

"Julian?" He's wearing a Pink Floyd T-shirt and faded jeans, both liberally sprinkled with construction dust. Black-rimmed glasses cover his face. He looks dirty and disheveled and unbearably attractive. Donna called him hot, and she was not wrong.

He gives me a small smile. "Sorry to show up without calling," he says as if the last time we spoke wasn't ten years ago. "I was driving by the health center, and I thought I'd see if you wanted to grab lunch."

At the fundraiser, he hadn't even said hello. Why this visit, why now?

Donna's gaze is boring into my back. Everyone is going to be talking about this. I just know it. The last time my personal life became a topic of discussion, I got fired. But Patricia is not Mrs. Caldwell, and I've just raised three million dollars for the health center. I doubt the same thing will happen here, but I still hate the idea of being the topic of gossip.

"Sure," I respond. "That sounds good. Let me grab my bag."

We walk into the parking lot. Julian looks down at his clothes ruefully. "I did not plan this very well," he says, his lips tilting up in a wry smile. "I'm really not dressed to eat inside. Is it okay if we grab sandwiches and eat at the park?"

It's a beautiful September day. Not too hot, not too muggy, not a single bug in sight. I would've worked through lunch and missed this glorious weather if Julian hadn't shown up. "The park sounds amazing."

"I don't want to get dirt on your upholstery. Shall we take my car?"

We get into Julian's truck and drive to Mama Lauro's, one of my favorite Italian restaurants. They do a brisk takeout business, so we order sandwiches and bottles of water. Ten minutes later, we arrive at the park and claim an empty picnic bench. I unwrap my eggplant parmesan sandwich and bite into it. It's *delicious*. Mama Lauro's always hits the spot. "This is way better than the instant noodle bowl I was planning to eat."

"I was going to eat the apple in my refrigerator," he says. "And some cheese, which might or might not have been moldy." He makes a face. "I should really go grocery shopping."

"Do you live in Highfield?" I blurt out. "Last time we talked, you lived in New York."

"I moved back just after Christmas."

Eight months ago. Highfield isn't a big town; it's a glorified village. I'm surprised I haven't run into him before.

"How did the fundraiser go?" he asks. "Did you raise enough money to buy your building?"

Seeing Damien and Julian at the fundraiser had been one hell of a shock. I'm feeling some of that same confusion now. *Why did Julian invite me to lunch?* They're not supposed to be here, either of them. In the last year and a half, Highfield has become my hometown. My brothers and I bought a home here, one we've spent a lot of time renovating. My life has a rhythm to it that I like. Go to work. Work out at the kickboxing gym in the evenings. I cook Mondays and Wednesdays; Simon cooks Tuesdays and Thursdays. Andre doesn't cook—he does enough of that at work—but he is in charge of clean-up. I block off Fridays for date night in a quest to find a guy before the time on my biological clock runs out. Saturday is the farmer's market, and Sunday is family dinner.

It doesn't sound very adventurous, and it isn't. But I'm not looking for adventure—that's what I've told myself. I'm looking to settle down and start a family of my own.

Damien Cardenas and Julian Kincaid are two rocks thrown into my placid pond. Waves ripple from the point of contact, disrupting everything.

"Yes, we did." Julian's name had been on the list of people who donated items to the auction. He offered up signed first edition copies of some of his comics. They had sold for a surprisingly large sum of money. "Official thank-you notes are in the mail, but thank you for your help." Did that sound grudging and churlish? I didn't mean it to. I just don't know what he's doing here. Or, as a matter of fact, what I'm doing here.

"It was nothing," he replies. "My publisher sends me thirty copies of every print edition. They just sit around in boxes in my office, gathering dust. It was the least I could do."

"Well, I certainly appreciate it. We needed to raise two million dollars, and I didn't think it was a target we'd reach, but we did."

"Is that what they wanted for your building?" He shakes his head. "I can't believe it. It was vacant for six years before you guys moved in. Real estate around here has gone crazy."

Are we going to make small talk for the duration of this meal? I have to bite my tongue to keep from blurting out, *Why did you invite me for lunch? Why didn't you say hello at the fundraiser?*

But I don't know Julian. Not at all. We had a one-night stand ten years ago. Any sense of connection I feel toward him—a connection I've always felt—is an illusion.

"You're probably wondering why I invited you to lunch."

It's as if he read my mind. *Spooky.* "A little bit, yeah."

He takes off his glasses, sets them on the table, and rubs his eyes. "I owe you an apology," he says. "I should have tried harder to contact you back then."

The sun beams down on us, but the air is ever so slightly cool. The warmth is pleasant, not oppressive. My sandwich is delicious. But at Julian's words, my sense of pleasure evaporates.

"Let me guess," I grind out through clenched teeth.

"Damien told you that my phone got disconnected, and you're here because you feel sorry for me. You don't owe me an apology, Julian. There's nothing to forgive. We slept together one night. We don't owe each other anything."

"Is that what you think?" His gaze holds mine. His eyes are vividly blue. "That's certainly what I told myself when I couldn't reach you. That we didn't owe each other anything. But it's not true." He leans forward. "That night was special," he says quietly. "It meant something to me. We might not have spoken any promises out loud, but we didn't have to. Our bodies knew the truth."

I stop breathing and stare at him, hypnotized by the raw edge of sincerity in his voice. *Our bodies knew the truth.* He's hit the nail on the head. That's why I've spent ten years feeling betrayed. Because I thought the three of us really had something. That's why, ten years later, I'm still angry with Damien. And why I was hurt that Julian didn't talk to me at the fundraiser.

That's why I'm here, having lunch with him.

And that's why I've agreed to teach Damien how to be a better person. Three times a week. As if I don't have anything else to do.

I'm a puppet, and these men hold my strings.

My emotions are too tangled, too close to the surface. I don't know how to respond. "Let's change the topic."

He looks like he's going to protest, and then he nods. "Of course. What would you like to talk about?"

I gesture at his clothes. "Are you building something?"

"I'm renovating a conservatory."

"Huh?"

"Sorry, my parents liked to be pretentious. They were diehard Anglophiles. It's a large greenhouse. I spent the morning pulling broken tile from the floor."

"Ugh." I've been there, and it's no fun whatsoever. "That's messy, dusty work."

He quirks an eyebrow. "That sounds like the voice of experience."

"My brothers and I bought a house when I moved to Highfield. The only reason we could afford it was because it was a wreck. We spent most of last year working on it." I have another question for him. "You kept in touch with Damien. Are you guys still friends?"

"Yes." He gives me an amused look. "I hear you're going to teach him how to be a better person."

"Evidently." I can't hide my disgruntlement. "Three times a week for the next month. I don't understand it. Damien Cardenas doesn't need me to teach him anything. What's his deal, anyway?"

He laughs out loud. "Is that a rhetorical question, or are you pumping me for information about my best friend?" He takes another bite of his meatball sub, and a big glob of marinara sauce lands on his T-shirt. "Oh, for fuck's sake," he swears. "I like this T-shirt."

"It'll come out in the wash if you rinse it out right away. Trust me, I know. I've had my share of marinara accidents at Mama Lauro's."

He eyes the bottle of water next to him. "It's worth a shot."

And then he pulls his T-shirt over his head, and his naked chest comes into view.

Oh. My. God.

My mouth goes dry.

Muscles. So many muscles. Julian is a writer. His job involves lots of sitting. He has no business having a body like this, with sleekly defined biceps and sculpted abs. It's impossible not to ogle, and I can't even be mad at him for taking off his shirt. *I suggested it.*

I try hard not to drool as he pours the bottle of water on the sauce stain. I fail *abjectly*.

He wrings the shirt out and lays it flat at the end of the table to dry. Then he sits down again. "I'm sorry," he says politely as if he hasn't set my every nerve on fire with his almost nakedness. "Where were we? Oh, right. You were interrogating me about my best friend."

"I wasn't," I deny. "Okay fine, I was a little. But you don't have to tell me anything. I don't mean to put you in an awkward situation."

He chuckles. "Damien's a big boy who can take care of himself. You want to know what his deal is? Here's what you need to know about Damien Cardenas. He's a compulsive workaholic who doesn't know how to take a break. Saturday night, after the fundraiser, he had a two a.m. conference call. It didn't even strike Damien that it's not normal."

Ha. I knew Damien was lying about his idle rich comment. "Why?"

"Why is he a workaholic? Because underneath that flippant, devil-may-care exterior, he has a very strong sense of duty. He is the oldest child. It was always expected that he would take over the family company. Everything he's done in his life has been in keeping with that goal. He went to business school. He joined a management consulting company to round out his experience. After a six-year stint there, he went to work for the Cardenas Group and made his way up the ranks."

I think about the phone that will not stop ringing. "And that includes two a.m. calls?"

"It wasn't always this bad," Julian replies. "His father died, and his mother remarried. She's the majority shareholder. She made her husband Tomas the CEO. Maybe she thought it would make Damien's life easier? I don't know. But Tomas Valera doesn't know a damn thing about running a conglomerate. Damien runs around, covering for him. Fixing his mistakes."

"Why doesn't he just tell his mother?"

"He'll tell you that's a waste of time. His mother has a stubborn streak, and she's going to do what she's going to do. But the real reason is that he likes Tomas and doesn't want to hurt his feelings."

Damn it. It's easy for me to hate the version of Damien Cardenas that got me fired. It's easy to hate the man who buys a house in Highfield without batting an eye. Who keeps a brand new SUV in a town where he doesn't even live because renting would be too much hassle.

But that's not the whole picture. The Damien that Julian knows is a lot more nuanced.

I don't like it.

It would be significantly more convenient for me to keep hating Damien. Significantly easier if I didn't feel *connected* to Julian. It would be much better for my peace of mind if I wasn't turned on at the sight of Julian sitting in front of me, biting into his sandwich with obvious relish. Much healthier if I wasn't still attracted to Damien.

DONNA STOPS me when I get back from lunch. "Who was that?" she asks, her eyes gleaming with curiosity.

"A friend," I say curtly.

She doesn't take the hint. "Back-to-back lunches with two hot guys. Some people have all the luck. Which one do you fancy, Sophia?"

"Seriously?"

She takes a look at my annoyed expression and raises her hand. "No need to get offended. It's just a joke."

"Do I look like I'm laughing?" I don't care if I'm being a bitch. People gossiped about me once before, and I lost my job. I am *never* going to let that happen again.

But Donna's question lingers in my mind all afternoon.

Which one of them do I fancy?

The answer has always been *both*.

And that's the real problem.

Just as I'm leaving for the day, my phone rings. It's not Damien. Not that I was waiting for his call or anything.

It's a number I don't recognize. I answer, and a woman asks, "Hello, is this Sophia Thorsen?"

"Yes, it is."

"This is Laura from the Collins Fertility Clinic," she says. "I'm just calling to confirm your appointment with Dr. Hernandez at one o'clock tomorrow."

The reminder is the cold bucket of water my libido needs. I'm not twenty-five any longer. I'm a grown woman who is getting older every day. Already, I'm considered to be of advanced maternal age. Every year I delay, it becomes harder for me to get pregnant. The risk of pregnancy loss increases. The odds of fetal chromosome abnormalities are higher.

I don't have time for Julian and Damien. I have goals for my life.

And those goals don't involve getting swept up in their net again.

"Yes," I reply. "I'll be there."

9

SOPHIA

Patricia was out sick Monday and Tuesday, courtesy of a stomach bug. She comes into my office first thing Wednesday morning, still looking a little exhausted from her bout of illness, but her eyes shine with excitement.

"Sophia," she exclaims. "I opened my email last night and saw your note about the donation from Damien Cardenas. A check for a million dollars? I can hardly believe it."

Yeah, me neither.

"How did you manage this?"

Crap. With everything that has happened since the fundraiser, I forgot to come up with a cover story for this donation. I like my boss, and I don't want to lie to her. "Umm..."

"I looked him up, of course," she continues. "He's the Chief Operating Officer of the Cardenas Group. The company supports quite a lot of community health care in South America, Asia, and Africa but doesn't do much in North America. I don't understand how we ended up on their radar."

Patricia has a dozen photos of her grandchildren on her desk. On the back of her office chair hangs a sweatshirt that says 'Cat Mom.' Someone meeting her for the first time might be excused for underestimating her, but I know better.

She's looking to me for an explanation, and I don't have one to offer her. I don't know why Damien gave our organization that money unless it was to spend time with me. But that's insane.

I settle for a version of the truth. "Damien is an old friend," I respond. "He was at the Summit fundraiser, and I guess he thought we were a worthy cause." He's also rich enough that a million dollars is a drop in the bucket. If Patricia looked him up, she'd already know that.

"Such a generous gesture," she gushes. "Sophia, we must thank him."

"I sent a note."

"No, no, no." She shakes her head emphatically. "That doesn't seem sufficient. We must take him out to dinner. An old friend, you said? Perfect. Can you set it up?"

More time with Damien, just what I need. Fantastic. Just fantastic.

I LEAVE work early and head to my appointment at the Collins Fertility Clinic. My appointment is with a Dr. Mark Hernandez.

Dr. Hernandez looks like he's in his late forties. He has olive-brown skin and brown eyes. "What can I do for you, Ms. Thorson?" he asks after the initial exchange of pleasantries.

"I want to get pregnant," I reply. "I'm thirty-five, single, and painfully aware that I'm running out of time. I want to explore my options." I take a deep breath. "Like donor insemination."

"Have you been trying to conceive?"

He's asking me if I'm having regular sex. I wish. "No, I haven't," I reply. "I've done a little bit of research, but I thought I'd schedule this appointment to see what the process is."

"Certainly," he answers readily. "The first step is to make sure that you have no fertility issues that will complicate donor insemination. Once that's done, the next step is to pick a donor. Some people choose to use the sperm of a friend or an acquaintance. But I'll caution you that there are some legal liabilities to consider in that situation."

Even if I could find somebody to be a sperm donor, I would never take that risk. They might try to assert custody over my child. I would never let my baby experience what Denise put us through.

"I'll be using a sperm bank, Doctor."

"Excellent. We work with several. Laura will give you a list on your way out. She'll also give you information about the differences between anonymous, semi-open, and open donors. Once you have a donor picked out, we move on to the insemination cycle. There are three ways to do this: intracervical insemination, intravaginal insemination, and intrauterine insemination. It typically takes anywhere from three to five rounds for fertilization to happen."

My head is spinning, and it's only been a few minutes. Some of what I'm feeling must be visible on my face because Dr. Hernandez gives me a thoughtful look. "Fertility testing and treatments can be stressful," he says. "Not to mention expensive. We can start the basic fertility screening today, but as you move forward in this process, I recommend counseling."

Some clinics don't welcome single women, but the Collins Fertility Clinic isn't one of them. I looked them up online, and several reviews mentioned how welcoming and supportive they were toward single parents and same-sex couples. Dr. Hernandez isn't trying to discourage me from having a baby; he's treating it like it's a major, life-changing decision.

Because it is.

I have good health insurance, but it doesn't cover fertility treatments and barely covers therapy. I used up most of my savings to fix up our house. Do I want a baby so much that I'm willing to go deep in debt?

Yes. *Yes, I do.*

"If counseling isn't an option, one of our volunteers runs a support group. I believe they meet once a week. Laura can give you the details." He looks up from his notepad. "If you're ready, we can begin the first part of your fertility testing today."

ONE UNCOMFORTABLE PAP SMEAR LATER, I'm at the front desk. "The doctor said you'd give me some information?" I ask Laura.

"About sperm banks, right? Hang on, I'll print a list of places we typically use." She stuffs a dozen brochures into a binder and hands it to me.

"Dr. Hernandez also said something about a support group."

"The group Nadya organizes? Yes, she left a flyer here somewhere." She hands me a sheet of paper. "They're meeting tonight."

"Tonight?" I can't do that. That's too soon. Plus, I have other things going on this evening. Things like coming up with the curriculum for Damien's How to Become a Better Person course. I should have done it yesterday, and I started to browse the Internet for ideas, but I fell asleep on the couch instead.

But Damien's only in town for four weeks, and he's held up his end of the bargain. No matter what I think of his motives, his gift was exceedingly generous. I need to do my part.

"I don't think tonight is going to work," I tell the receptionist. "I'll just attend their next meeting."

BEN, my oldest and most responsible brother, calls me as I'm driving back from the clinic. "Papa's birthday is coming up," he says. "He's had his eye on a set of golf clubs, but they're not cheap. Do you want to go in on it? I talked to Andre, and he's in. So is Aurora. I left a message for Simon."

In true contractor fashion, Simon only checks his messages twice a week. *If that.* "Good luck getting a reply," I tell Ben. "The house that he's working on is giving him problems. He's there fourteen hours a day."

"He works too hard," Ben says disapprovingly.

"As if you're any better. Yeah, count me in on the clubs. I'll tell Simon about them if I see him tonight."

"Thanks, I'd appreciate that." He's about to hang up when he remembers to ask, "What's going on with you, Soph? Are you really thinking of doing the pregnancy thing?"

"I'm on my way home from the fertility clinic. I had my first appointment today."

He whistles softly. "You're moving quickly."

"I don't have a lot of time to waste," I point out.

"Hmm. There's no guy in the picture, then? No one you want to do this with?"

For some inexplicable reason, I think about Julian and Damien. And then I laugh at my imagination. Damien and Julian as parents? Julian might be father material, maybe, but Damien? Hell, no. I would never have a baby with somebody that wealthy. If there's any custody dispute, he'd be able to steamroll over me. "No," I tell my brother. "There's nobody in the picture. Why do you ask? You don't think I should have a baby via sperm donor?"

"You should do whatever you want," he replies immediately. "Whatever makes you happy." He hesitates. "Do you know my friends Tony and Leela?"

"I've heard you talk about them. Why?"

"They've been trying for a baby. Leela did fertility treatments last year. It wasn't good. They'd get their hopes up with each cycle, and when it didn't work, their hearts would shatter." His voice turns sad. "This year, Leela desperately wanted to keep trying. Tony didn't. They can't figure out how to get past it. They're separated now. Probably getting divorced."

"That's brutal." The car in front of me stops abruptly, and I have to slam on my brakes to keep from rear-ending him. Blissfully unaware, he turns right. Asshole. Ever heard of a turn signal? "The doctor suggested a support group."

"You should go, Soph. Make sure you know what you're getting into."

I EMAIL the support group when I get back home. Nadya, the organizer, writes back almost immediately. "There is a meeting tonight," her email says. "We meet at Grounds for Thoughts, the coffee shop on Main Street."

Attached to her email is a schedule of their upcoming meetings. I'm about to reply saying I can't meet tonight when I notice that they aren't meeting next week.

And next week I'm meeting with Dr. Hernandez again to discuss the results of my fertility tests.

Crap. So much for Damien's curriculum.

There are five women at the coffee shop, all roughly the same age as me. I walk up and introduce myself. I'm not naturally extroverted, but my job makes me good at faking it. When you routinely have to ask people for money, you learn to get over any sense of embarrassment.

There's Nadya, Poppy, Jennifer, Felicity, and Malia. After some initial chitchat, everyone goes around the table to talk about what they're struggling with. Felicity, a freckled redhead, is the only woman apart from me who is single. "I went on a date last night," she says when it's her turn to share. "It was weird."

"Why?" Jennifer asks.

"It's the first time I didn't tell a date I was planning on getting pregnant." She turns to me. "Sophia, you'll probably run into this too. Dating is hell when you're trying to have a baby."

I think about my string of bad dates. "Isn't dating hell all the time?"

She gives a short laugh. "You would think, right? But as bad as it is out there, it gets so much worse once you're on this journey. Most guys you go out with think you're looking for a father for your child and that you want to trap them into marriage. I tell them the truth because I believe in disclosure, but then they end up ghosting me. Or I get the weirdos. I went out with a guy that told me I didn't need fertility treatments. He would breed me."

"That sounds delightful." Ugh. Is this what my future

holds? Matthew Barnes, my most recent horrible date, sounds positively charming in comparison.

"Anyway. . ." Felicity's expression turns embarrassed. "I ended up sleeping with the guy last night. We used a condom, of course."

"Do it while you still can," Poppy replies. "When Tom and I had Grant, things weren't right down there for ages. I don't think we had sex for two years after the baby was born."

Malia looks aghast. "Two years? I had a nine-month dry spell once, and that was bad enough."

"Grant wouldn't sleep," Poppy explains. "I had no sexual desire. None whatsoever. My fantasies were about getting a hotel room, soaking in the utter quiet, and getting a good night's sleep." She shudders at the memory. "It was rough. Tom and I almost broke up over it." She makes a face. "And we're doing it again. Yippee."

If the support group meeting is supposed to make me feel better, it fails miserably. I go home to an empty house. It's my turn to cook, and I decide on pasta for dinner. I chop veggies while the water boils, my thoughts dark. Let's assume it takes me a year to get pregnant. If I add in almost another year of being pregnant and two years of post-baby celibacy, à la Poppy, I'm looking at a dry spell of *four* years.

My pussy is already growing cobwebs. And the prospect of not seeing any action for the next four years? I really don't like the sound of that.

Aurora calls me when I'm adding dressing to the lettuce. "Did you go to your support group meeting?"

"I see you talked to Ben. Is nothing private in our family?"

She laughs. "Come on, Sophia, you already know the answer to that. So, did you go? How was it?"

"Do you guys do it?" I blurt out. "There was a woman there who said it took two years after she had her baby for her and her husband to have sex again."

"I've heard worse," Aurora replies calmly. "It took us six months after Dawn."

My mouth falls open. "Really?"

"Think about it, Soph. I pushed a baby out of my vagina. Dawn was the size of a pumpkin when she was born. There was tearing. There was leakage. Nobody tells you that part because if they did, women wouldn't put themselves through it. I didn't feel right for a very long time, and I certainly didn't feel sexy."

"Oh."

"But it doesn't have to be the same for you," she says. "You could have an entirely different experience. And anyway, why are you worrying about this? Are you really that interested in sex? The only time you mention guys is to complain about them."

I blink in confusion. "Of course, I'm interested in sex. I love it."

Am I lying? Is Aurora right? Sex is nice, and it is pleasant, but the only time it's ever really blown my mind...

Was the night I had a threesome with Damien and Julian.

Fuck.

"You do?" Her voice is dubious. "If you say so."

"Felicity said that every guy she's gone out with thinks she's looking for a father for her child."

"You know what you need? A fuck buddy."

"What?"

"Do I have to explain the concept to you? Friends with benefits. Netflix and chill. Forget dating. Go on Tindr and find yourself a boy toy."

"How do you know about Tindr?" I demand, laughing despite myself. "Aren't you a happily married woman?"

"Of course I am. But I don't live under a rock." I hear a shrill shriek in the background. My niece is home. Sure enough, Aurora says, "Soph, I have to go. JP and Dawn are here. See you Sunday?"

I don't want to go on the Internet to find a sexual partner. I want good sex, and despite what Aurora might think, that's not easy to find.

You already know where you can get good sex. No, not good. Great sex.

Never going to happen.

I POUR myself a glass of wine after dinner. I light some candles and run a bath. Sinking into the steaming hot water is a blissful contrast to the cool night air that blows in through the window.

Then I close my eyes and allow myself to fantasize about Julian and Damien.

They're naked. Julian's hair is tousled. He's taken off his glasses, and I can see the heat in his eyes. He positions me on the bed so I'm on my back with my head tilted backward, and then his cock is at my lips.

I open them, and he slides into my mouth. His hands squeeze my breasts and pinch my nipples, setting me alight with desire. He grunts in pleasure as I swallow, my throat bobbing on his length.

Damien spreads my legs wide. He dips his head between them, zooming unerringly to my clit. "If you're good tonight," he says, his voice smooth as silk, "You can have both of us." He thrusts two fingers into my dripping pussy. "Whose cock do you want in here?"

His thumb glides over my anus. A shiver of anticipation wracks my body. "And whose cock do you want here?" He pushes in, and my muscle yields. I whimper. "Tell me, Sophia."

Memories fade and blur, and try as I might to forget, I remember everything about that night. Every whispered promise. Every growled order. My fingers glide down my body. I spread my folds and trace a soft circle over my clit, shivering despite the heat of the water.

"I can't decide," I remember whispering.

"You can't?" Julian said, his expression wickedly amused. Then he wrapped a blindfold over my eyes so I couldn't see. A cock thrust into my pussy, and another speared my ass. With my vision cut off, I could only feel.

My body throbs with the memory. My fingers move over my clit, faster and harder. My wine is forgotten. The water cools. None of that matters. I chase my pleasure with ruthless focus, and then I'm tipping over the edge.

They would be good fuck buddies. Really good.

Oh please, the practical side of my brain scoffs. *Damien got you fired. At the fundraiser, Julian didn't even come and say hello.*

But in the aftermath of my orgasm, I find it hard to summon up the same ire that I felt as recently as yesterday.

I clean up the bathroom and take myself to bed. Sleep has almost claimed me when an unpleasant thought jerks me awake. I was supposed to work on the curriculum tonight, and I didn't.

And my first lesson with Damien is tomorrow.

10

JULIAN

Shaun had not been exaggerating. The team that bought *Revenant* is *extremely* eager to get going. Thursday evening, I fly to Los Angeles, and Friday, I have lunch with the producer, Kyle Donovan. He's accompanied by another man he introduces as Francisco Flores.

Donovan is enthusiastically, embarrassingly happy to meet me. "I am a huge fan of your work," he says. "Have been for years, ever since *Kingdom Night*."

Kingdom Night was my first breakout comic. Kyle Donovan might or might not be a fan, but he's done his research. I'm impressed and more than a little flattered. "Thank you," I mumble.

"It's a pity Shaun couldn't be here," he continues. "But don't worry, I'm not going to discuss contracts today. I really just wanted to meet you and introduce you to Francisco."

It turns out that Francisco Flores is a well-known screenwriter. "I want the two of you to work together," Kyle says. "Francisco will take your vision and translate it for the screen, but Julian, I want you to be involved. No, more than that. I want you to be in charge."

I happen to catch the look on Flores' face when Donovan says that. He's clearly not thrilled by the idea.

While I wait for my flight back home at the airport, I call Shaun and ask him about the arrangement. "I looked up Flores. He's an experienced screenwriter, but Donovan seems to want me to be in charge. Is it typical?"

"Usually, no," Shaun replies, confirming my suspicions. "Only the really big-name writers get a say in the script. If you're J.K. Rowling, if you're E.L. James, you can have an opinion. Everyone else, no. And that's a good thing, trust me. After all, you wouldn't take advice from Donovan on how to make a comic."

"So why am I even involved?"

"Because Kyle Donovan wants you to be, and he's the producer."

This has disaster written all over it. "Shaun, I don't think Francisco Flores is looking forward to this collaboration."

"It is what it is. Work with him and don't make waves. Francisco might be annoyed, but he's a professional. He'll get over it."

The film company paid for my flight, but they put me in coach. Donovan might be a fan, but he's not wasteful of his money. Normally, I'd pay for the upgrade, but with my house needing extensive maintenance, I hold off. It was fine on the way to LA, but the return journey is hell. The plane is packed, and unfortunately, I get stuck in the middle seat. I'm six feet tall, and there is no legroom.

And when I get back home, I find that there's been a freak storm in my absence. I covered the roof with a tarp, but it wasn't enough. The hothouse floor is dotted with puddles of water.

There won't be any tile removal today, not until I get this floor mopped.

I've just started the shop vac when Hannah calls. "Hey Julian," she says cheerfully. "I know we talked about doing the wedding at the house, but I wanted to check in and see if you're still good with it."

"Yes, of course."

"Because I was talking to Jamila," she continues. "You remember her, don't you? She still lives in Highfield. I asked her to be my maid of honor, and we got to talking. She was pretty surprised when I told her where I was getting married."

Crap.

"She said the house wasn't in great shape. She called it a wreck."

I run my hand over my face as I think about how to respond. "It's not in the best of shape, no," I say carefully. "But I have a plan. I thought we could have the wedding in the greenhouse. It's a big, bright space, and it's large enough to accommodate your guests."

"Oh, I like that idea," she exclaims. "We used to feed the fish there, remember? And it's in good condition?"

Far from it. "It needs some maintenance," I hedge. "But the damage isn't too extensive." *Lie.* "I'm looking for a contractor, but even if I can't find one, I don't have a lot going on right now. I have time to work on it myself."

Another lie.

"I trust you," she says. "You'll handle it. But you have to tell me what it costs, Julian. If you're renovating the place because of my wedding, I should pay for it."

I have no idea where her faith in me comes from, but I'm determined not to let her down. As for me sending her a bill? Yeah, that's never going to happen.

I make a noncommittal noise. Thankfully, Hannah's in wedding-planning mode, and she doesn't register it. "Can I come take a look at it?" she asks. "Samir's sister Priya is a florist, and she's offered to do the flowers for the wedding. I promised I sent her some pictures of the space."

If my sister sees the greenhouse in the shape it's in right now, she's going to hold her wedding somewhere else. I cannot disappoint her. I need to buy myself some time.

"I have a deadline," I lie. Again. "It's going to keep me busy for the next few weeks. How about the second week of October?"

That'll give me just over five weeks. It's not a lot of time, especially with the developments around *Revenant*. But hopefully, it's long enough that I can fix the worst of the mess.

Once Hannah hangs up, I look around the hothouse again. This time, without rose-tinted glasses. Then I get on the phone with Damien.

"Julian, it is eight in the morning on a Saturday, for fuck's sake."

Ouch. So it is. Hannah must have gotten an early start on her day. "Sorry."

"What's the matter?"

"Are you doing anything today?" I ask him. "I need your help."

11

SOPHIA

I have to cancel on Damien on Thursday. We have to make the formal offer for our building, and Patricia wants me to go with her. "I'd like someone to double-check the paperwork," she says. Her lips twist into a wry smile. "Also, if I'm being honest, I'd like you there for moral support. I didn't think this day would ever come."

Me neither.

Damien is not as annoyed as I expect him to be. I stammer out my apologies, and he listens to me patiently. "Okay," he says when I'm done. "When do you want to meet instead?"

He's been in town for a full week already, which means he only has three weeks left. I don't have a plan yet. I have no idea what to teach him.

And you're acting like this class is a real thing. Like Damien really wants you to teach him to be a better person. You're acting like this is not some kind of weirdly twisted game that he's playing.

"How about this weekend? I have plans on Sunday, but I'm free on Saturday."

"Hot date?" he asks. "I never did ask if you were seeing someone."

It's none of his damn business if I'm dating someone or not. I should be irritated by his question. *But I'm not.*

"I have dinner with my family on Sundays." My grip on my phone tightens. "What about you?"

I hold my breath as I wait for his answer, scolding myself at the same time. Why does it matter if Damien is seeing someone? Or worse, if he's married? It shouldn't matter. He's a part of my past, and that's where he needs to remain.

"No, I'm not," he replies. "Not married, not engaged, not seeing someone."

I release the breath I didn't know I was holding. *Why not?* I want to ask, but that would be incredibly nosy, and despite what I told Patricia, Damien is not my friend. "Okay, I'll see you Saturday. How about ten?"

"As long as you pour a couple cups of coffee into me when you get here, ten is fine."

I LEAVE work early on Friday to do the second part of my fertility test. This one is a specialized ultrasound. A technician rolls a condom on a wand, smears it with lube, and pushes it into my vagina. She then proceeds to poke and prod me for almost an hour. It's not painful, but it's definitely not comfortable.

She hands me a box of wipes when the exam is complete. "When will I get the results?" I ask.

"Next week," she replies. She gives me an encouraging smile. "I didn't see anything concerning. You should be able to get started right away."

Relief spreads through me. I've been more nervous about this examination than I was willing to admit. The women in the support group shared so many horror stories about how difficult this process had been for them. I've been trying hard not to think about what will happen if I can't get pregnant. Dr. Hernandez might talk about multiple rounds of treatments, but I can't really afford years of trying and failing.

Maybe I won't have to face that. "No cobwebs down there?" I quip, relief loosening my tongue.

The joke goes over her head. "What?"

I wince. She's an older woman, and her expression right now reminds me faintly of Mrs. Caldwell. "Nothing," I murmur. "Thank you."

I PROMISED myself that I'd spend Friday night coming up with a game plan for Damien, but once again, I get nowhere. I google 'How to be a Better Person,' and the first thing that comes up is a list of fifteen suggestions. Two of those catch my eye.

Let go of anger.

Practice forgiveness.

Ouch. Maybe I'm finding this so difficult because Damien is actually quite a good person. He wrote the health center a check for a million dollars, didn't he? When I knew him, he always treated everyone around him with impeccable politeness. He never did anything to make me think he wasn't a decent person.

Maybe I wasn't fair to him at the fundraiser. Maybe he's right, and he didn't get me fired. Besides, I'm the one who avoided their phone calls. I'm the one who ignored their voicemails and deleted their texts.

Simon gets home unexpectedly early. I'm curled up on the couch in a pair of faded shorts and a T-shirt that has seen better days. "It's done," he says, a wide smile on his face. "99 Canter Lane is finally done. The homeowners did their final walk-through today. They love it, thank fuck. I will never have to see that damn house again." He looks down at me. "Get changed, Soph. We're celebrating."

Introspection is uncomfortable, and Simon looks so happy I tell myself I can't turn him down. We go out to our local bar and end up running into some of his friends. A new escape room has opened up in Gracemont, and they want to try it. One drink becomes three. By the time we get back home, I'm fighting to keep my eyes open, and it's far too late for lesson plans.

Shit.

Saturday, I'm supposed to meet Damien at ten in the morning. I call him at nine-thirty. "I don't have anything," I admit, my cheeks hot with shame. "I'm sorry. It's been a stressful week. I'm not blowing you off, I promise."

I wait for him to make a joke about me blowing him off, but it doesn't happen. Good. I tell myself I'm glad.

"However," I continue. "The community garden always needs volunteers. It's not the best idea I have, but—"

"If you don't mind getting your hands dirty," he interrupts. "I have a suggestion."

"You do?"

"Julian is renovating his house, and he's running a little behind. Helping a friend, that's supposed to make me a better person, right? I thought I'd go over and pitch in. Want to join me?"

I try to picture the elegant, suave Damien Cardenas with a screwdriver in his hand. My imagination is not that good. "Have you ever done anything like this?" I ask him. "Do you know how to use a power tool?"

Okay, fine. I admit I'm deliberately baiting him. I want

him to murmur something about how good he is with his hands. How he's never had any complaints about his power tool, and since I appear to have forgotten, would I like a reminder?

Once again, he doesn't react to the innuendo. *Not at all.* "Oh, no," he admits cheerfully. "I'm completely clueless. Julian knows what he's doing, more or less, and I'm going to be manual labor. As long as I get back with my fingers and toes intact, I consider it a win."

God, he can be so charming. The wry, self-deprecating note in his voice. The ready acknowledgment that he doesn't know what he's doing. It's so *maddeningly* attractive that I want to strangle him.

Admit it. You want to go over. You want to see them again. Both of them. You want to see Julian and Damien with their shirts off, dripping with sweat, reaching for you, closing the distance between our bodies...

I slam the door shut on that train of thought. "It's a good thing I'm reasonably handy then," I tease. "Someone has to keep you from getting into trouble."

He laughs. "Yes, Julian mentioned that you renovated your house. Are you in, then?"

They discussed me? Pleasure fills me, followed rapidly by curiosity. Why were they talking about me? What did they discuss, and what does it mean?

"Yes. Yes, I'm in."

12

DAMIEN

What the fuck am I doing?

Ever since I found out how hard Sophia's life became after being fired, I've been consumed with guilt. And yes, I know it's not rational. But Sophia was important to me, and I can't help feeling like I let her down.

She *is* important to me. And that's the rub, isn't it? One look at her, and I can't stop remembering that night. I can't stop wondering what my life would've been like had we not gone our separate ways. I can't stop wondering what my life would be like if she were a part of it.

I *want* her.

But if there's to be anything between us, I have to end this arrangement. I was so annoyed at the fundraiser that when I told her to teach me how to be a better human being, I was mostly being snide. Julian called it a dumb idea from the start, and he was right. I cannot have Sophia feeling beholden to me. The million-dollar gift to the community center needs to be just that. A gift. No strings attached.

She called me Thursday morning, asking if she could reschedule. I should have called off the whole thing then, but I hadn't. Something stopped me from uttering the words.

I know why I've kept silent. If I tell her to forget about this class, then there's nothing holding us together. Nothing connecting us. We'll have no reason to keep in touch, and I might never see her again. She lives in Highfield, and I don't.

Julian lives in Highfield.

That thought sends an unexpected stab of jealousy through me.

A threesome is a funny thing. Ten years ago, I suggested it to Sophia on a whim. She'd obviously been interested in Julian and me, and I was open to seeing where it went. I didn't really think it through.

Now though? I'm ten years older. I've seen more of life. A few of my friends are in polyamorous relationships. Brody, Adrian, and Fiona have been together for a couple of years. Maddox and Kai are involved with Avery, and Hunter and Eric are with Dixie. The older I get, the more I understand it. Relationships come in all shapes and sizes. The configuration isn't as important as the bond that holds them together.

I had dinner with Hunter, Eric, and Dixie last night. It's a new relationship, but it was obvious that the three of them were a team. It wasn't like there was a primary couple, and the third person was an add-on. The three of them were completely, irrevocably, *together.*

The idea of both Julian and me being in a relationship with Sophia doesn't bother me. But if the two of them started dating, it would.

And you can cross that bridge when you come to it.

She calls me Saturday morning, and I have an opportunity to call off the whole arrangement. Once again, I don't do it. Instead, I ask if she wants to help Julian out.

The three of us haven't been alone together in a very long time.

What do I think is going to happen? What do I *hope* will happen?

I remember what Julian said to me at the fundraiser. *You're generally sensible, but every so often, you do something profoundly stupid.*

I really hate when he's right.

13

SOPHIA

Damien gives me his address. At ten, I pull into his driveway. I don't know what I expect his lake house to look like, but if I had to guess, it would be large and grand.

This is neither. The view of the lake is spectacular, but the two-story brick house looks cozy and welcoming. Large planters flank the front door. The windows are thrown open, Reggaeton spills out and hang on. Is Damien singing along?

I *love* it.

He must hear me pull in because he opens the door before I knock. He's wearing faded jeans and a gray T-shirt that looks like it's been through the wash dozens of times. He looks good enough to eat. Hunger grips me. I want to pull down those jeans and wrap my lips around his cock. Right here, in the doorway.

How would he react? Would he be horrified? Or would heat flare in those dark eyes? Would his fingers tighten in my hair, would he tug me closer? Would he thrust down my throat and cum in my mouth, or would he erupt over my breasts and make me lick up the mess?

Where the hell did that come from?

I stopped on the way for coffee. Damien's eyebrows rise as I hand him a cup. "Should I be suspicious that you're being nice to me, Sophia?"

"You said you didn't really wake up before two cups of coffee. We're handling power tools today, aren't we? I figured it would be safer this way."

His lips quirk. "Thank you. I'd invite you inside, but we should go. Julian is wielding heavy machinery on less than three hours of sleep. Someone should probably keep an eye on him." He steps out and shuts the door. "Do you want to ride with me or follow along in your car?"

The sensible answer would be to follow him. That way, I'm not riding along with Damien. Damien Cardenas exudes sex appeal. Always has. The last time we'd been in the enclosed space, I'd been mad at him, and even so, I'd been only too aware of him. Now, when I'm a mix of confusion, regret, and horniness? Damien is my kryptonite.

And I've never been able to resist. "I'll ride with you."

If he's surprised by my answer, he doesn't show it. "Let's go."

Julian's house is huge. It's not as large as Xavier's castle, but there are turrets and rolling lawns, for heaven's sake. My mouth falls open as we pull up to the front. "This is where Julian lives?"

Damien turns off the engine. "Let me guess, you've driven past this place dozens of times, but you thought it was abandoned."

"Pretty much, yes." This place doesn't seem to be Julian's style. Then again, what do I know? The night we were together, we didn't exactly discuss our architectural preferences. We had hot, raw, passionate sex. "It's just Julian here? This is a lot of house for one person."

He gives me a sidelong glance. "Are you asking if Julian is single? The answer is yes."

My cheeks heat. I was probing, true, but I thought I was subtle about it. Damien saw right through me. "Julian's father died last year and left the family home to him." He grimaces. "Julian hates this house."

"Why?"

"The short version is that Julian's parents weren't the nicest people. His plan was to fix it up and sell it, but he just hasn't had any time to work on the place. His father left things in quite a mess, and Julian has spent much of the last eight months juggling his work, his father's estate, and basic maintenance."

Ouch. Poor Julian. I've been there. Simon, Andre, and I worked on our house every spare moment we got, making it into a warm and welcoming home. There had been three of us, and Simon was a professional, but it had still been exhausting.

"You said on the phone that Julian was running behind. Does he have a buyer? Is that why there's a deadline?"

"No, Julian's sister Hannah wants to get married here. It's a Christmas wedding."

I open my mouth to tell him that that's just four months away, but it's not as if he doesn't know that. "Has Julian thought about hiring a contractor?" I assume he can afford it, but maybe I'm wrong.

"Trust me, he's tried. Finding a contractor in Highfield seems impossible. Julian tells me he's left messages for fifteen different contractors in the last week. Only two have called him back."

Yikes. I wonder if Simon was one of them. I have to get my brother to check his messages.

"Anyway," Damien says, opening his door. "The wedding is in the greenhouse, so that's what we're working on. Shall we?"

Julian opens the front door, a harried expression on his face. "Thank fuck you're here," he says. "I'm still drying the place out. Stupid freak storm." Then he catches sight of me, and surprise flashes over his face. "Sophia, what are you doing here?" He winces. "Ouch, that sounded rude. Let me rephrase that."

I have to laugh. "I'm not offended. I'm teaching Damien how to be a better person, remember?"

"And that involves pulling up tile?" he asks dryly. "Tough class. Come on in."

The foyer makes me gasp. I step inside and am greeted by two curving marble staircases. A glass chandelier drops from the soaring ceiling. Once upon a time, it would have looked magnificent. Now, the marble is stained yellow, and cobwebs drape the dull crystals of the chandelier. It still takes my breath away.

Julian catches sight of my face. "I know, it's ridiculous," he comments. "My great-great-grandfather built this house. Probably so all his neighbors could see how important he was." His lips quirk. "He named it Kincaid Castle. He had delusions of grandeur." He leads the way through sparsely furnished rooms to a side entrance. We're moving too quickly for me to gawk, but the impression I get is that the home is largely empty of furniture. "It's too large," he continues. "The roof leaks, the place is impossible to heat in the winter, and there's no hot water." He opens the door to the outside, and we step onto a curved pathway. "And then there's the infamous greenhouse."

I stare at the large glass building in front of me. The space is massive, easily five thousand square feet. It is bigger than my house, for crying out loud. "Oh, wow."

"My mother liked to garden," he says. "There were always roses here, even in the dead of winter."

"I love roses," I murmur absently as we step inside. Part of me is wondering if I can talk Simon into installing a greenhouse in our backyard. The other part of me is horrified at how much work Julian will have to do to get this place wedding-ready. The floor tiles are cracked and chipped. Multiple glass panes are broken. Radiators line the insides of the walls, but they look like they're a hundred years old. "When's your sister's wedding again?" I ask, even though I know perfectly well what the answer is.

"December." Julian runs his hand through his hair, his expression wary. "It's an aggressive timeline, I know."

Aggressive? Think impossible. I'm not an expert by any means. Simon is the contractor in the family, but even I know that one person can't do this in four months. Of course, Julian probably knows it too. So, I give him a bright smile rather than rub it in. "What's the plan for the day?"

"Finish prying up the floor tiles," he replies. "And, if there's still enough time left, take it to the dump. I need to get the tile off to look at the underfloor heating. It isn't working, and I have a guy coming on Monday to deal with it. Fingers crossed, I won't also have to bust open the concrete slab underneath."

"That's how the space is heated? The radiators plus the underfloor heating?"

He nods. "There's a boiler for the greenhouse and one

for the house. The one for the house works sporadically. This one hasn't worked in a long time."

We put underfloor heating in our bathrooms. It's so nice. Nothing is more luxurious than a warm floor in the middle of winter.

"Okay, bust up the tile," Damien says cheerfully. "Got it. What do you want me to do?"

Julian glances at me. "Sophia, this is messy work. Damien volunteered, but if you don't—"

"Julian," I interrupt. "I'm here to help, and unlike Damien, I even know what I'm doing. Do you have a spare set of safety glasses and some earplugs?"

His eyes hold mine for a long instant. "Thank you," he says softly, his expression warm. "Yes, there's safety gear in the kitchen. Where there's also a pot of coffee and a box of donuts." He gives his friend an amused glance. "Get your caffeine fix in. It's going to be a long day."

DAMIEN WASN'T LYING when he said he didn't know what he was doing. But he's a quick learner. He watches Julian operate the tile breaker, his expression focused. He tries it once, adjusts what he's doing, and then has the hang of it. It's *deeply* annoying.

I find it unexpectedly relaxing working with my hands. I've been so stressed the last few weeks. The threat to the health center and long hours spent on the phone and hunched in front of my computer have taken a toll on me. Now add in the appointments at the fertility clinic and the meeting with the support group, and I feel ready to burst.

Scraping tiles off the floor is cathartic.

Damien and Julian talk while they work. They've been friends for a long time, and it shows in their banter and the good-natured insults they throw at each other. I see sides of both men I haven't seen before.

It only makes them hotter.

The work is messy and dusty, and it does nothing to quench my inconvenient lust. I am incredibly aware of the two men as I work all day. Aware and attracted. I notice them move. I home in on every smile. My nerves tingle to life when their gaze rests on me.

The physical labor feels like foreplay.

I tried to remember why it would be a bad idea to fall into bed with them, but all the reasons I listed earlier elude me. All I hear is Aurora's voice telling me, "You should have sex."

On Wednesday next week, Dr. Hernandez will discuss my fertility test results with me. If everything looks good, I pick a sperm donor, obtain vials of semen, and then we're off to the races. Even if my follicle count is low, Dr. Hernandez has assured me that I can take drugs to increase my fertility.

Soon, I'm going to be a hormonal mess. I have a short window here. There is a clock, and it's ticking. And Damien is only in town for a month.

What's the harm, really?

EIGHT HOURS OF MESSY, exhausting work later, it's done. My nails are caked with dirt, my T-shirt is covered with dust, but every last tile has been pried up. "Thank you," Julian says, his voice vibrating with sincerity. "Thank you both so much. I can't even tell you how grateful I am, but please, let me buy you dinner. It's the least I can do."

Damien tilts his head to the side. "Sophia?" he asks. "I'm your ride. What would you like to do?"

I don't want this day to be over. Well, I do want the hard physical labor part of the day to be over—every muscle in my body aches—but I'm not ready to leave. All-day, anticipation has been building up inside me. To leave now would be anticlimactic.

"I never say no to a free meal." I glance down at myself. I'm a mess. We all are. "Then again, I can't go out looking like this. Maybe we should get pizza again?"

"May I suggest an alternative?" Damien says. "Why don't we head back to my place? We can shower, get cleaned up, and I can put a couple of burgers on the barbecue." He flashes me a grin. "Unlike Julian, I have hot water."

Julian makes a face. "It's a wreck, I know."

"Don't let him give you grief," I tell Julian. "It's not easy juggling a job and renovations. It took us a full year to fix our house."

Damien's offer hangs in the air. Dinner with them. The three of us, alone in his home. Nobody else around. Nobody to stop me from my impulses. Would we open a bottle of wine? Undoubtedly. Knowing what I do of Damien, it'll be something delicious. I'll drink a glass or two, and then what?

There is food in my refrigerator. I should decline his offer and go home.

But I don't.

I take a deep breath and commit to the evening. I acknowledge my desire instead of denying it. For the first time, I admit I want this. I want *them*. I want to be open to the possibilities that scent the air we breathe. I want to see what might happen between the three of us.

"Let's do it."

14

SOPHIA

Damien and I ride together on the way back. Julian elects to follow us in his truck.

For a few moments, we sit in silence. I'm finding it difficult not to stare at him. It's dusk, and we're still rural enough that Damien has to watch out for stray deer. Convenient for me. I keep sneaking looks over while his attention is on the road.

Are you doing this, then? If the opportunity presents itself, are you going to revisit the past?

I don't know what is wrong with me. Sometime in the last week, I have evidently decided that Damien getting me fired is no longer an issue. Seeing him again, I've finally been able to let it go.

And I really want to sleep with them again.

Maybe it's because of the soon-to-happen fertility treatments. Maybe it's an awareness that I'm running out of time. Or maybe the prospect of multiple years of celibacy has me throwing myself at the nearest available guy.

The nearest available guy? My subconscious scoffs at me.

If Matthew Barnes, your last blind date, was here, would you sleep with him?

Okay, fine. I reluctantly admit that it's not any available man I want. It's these men.

I sneak another look at Damien. He's not wearing his sunglasses any longer. His left hand is on the steering wheel, and his right hand is on the gear stick, even though the car has an automatic transmission. "Are you used to driving a manual transmission car?" I guess.

"Yes. Is it that obvious?"

Only if you're paying very close attention. "My car has manual transmission as well," I tell him. "I like stick shifts."

It's a perfect opening for Damien to respond with some sexual innuendo. Surely there's enough to work with there. A quip about how I enjoy stroking a shaft, maybe? Something, anything.

But he doesn't react. *Again.*

God, this is cringe-worthy. I'm being so fucking obvious, and he's politely ignoring it. Is he even interested in me? I thought he was. When we had lunch at Taco Gus, I would have sworn that he would be quite happy to pick up where we left off.

But ever since then, he's pulled away.

And Julian? Julian's even more of a closed book. I have no idea what he's thinking.

If I want them, I'm going to have to make the first move. And the thought of putting myself out there, leaving myself open to rejection, makes me want to break out into hives.

Ugh.

THE INSIDE of Damien's lake house is comfortable, cozy, and welcoming. An oversized sectional in the high-ceilinged living room faces a window offering a spectacular view of the lake. The kitchen is brightly lit, open concept, and surprisingly colorful. Buttercup yellow cabinets and a turquoise tiled backsplash provide a cheerful contrast to the stainless-steel appliances. On the other side of the room, six blue chairs surround a somewhat battered dining table.

Everything here was chosen for comfort. It's not what I expected at all. But the moment I see it, I know that no matter where Damien lives—whether it's Peru or Manhattan or Hong Kong or Toronto—this is his refuge. This is his home.

"You want to shower before dinner?" he asks me.

"Yes, please."

"I'll find you a towel. Julian, you know your way around."

Damien leads the way up a flight of stairs. Family photos line the wall. I don't have time to take them in—he's moving too fast for that—but one thing is obvious. The Cardenas are a good-looking family. Everyone is drop-dead gorgeous.

Nothing to feel insecure about here. *Nothing at all.*

The stairs end in a landing. Damien turns left and stops in front of a closed door. "Can we talk for a moment?"

He has an uncharacteristically serious look on his face. My heart starts to race. I wipe my suddenly sweaty palms on my jeans. "Sure?"

"At your fundraiser, you said you weren't going to sleep with me."

"Yes," I whisper. How could I forget that conversation? His response is etched in my memory. *Do you really believe I think so little of you?*

"I deeply regret what I did," he says quietly. "I shouldn't have made my donation to the health center conditional on you teaching me how to become a better person." He takes a deep breath. "There have been times in the last couple of days when I've thought. . ." His voice trails off. "The money is the health center's to use as it sees fit. No conditions, no strings attached. I would like to see more of you, Sophia, but only if you want to as well."

"Oh." My head spins. "Okay?" He quirks an eyebrow at my reaction. "Should I leave?"

He blinks. "Do you want to go?" He takes a step toward me, closing the distance between us. His voice dips lower. "Because it doesn't seem like it. Unless I'm reading your signals all wrong?"

So Damien has noticed I've tried to flirt with him. I swallow hard. His nearness is melting my mind. "I should shower," I stammer.

"Of course." He throws open the door, the beginnings of a smile tipping the corners of his mouth. "Guest bedroom," he says in explanation. "There's an attached bathroom." He vanishes for a moment and returns with a folded towel. "If you'd like, I can put your clothes in the wash."

My brain takes in the bed and short-circuits. My mind fills with images of the three of us, bodies naked, limbs entwined. It takes me a moment to focus on Damien's words. "But then I'd have nothing to wear," I say stupidly.

He chuckles, warm and smooth and oh-so-sexy. "You can borrow one of my shirts." His eyes sweep over me, and I feel his gaze like a touch. My heart jolts, and my pulse pounds. "Do you want to hand them to me?"

The air around me seems electrified. I remember this feeling from ten years ago. I felt the same excruciating mix of awareness and anticipation when I followed Damien to Club M.

And now? He's waiting, watching me with an unreadable expression in his eyes. I almost open my mouth to ask if he wants me to undress in front of him but stop myself. What the hell am I doing? This is madness. I'm having a temporary attack of insanity.

"Give me a second." I dart past the bed into the attached bathroom and shut the door. I strip naked and open the door a crack, just wide enough to hand him my jeans and T-shirt. "Here you go."

His laughter is soft and knowing. I hold my breath, almost giddy with lust, but he doesn't say anything. After a long moment, I hear his footsteps recede.

THE SHOWER IS BLISSFUL, and I linger under the hot water for a long time. I come downstairs, my hair damp and only dressed in Damien's white linen shirt, to see it's just Julian in the kitchen.

He takes in what I'm wearing, and his eyes flare with heat. I haven't bothered with a bra, and his gaze lands on my chest. My nipples start to pebble. My mouth goes dry, and I instinctively take a step toward him.

He drags his eyes back to my face. "Damien had a work emergency," he says. "He promised to be quick."

"A work emergency? It's Saturday night."

"We're talking about Damien Cardenas," Julian responds. "He doesn't have an off button." He holds up a bottle of wine. "Would you like something to drink?"

I'm not exactly a lightweight, but I don't like to drink and drive, even if I've only had one glass of wine. It's just not worth the risk. If I take Julian up on his offer, I'm either spending the night here or, at the very least, I'm staying for a very long time.

It would be more sensible to drink water.

Except I don't want to leave.

"Wine sounds good."

He pours me a glass. "I want to talk to you about something," he says.

Not Julian too. I'm still reeling from Damien's declaration earlier. "Umm, okay?"

The smile that ghosts over his lips doesn't quite reach his eyes. "There's chemistry between you and Damien, and I don't want to make any assumptions based on something that happened a decade ago. Do you want me to leave?"

Whatever I thought he was going to say, this wasn't it. We had lunch earlier this week. Did he not notice the way I was staring at his naked chest? I've masturbated to him spilling marinara on himself. Except in my fantasies, it's chocolate, and I lick it off him.

A wave of uncertainty washes over me. "Do you want to go?"

"What I want doesn't matter."

Huh? What's this about? "Of course it does," I reply, puzzled. Julian might be quieter than Damien, but he's never struck me as the shy, retiring type. At Club M, he was the more dominant of the two. He was the one with the fiendish imagination. The one who tied me up, spread my legs wide, put a vibrator between my legs, set an hourglass in front of my face, and told me that I had to hold back my orgasm until the sand had fallen to the lower bulb. What's changed now? "Why do you think your needs aren't important?"

He doesn't meet my gaze. He chops a tomato with swift, efficient strokes and then moves on to a cucumber, dicing it into squares. It's clear that he knows his way around a kitchen.

It's also clear he's not going to answer my question.

"I don't want you to go."

He looks up. "Are you sure? There's a lot of chemistry between you and Damien."

Okay, that's quite enough of that. He's being remarkably dense for some reason, and if I have to hit him on the head with it, I will. I don't want one or the other. Call me greedy, but I want both. "Julian, I don't enjoy ripping up tile, and yet, I spent all day doing it. Also, in case it wasn't obvious, we had lunch, and I couldn't stop staring when you took off your shirt."

His lips quirk. "It was a little obvious."

"Let's call it what it was. I was drooling. I want to have dinner with Damien *and* you." I want a lot more than that. *I want them.* My cheeks are on fire. I'm going to need a glass of water to cool off. A bucket.

Damien comes downstairs at that moment. He's showered too. He's wearing a pair of gray linen shorts and a black T-shirt. His eyes travel from Julian to me. "Is everything okay?"

"Everything's fine," Julian replies calmly. "Shall we eat? There are French fries in the air fryer, burgers on the barbecue, and I just have to dress the salad."

"How long was I gone for?" Damien asks ruefully. "Never mind, don't tell me. Sophia, can I get you a drink?"

I hold up my half-empty glass of wine. "Already have one."

Damien smiles slowly. "Well then. I'll have to hurry if I'm going to catch up."

WE EAT DINNER OUTSIDE. The light is waning, a gentle breeze blows in off the lake, and the view of the sunset is spectacular. Not that I really look. My attention—my focus—is on Julian and Damien.

There are a lot of long, lingering looks exchanged during the meal. Our fingers brush. Under the table, our knees collide. We make conversation, but if you ask me what we talked about, I couldn't tell you.

The night grows darker. One glass of wine becomes two. Like I said before, I'm not a lightweight. It's not the alcohol that's making me feel fluttery and breathless. It's them.

My body trembles in painful anticipation.

After dinner, I offer to help Damien with the dishes, but he declines. Julian and I end up in the living room while Damien clears up. He pours the last of the wine into my glass and then sprawls on the sectional. He looks relaxed, but there's a predatory gleam in his eyes that sets my heart racing. "Come here, Sophia," he says, patting his lap.

"Oh God, yes," I blurt out. "I thought you'd never ask."

He chuckles softly. "You know what I like about you? You're not coy. You're never coy. It's refreshing."

I could tell him that women are coy because when they express their desires, society calls them sluts. Then again, I actually want to get laid tonight, so instead of saying something indignant about the patriarchy, I move closer to Julian.

He tugs me onto his lap.

Damien looks up. "Should I leave?"

Not this again. "What is the matter with the two of you?" I demand. "First, Julian asks if he should go, and now it's you. Do I have to spell it out?"

It was a rhetorical question, and I didn't expect Damien to answer, but he does. "The last time we had a threesome, you stopped talking to us. You wouldn't pick up your phone. Sure, I could have found you, and Julian could have as well. But there's a fine line between persistence and stalking, and I would never want to make you uncomfortable. For ten years, I thought the reason you disappeared was that you regretted what we did." His eyes are on mine. "This time, I don't want to make any mistakes."

Julian strokes my neck as Damien talks. Heat coils through my core as his fingers tangle in my hair. His touch is maddeningly light, and I want more. So much more. There's no point pretending I don't want them because I do. My nipples are hard, my pussy is wet, and I *ache* for them.

I force my brain to cooperate. "But now you know it wasn't the threesome. That's not why I avoided you."

"I do," Damien agrees.

Julian undoes one of my shirt buttons. His fingers brush my nipples through the fabric. I bite back my moan and lean into his touch. "More," I whisper. "Please..."

Damien's still in the kitchen. What the hell is he waiting for, a handwritten invitation? "Are you going to join us, or are you just going to watch?"

He *finally* moves. "Fuck the dishes," he replies, stalking over to the couch. His smile turns hungry, *feral*. "I want to watch," he growls. "I want to participate. I want *everything*."

I tilt my head back and look up at Damien. The air between us is charged with tension. For a long moment, he stares at me as if he can't quite believe I'm here, and then his lips crash into mine.

Oh fuck yes.

He kisses me as if he can't get enough of me. As if he's been wandering the desert, and I'm his oasis. I've seen Damien's dominant side. This is something else. This is predatory in the best possible way. This is a claiming.

He nibbles my lower lip and licks the seam, demanding entrance. I open my mouth with a hum of pleasure, and his tongue slides in as if he *belongs* there.

Every nerve in my body is ablaze. A shiver runs through

me. I sit on one man's lap and kiss another, and it's hot and filthy and perfect.

Julian unbuttons my shirt and spreads it open. His hands cup my aching breasts, squeezing them hard. He rolls my nipples between his fingers, and I arch in response and whimper into Damien's mouth.

Damien pulls back with a groan and surveys me with hot eyes. I'm not wearing a bra underneath the shirt, but I wasn't brave enough to forgo my panties. From the expression on his face and the way he's drinking me in, it doesn't seem to matter.

Then he looks up at Julian. "Can you hold her legs open?" he asks, his voice deliberately casual. His lips curve into a wicked grin. "From what I remember, she likes to clamp them shut when she's close."

He's speaking about me like I'm not there, and fuck me, that's hot. So hot I almost don't register his actual words. "You remember that about me?" I ask, shocked. It's been ten years, after all.

"I remember everything about that night," Damien responds. He tugs me closer, moves the coffee table out of the way, and kneels in front of me. Julian puts his hands on my thighs and spreads me open. Damien pushes my panties aside, and then...

And then his fingers part my folds. His mouth is on my pussy, and all thought flees my brain. Nothing is left except sensation and blistering hot pleasure.

Julian wraps his big, callused hand around my neck. Desire jolts up my spine. He's not squeezing my throat, and I trust him not to do anything that would put me in danger.

But if he wanted to, he could.

Is it messed up that that turns me on?

Damien's tongue laps my slit. "So wet already," he

breathes. He pulls his head back, watching me with an openly appreciative look on his face. "So fucking wet, and we've barely started."

With one finger, he slowly rubs circles around my swollen clit. A shudder of arousal runs through my body.

I moan softly, and Julian chuckles, his breath warm against my ear. "Damien wants to hear you scream," he murmurs. "But I think you should make him work for it." He tilts my head, and his lips find mine. His tongue slides into my mouth, and he swallows my moans.

"I'm up for the challenge," Damien replies, a thread of laughter running through his words. "Bring it on."

Again, oh fuck yes.

Damien yanks my panties down my hips. He bends his head back to my pussy, and his tongue works with a vengeance. He licks me and sucks my clit. I have to grit my teeth to keep from crying out. "Yes," I whimper into Julian's mouth. This is so hot. So filthy. "Don't stop—"

Julian's hands squeeze my breasts; his fingers pinch and pluck my nipples. He pulls away from my mouth long enough to ask a question. "How hard do you want it, Sophia?" he growls. "How rough do you want me to be?"

A shiver runs through me as I remember that night at the club. Julian might look easy-going and mild-mannered, but I learned at Club M that he has a wicked, twisted imagination.

And I loved *everything* he did to me. "Hard. Don't go easy on me."

He rubs an engorged nipple between his thumb and forefinger. "Like this?"

"More."

He squeezes harder, and delicious pain winds through my body. Damien thrusts two fingers into my dripping pussy, and I moan louder. His tongue... his fingers... A hot wave of arousal washes over me. He twists his fingers inside me, searching for my G-spot, and when he finds it, I nearly explode. My muscles clamp down on him. The sensations are exquisite.

Julian seems to decide I can keep my legs spread open on my own and transfers his attention to my breasts, his rough hands squeezing them. His fingers pinch my nipples, hard enough to make me gasp, soft enough to make me beg for more. Damien's tongue presses down on my clit, and I see stars.

A white haze of desire envelops me. Pleasure assaults me from every direction. I writhe on Julian's lap. I can feel his erection against my ass, and I grind on it, shameless in my need. I'm falling into a familiar, tight spiral. Each time Damien's clever tongue flicks my clit, relentless pressure builds inside of me.

"You want to come?" Julian demands. "Ask for permission."

My nerve endings are on fire. I am a river of need. Lust pounds through me, a relentless drumbeat. I can't hold this orgasm back. I cannot. I will shatter. "Please," I gasp. "I need—"

Damien adds a third finger, stretching me in an almost painful way. He sucks my clit between his teeth, and that pushes me over the edge. I barely hear Julian's voice telling me to come, and I explode.

I SLUMP against Julian's back, absolutely drained. It takes a few minutes before I can make myself move. I start to get up, and Julian's grip around my waist tightens. "Going somewhere?"

There's an unspoken question there. "I'm not leaving, if that's what you're asking me," I retort. "Damien just went down on me. I thought I should return the favor." I give him a cheeky grin. "Unless you don't want to wait your turn."

Julian's lips tilt up in a smile. There's a gleam in his eyes that bodes trouble for me. "Don't worry about me," he says, his tone innocent. "I can keep myself occupied."

"Why do I have a feeling you're planning something?"

Damien laughs out loud. He moves back to the couch, his cock straining against his trousers. "Because he is, Sophia." His eyes meet mine. "If you're up for it, that is."

I look at Julian. "What do you have in mind?"

He tilts his head and surveys me thoughtfully. "Some light bondage. Some sensation play. You can tell me to stop anytime you want, and I will."

I just came. I should be orgasmed out. But when Julian quirks his eyebrow at me, fresh heat curls through my body. "Sensation play," I whisper, my throat dry. "Like a riding crop?"

Damien shakes his head. "I don't have a collection of toys here," he says. "But Julian will undoubtedly improvise."

No collection of toys. Does that mean he doesn't bring women back here? I don't know why that thought fills me with pleasure. I shouldn't care what either of them does. We're not in a relationship; I have no business feeling possessive.

Julian's waiting for me to respond. Why am I even hesitating? There's not the slightest bit of doubt in my mind. I want this.

"Count me in."

His eyes gleam with anticipation. "Good," he says, lifting me off his lap and setting me on the couch. "Don't go anywhere. I'll be right back."

He disappears up the stairs, leaving me alone with Damien. The moment has the potential to get awkward, but Damien being Damien, doesn't let it. "Sophia," he says with a groan. "I'm having the world's biggest case of blue balls. Help me out here, baby."

A thrill shoots through me. "Are you telling me to suck you off?"

"I'm asking," he corrects. "Very nicely."

I slide off the couch and get on my knees. Damien kindly offers me a cushion, and I give him a suspicious look. "Why are you being nice?"

"I'm a considerate guy," he says, his lips twitching. He strips off his clothes, quickly and efficiently. I try not to drool as his thick erect cock bobs into view, but it's hard.

"Also," he continues. "You're going to have my cock in your mouth, and you have teeth. Best not to take any chances."

I giggle like a teenager. This feels so good. The orgasm was amazing, and, don't get me wrong, amazing orgasms are hard to find, but so is joking during sex. I don't know why I feel so comfortable with Damien and Julian. I don't know why I feel so safe with them.

But I do, and it was the same ten years ago.

I kneel on the cushion and settle between his legs, openly ogling his thick cock. He's leaned back on the couch, his big thighs splayed open, his erection jutting straight up. A drop of precum beads on the head, and I lick it up with the tip of my tongue.

Damien groans out loud. "Sophia," he grinds out. "You're killing me here."

The ragged edge in his voice makes me feel powerful. Makes me feel like a goddess. "Good." Then I lean forward and slowly, delicately, take him into my mouth.

He throws his head back. "Oh fuck yes," he hisses. "Do that again. Wrap your pretty lips around my cock."

I lick his head again like I'm licking an ice cream cone. "That sounded more like an order to me." I look up at him through my lashes. "I like when you order me around."

Heat flares in his eyes. "Is that so?" he says silkily. "I'll have to remember that." He wraps his hand around the back of my head and tugs me forward. "Now, Sophia."

He slides into my mouth. I open wide and take him deeper, tracing my tongue up his shaft before pulling back and trailing small kisses all over his length. Then, when his hips are thrusting in the air and his hands are fisted at his sides, I lick the underside from the base to the head and suck him in as deep as I can, hollowing my cheeks to increase the suction.

His breathing is shallow, uneven. His face is etched with arousal, and his hands grip my shoulders. He looks the way I feel. Feverish with lust, *undone* by it.

I hear footsteps. "Well, well," a low, intent voice says. "I see you couldn't wait."

Oh shit. *Julian.*

I whip my head free and stare at the other man.

Is he annoyed?

15

JULIAN

Sophia looks so startled that I have to fight not to laugh. I do my best to keep a poker face, but my amusement bubbles through.

"Oh," she says, relieved. "You're not mad."

I raise an eyebrow. "It's almost like you want me to be, Sophia. Is this a fantasy of yours, sweetheart? You want to get caught?" The excitement that flares in her eyes is answer enough. "You do, don't you? Bad girl."

I move closer to her. The shirt she's wearing is falling off her shoulders. I tug it free and toss it aside, drinking in her body.

She's so beautiful. Her blond hair falls to her waist in gentle waves. Her lips, wiped free of lipstick, are deliciously swollen. Her pink nipples are erect with need. Her pussy is dusted with blonde curls, and fuck me, I need to taste her.

But first, her fantasy.

"I *am* a bad girl," she whispers, a shiver running through her. "Are you going to punish me?"

"Oh, you're definitely going to get punished, baby. Put your hands behind your back."

She obeys. I pin her wrists in place and bind them together with Damien's silk tie. She tests the bindings experimentally, but I know what I'm doing, and she's not getting free of them anytime soon. Not unless she asks.

"You were sucking Damien's cock, weren't you?" I demand, twining my fingers through her hair and pushing her face toward his lap. "Did he give you permission to stop?"

She inhales sharply. "No, he didn't."

"What are you waiting for? Open your mouth and take it." I push her head forward so she's forced to swallow more of his length. My fingertips trail over her curves and move to her pussy. She's drenched. Hot and wet and fucking perfect, and fuck me, if I don't do something to distract myself, I'm going to shoot my load right here, right now.

She bobs on Damien's length. "Deeper," I order. "In fact. . ." I push the coffee table closer to the couch, lift Sophia up, and place her on it—stomach down with her round, delectable ass in the air. Half her body is on the coffee table, and the other half is in Damien's lap. Her hands are tied behind her back, and she can't hoist herself up. Gravity is pushing her mouth deeper onto Damien's erection.

And she's drenched.

"You like that, don't you?" I lightly graze my fingernails down her back before squeezing and spanking her ass. She moans in pleasure at the contact. "Do that again," she mumbles around a mouthful of cock. "Please."

"Ah, Sophia, you know you don't get to tell me what to do." I shove two fingers into her dripping pussy, and she whimpers and squirms. She's so fucking hot that I can't breathe. "Do you like that?"

"Fuck, yes," she hisses.

Damien has his head thrown back, his eyes clenched

shut. I lick Sophia's juices off my fingers and spank her again, a little harder this time. How stupid were we ten years ago? Why the fuck did we let her leave our lives without fighting for her?

"Ready for more?"

16

SOPHIA

"Ready for more?"

Julian's question hangs in the air.

For a decade, everything about that night with them has played in a non-stop loop in my memory. Even when I was hurt—even when I was angry—I haven't been able to forget about my threesome with them.

And now, I get more of it.

"Yes," I choke out around Damien's cock.

Julian's nails rake down my back again. "And how hard do you want to play, Sophia?"

They'll stop the second I want them to. Julian and Damien would never do anything to make me uncomfortable. They might inflict pain, but it will always be a pain I crave. They might spank my ass, but I will thrill after each harsh stroke. Their cocks might choke my throat, but only because I want it. They might make me cry, but the tears, when they fall, will be cathartic. I know this with every fiber of my being.

I hoist myself off Damien's cock long enough to say, "Do your worst."

Damien chuckles softly, and then his voice turns steely. "Did I give you permission to move your mouth from my cock?"

A thrill shoots through me. I'm such a sucker for that tone. They only have to order me around, and I turn into a wet, whimpering mess. And they know it.

Something hot drops on my spine. For a second, fire blooms at the point of contact. I exhale in a rush, and another drop falls on my back.

It's a candle, dripping wax on my skin.

Oh, God, yes.

I start to turn, trying to see Julian's face, but Damien shakes his head. "No, sweet Sophia," he says. There's no give in his voice, none at all. The easy charm and the quick smiles are hidden under a layer of sternness. "I want your attention on my cock."

I'm so turned on that I can't breathe. I can't think. My mind is lost, submerged under a haze of need. I suck Damien's cock into my mouth again. "Good girl," he says approvingly.

His fingers tangle in my hair, but he's not fucking my throat as much as reminding me that he can.

Julian rakes a path down my back with his nails and immediately follows it with a drizzle of hot wax. I squirm as relentless pleasure winds through me. The heat fades quickly as the wax hardens, but inside me, an inferno blazes.

Then something cold and wet trails over my skin.

Ice.

"I want you to feel every minute of this, Sophia," Julian says. "I want you to take everything I'm giving you, and I want you greedy for more."

"Yes," I sob around Damien's thick cock. "Yes, please, yes."

"You need my permission to come," he adds with wicked amusement. "Got it?"

I wanted to be pushed, and I'm going to get my wish. I'm not going to survive this.

I suck Damien's length into my mouth. The tension rises. I'm drunk with the sheer eroticism of the moment. I've never been so wet, so swollen, so desperate.

Hot wax. Cold ice. Julian is a master craftsman, these are his tools, and I'm the lucky recipient of his fiendish imagination. Fire and ice. Pain and pleasure. I'm balanced on a knife's edge, aching and needy. Lust builds inside me, filling me to the brim, and I bob my head faster on Damien's cock, focusing on his moans and grunts to keep my orgasm at bay.

"Of course," Julian continues. "You've already come once today, haven't you? So you can ask for permission, and you can beg, but you won't be allowed to orgasm before Damien does."

Damien chuckles, a strained edge in his voice. "Damn you, Julian," he grinds out. "Okay, fine. Let's make this interesting."

Interesting? They're jerks, both of them. Damien was close. Now he's determined not to come, and I have no doubt he has awe-inspiring levels of self-control.

"Julian, please," I whimper around the thick cock in my mouth. "I can't..."

"Do you know how wet you are?" he growls. "You're drenched. Soaked. Spread your legs for me. That's a good girl. Bend your knees. Yes, just like that."

Julian wraps another of Damien's silk ties around my ankles. He feeds one end of the improvised rope through the restraints at my wrists, tying them together. His hands are on my knees, spreading them apart, wider and wider, until I feel cool air on my pussy.

Oh, fuck. Julian isn't going to...?

Yes, he is.

A drop of wax lands on my swollen pussy.

I yelp. It's an instinctive response. I brace for a wave of pain to overtake me, but it doesn't come. Instead, there's just more pleasure. More heat, more intensity. More *everything*.

Fuck me. What do I have to do to get Damien to come? I suck in my cheeks and bob my head faster. I need him to erupt. If he doesn't come, neither will I, and I'm desperate. If my hands were free, I'd stroke his balls and do my best to speed this up, but of course, my hands are restrained.

I feel liquid being drizzled in the crack between my cheeks. Oil, not wax. It's slick, and it's warm, and I squirm again. "You want both of us, Sophia?" Julian's fingers work the oil into my tight hole, loosening me. *Preparing me for his cock. Preparing me for both their cocks.*

Damien plays with my nipples, plucking them between his fingers. He squeezes my breasts, using them as a lever to force me deeper onto his cock. He's fucking my face now, and I love it.

A fresh wave of pure arousal washes over me. I start to clench. A familiar tension builds in my core, and I clamp down on Julian's finger...

He yanks it away. "Were you going to come without permission?" he asks with cool interest.

"I'm sorry," I whimper through a mouthful of cock. I've only done this with Julian and Damien. I've only lost control this way around them. They're watching me unravel—no, they're *making* me unravel—and it's so deeply intimate. This is not sex; it's so much more. They're squeezing every bit of pleasure from my body, and I love it.

I hear the sound of a condom wrapper tear. "Sophia?" Julian asks. "Yes or no?"

I don't know if he wants my pussy or my ass, but either way, the answer is an enthusiastic yes. I spread my knees open in deliberate invitation. Julian groans out loud and slams into my pussy. Lightning explodes behind my eyes. I suck Damien's cock between my lips as the other man plows into me, his strokes deep and hard and powerful.

Each thrust pushes me deeper onto Damien's cock. I'm tied up. Spread open. I can't move, even if I wanted to. It's wild and uncontrolled and a little scary, and it's the hottest thing I've ever done.

Shivers roll through my trembling body. Julian's fingers grip my hips as he pounds me. His nails rake down my back again, and bits of hardened wax fall from my skin. Damien's fingers work their magic on my tender nipples. I know I'm supposed to ask for permission. I know I'm not supposed to come. But I don't think I can hold off. My climax is hurtling toward me like a tsunami, and there is nothing I can do to stop it.

Damien's thrusts speed up, his self-control finally fraying. "If you don't want to swallow, now's the time to say something," he says, sounding strained. His expression is one of raw need. In response, I lick the underside of his cock and take him down my throat. I want him; I want this.

He erupts in my mouth. I swallow his cum, my entire body ablaze. I need... I want... I cannot hold on...

Julian's fingers find my swollen, throbbing clit. "Such a good girl," he breathes. "Come for us, sweet Sophia."

For the second time that evening, I fall apart.

. . .

"I thought you were going to fuck my ass," I say to Julian when I've caught my breath. They've untied me, and I'm sitting on the couch, naked, next to a just-as-naked Damien Cardenas. I feel deliciously satisfied. Decadently sated.

"It was tempting," he says. His cock is jutting out, stiff and proud, the condom glistening with my juices.

"And you didn't come."

He laughs softly. "Again, it was tempting." He gets to his feet and grabs three bottles of water from the refrigerator. Good idea. I take the bottle he offers me and drain half of it in one gulp.

"Why didn't you?"

This time, it's Damien who responds. He gives me a truly heart-stopping smile. "You don't think we're done, do you? It's been ten years, Sophia. I hope you don't plan on sleeping tonight because we're just getting started."

Sunlight streams in through the window when I wake up. Damien is nowhere to be seen, but Julian is fast asleep.

I tiptoe out of bed, shower quickly, and get dressed in my freshly laundered clothes. I head downstairs, following the smell of coffee to the kitchen. Damien sits at the table, laptop open and notes strewn all around him. He looks up when I come in and gives me a blinding smile. "Good morning, Sophia. Did you sleep well?"

"Not at all," I tell him. "I was with two really hot guys, we were having amazing sex, and they kept me up far too late."

His lips twitch. "Sounds like you need a cup of coffee."

He starts to get up, and I wave him back into his seat. "I can grab this." I glance at the piles of paper. "Do you find it difficult, working remotely?"

"It shouldn't be," he says. "It's complicated. It's a family company. When my father died, my mother wanted to retire. Except she's not good at letting go of the reins. She says she doesn't want to be involved, but she wants me to do things the way they've always been done." He grimaces. "I love my mother, but she can drive me nuts sometimes."

"You're not the CEO, though, right?"

"Correct. That's Tomas, my mother's husband."

I tilt my head to the side. "Julian said you run around covering for his mistakes."

"Did he?" he asks dryly. "Julian's one to talk."

I don't know if this is a sensitive topic, so I change the subject. "He's still asleep. He looked pretty dead to the world."

"He would be. He said he didn't get much sleep on the red-eye."

"Red-eye?"

"He flew in from Los Angeles yesterday morning. He couldn't have gotten more than a couple hours of sleep on Friday night, and then there was last night." He gives me a cheerful smile. "I've never been happier to pull an all-nighter."

My cheeks heat. Last night was. . . let's just say I'm *very* well-fucked. "What was he doing in Los Angeles?" I'm being nosy, but I want to know everything about the two men.

"One of his comics got optioned, and it looks like they're going to film the pilot this year. The producer wants Julian to co-write the screenplay." He winces. "Poor Julian. The timing is terrible. He's got the house to finish, another comic that's due, and now this screenplay." He glances at me. "What were you two talking about last night?"

His tone is a little too innocent, a little too casual. Hang on, is Damien jealous? Oh, I'm going to enjoy this. I take a sip of my coffee and lean back against the counter. "Wouldn't you like to know?" I tease.

"It's none of my business," he says hastily. "Sorry. Pretend I didn't ask."

I roll my eyes. "I already told you what we talked about," I tell him. "Julian said there was obvious chemistry between you and me, and he asked if he should go. I'd just finished telling him I wanted both of you when you came downstairs and asked me the same question." I give him an exasperated look. "I was starting to wonder what it takes for a girl to get a threesome around here."

He laughs out loud. "You just have to ask for what you want."

I did. Several times. "You looked surprised when I did."

"You have to admit that it's not exactly the conventional choice," he responds.

Oh, I am *enjoying* this. I quirk an eyebrow. "Are you calling me boring and sexually unadventurous? Damien, I think I'm offended."

"Ouch." A look of chagrin washes over his face. "In my defense, I've only had one cup of coffee so far. I can't be held liable for what comes out of my mouth."

The poor guy. I should stop busting his balls. His mug is empty, and I refill it. "I'm adopted," I tell him. "My parents are a gay, interracial couple with five kids. I'm used to being perceived as unconventional. If I had a dollar for every person who clutched their pearls at the thought of two men adopting a child, I'd be on a yacht somewhere. Or diving into a pool of money."

"You were adopted?" He gives me a curious look. "But same-sex marriage has only been legal in the United States since 2015."

Same-sex marriage has been in popular culture and in

the news so long that most people forget how recently they were granted that right. I give him a questioning look. "How come you know that?"

"My brother Cristiano and his partner Magnus want to get married and have kids," he says. "Unfortunately, it's not legal in Peru, so they moved to New York earlier this year."

"Ah, okay. You're right. It wasn't legal when I was growing up." I try to keep the bitterness from my voice, but I'm not particularly successful. "My biological mother, Denise, was a shitty parent. When I was two, she dropped me and my brother Ben off at her brother Lenny's house and took off. Lenny and his partner Hank brought us up. We only saw Denise when she wanted money. She'd show up and threaten to take Ben and me away unless my fathers paid her off." I take a deep breath. I haven't seen Denise in years, but I will never forgive her for threatening to remove me from my home and family. I can never forget the fear I felt every time I opened the door to see her there. "I don't give a fuck what the world says. Dad and Papa are my parents, not Denise."

"That had to be a difficult way to grow up."

"I had a great childhood, Damien."

"Except you always knew it could get taken away from you."

Oh. *Oh.* All my life, I've been conditioned to think good things can be ripped away from me at a moment's notice. If my custody had ever become a matter for the courts, they would have recognized Denise's claim over me. They weren't going to protect me from her. Lenny and Hank wouldn't have found justice in the legal system.

That's why I was so ready to believe that Damien got me fired.

Oh, wow.

Julian comes downstairs just then. "You shouldn't have let me sleep in," he grumbles. "Good morning, Sophia." He pours himself a cup of coffee and joins us at the dining table. "I didn't mean to interrupt your conversation."

"You didn't," Damien replies. "Sophia was telling me about her complicated childhood." He gives Julian a sidelong glance. "A familiar topic for you."

"It was Hannah who had a shitty childhood, not me." He looks at me. "My parents favored me over my sister. It was not pleasant."

That's why renovating the greenhouse is so important. That's why Julian is working flat out. He's making amends.

Damien's phone beeps. He glances at it and sighs. "I have to take a call in ten minutes," he says. "Sophia, I'm so sorry—"

He has a meeting on Sunday morning. The poor guy. "That's okay. I should head back home anyway."

He puts his hand on top of mine. "In case there's any doubt about it, I want to see you again." He glances at Julian. "We both do."

Ten years. I can't help feeling like I wasted so much time. I'm determined not to let it happen again. "I want to see you too."

"Have dinner with us on Wednesday?" Julian asks.

I pull out my phone and open my calendar. My only appointment Wednesday is with Dr. Hernandez to discuss the results of my fertility tests.

Fuck. I forgot all about that.

This doesn't feel like a fling. This feels real.

Is it, though? Damien is leaving in three weeks. Julian wants to sell his house as soon as he can. And you're thirty-five. Can you take a chance on a new relationship, knowing that with each passing day, your odds of having a baby get lower? Can you afford to wait?

I should tell them about my sperm donor plans, but I find myself hesitating. It's very early days. I don't even know if this is a relationship. We haven't talked about exclusivity. We've had one night together, that's all.

I can't throw this at them. It's too soon. What would that conversation be like? *I need to know if you're serious because I want a baby.* Hell, no. If I lead with that, all I'll accomplish is chasing them off.

"Yeah, I can do that."

Will this blow up in my face? Maybe. But I can't cancel my appointment. I can't afford the risk. I *refuse* to let one night of glorious sex alter my life plans.

17

DAMIEN

I've been in Highfield for a little over a week and a half. In that time, I've attended thirty-seven meetings, answered hundreds of emails, and have worked at least eight hours a day every single day.

And I'm supposed to be on vacation.

Yesterday, I rebelled. I called Luis and told him that I was going to be unavailable. I put my phone in airplane mode and ignored my laptop.

It was *amazing.*

To be fair, much of my good mood this morning is not because of my day off. It's because of Sophia.

Last night was amazing. Truly special. And it's not the sex. Don't get me wrong—the sex was off-the-charts hot. In fact, if I think about it for too long, I'm going to get a hard-on. Which is something I'd like to avoid, given I have to talk to one of my employees, Rafal, in ten minutes.

What's much more important is the connection between us. It felt special. It felt right. And this time, I'm not going to let it slip through my fingers. I'm older now, and I know what a rare gift this feeling is. I won't let it go.

As tempting as it is to turn off my phone for the rest of the month, I cannot. Luis is probably already feeling the heat from my mother, Tomas, Gisele, and Victoria. From everybody. It's a shitshow, but it's not his shitshow to manage. It's mine.

Once Sophia and Julian leave, I take my phone off airplane mode. Emails start to flood into my inbox. Thirteen of them are marked Urgent. My mother has left me two messages, and Vicky has called three times.

Fuck me. I rub my chest. I turned off my phone for one day—on a Saturday when people shouldn't be working anyway. You'd think I disappeared for a year on from the way everyone is carrying. This is insane. This is unsustainable. This is exactly the sort of thing that got my father killed. He's been gone for three years, and I miss him every single day.

And I feel myself fall into the same trap that took him.

Rafal calls me at ten to give me an update on Acra. "The negotiations are almost done," he says tersely. "I just need your okay on the final numbers."

He's already sent me an email with the details, so this is at least a quick conversation. "I'm okay with them," I respond. He's usually cheerful and garrulous, so this terseness is unlike him. Unlike Jack Rutherford, I know Rafal well. We went to business school together. We've eaten in each other's homes. There's a certain stiffness in his voice that isn't normal.

"The meetings went well?" I probe. "Or were they being difficult?"

"They were fine."

Then what's wrong? Before I can ask, he continues, "Your sister has been sitting in on the negotiations all week."

"She has?" You have to be fucking kidding me. My lips

tighten. Damn it. I made it clear earlier this week that Rafal would be our point person for the Acra negotiations. Mama and I talked about it; I thought she agreed with me. I sent Rafal an email telling him to handle it. I copied my mother on that email. Tomas too. Vicky as well. Everyone knew Rafal was in charge.

And yet, Vicky couldn't let him handle it.

I'm so angry I see red. I cannot afford to lose Rafal. My mother might think that only family can be trusted, but she's wrong. I recruited Rafal Loyola personally. He's a star, and if he feels undermined, he will quit.

Cardenas Group is nothing without the people that work for us. Something my mother refuses to see.

And Victoria? She should have known better. I am incandescent with rage.

I rub my chest again and say something conciliatory to Rafal. Praise him for a job well done. Then I hang up and take a deep breath. I need to get my temper under control before I call my sister.

She calls me before that can happen. "Your phone was off yesterday," she snaps. "Ask me what I did yesterday, Damien. I sat in the most boring contract negotiation of my life. All day long."

She sounds pissed off, but it's nothing compared to how furious I am. "Why were you there?" I demand. "I told Rafal to handle it. I sent everyone an email saying he was in charge. I copied you on that note. I copied everyone, for fuck's sake. I wanted there to be no doubt that he could handle it. What possessed you to attend the negotiations?"

"Mama told me to go."

Of course she did. I'm exasperated beyond belief. There is a dull pain in my chest. I massage it absently. I shouldn't have eaten those burgers last night. Red meat isn't good for me. "I am the Chief Operating Officer," I snap. "The only person with authority to overrule my decisions is Tomas." At least Tomas doesn't interfere. "Not Mama. Whether she likes it or not, Mama is retired. She doesn't work in the firm any longer. You should have ignored her."

My sister laughs incredulously. "Really? Ignore Mama. Have you met the woman?"

That's fair—I can't dispute that. "I put Rafal in charge," I point out. "By showing up to the Acra meetings, you undermined him. By extension, you undermined me." I massage my chest again and get up to pour myself another cup of coffee. "Did Tomas interfere? No, he didn't. Because Tomas might not know anything about running this company, but he does know that the family can't do it alone. Not anymore. We're just too big for that."

She's silent a very long time, and then she sighs. "I'm sorry. You're right. I'm not good at dealing with Mama. She called me, practically in tears, and gave me a long guilt trip about how Papa sacrificed everything to build this company. And yes, she understood that you asked Rafal to do it, but he's only been with the company for three years and was I really sure we could trust him? You know how she can get."

I do. My anger drains away. "I'm not good at dealing with her when she gets that way either," I admit.

"Maybe if Cristiano were to do more—"

"Bullshit. Cristiano is the only one with any work-life balance. We both need to do a better job pushing back."

"Yeah. . ." Her voice softens. "She's not handling retirement very well."

"That's the understatement of the year." My parents had talked about retirement when my father was alive. They had planned to take an around-the-world cruise. My father's unexpected death shocked my mother into retirement, but it's not easy to reset old patterns. My parents were workaholics. Now that she's retired, Maria Cardenas doesn't know what to do with her spare time.

And so she meddles in the company.

"You have children. Just drop Felipe and Johan off with her. She's not doing enough grandmothering, clearly. Have her babysit your little monsters."

"She'll probably have them working in the mailroom."

"They're seven and nine, Victoria."

"And we're talking about our mother, Damien," she retorts. "Okay, I'll find Rafal and smooth things over, and I'll do a better job holding the line."

I hang up. I take another sip of coffee, but it's bitter in my mouth. Something I ate obviously didn't agree with me. I make myself get up and drink a glass of water. For safe measure, I swallow an aspirin.

Then, ignoring my laptop, I walk out to the deck and look at the lake.

It's a vivid shade of blue. The day promises to be beautiful and sunny, and the water calls to me. When I bought this house, I had illusions of jumping in for a swim every morning. There's a canoe in the boathouse, and I can count on one hand how many times I've gone out on it.

I never seem to have any free time. My calendar is always packed with meetings. There's always an endless flood of work.

Resentment prickles through me, not for the first time. I've worked hard all my life. I've done my duty to the family. I went to business school, spent four years as a management consultant to broaden my experience, and then joined the firm and worked my way up the ladder. When do I get my reward?

Don't get me wrong, I'm extremely privileged and very

aware of it. I am financially stable. More than stable, I am wealthy. But what's the point of all that money if I can never take a weekend off? If I never get any time to enjoy it?

Stop throwing yourself a pity party. If you want things to change, then do something about it.

I close my eyes and bask in the sun. I need a better work-life balance. We all do. It took Magnus leaving Cristiano for my brother to realize what was truly important.

I don't want to learn that lesson the hard way. Last night with Sophia has brought my discontent to the forefront. I wanted to spend time with her today, but I had meetings. I wanted to eat a slow, leisurely breakfast, but I knew people needed me. I wanted to drag her back to bed and spend the afternoon making love to her, but my mother panics if she can't reach me.

Something needs to change.

For a minute or two, I allow myself to fantasize about the future. If we were in a relationship, I would move to Highfield. I can work out of the Manhattan office two days a week and work remotely the rest of the time. Sophia clearly loves her job, and Julian already has a home here. I know he's talked about selling it, but if his relationship with his sister improves, he might decide to hang on to Kincaid Castle. It makes sense for me to be the one to move.

I want the fantasy so much it *hurts*. I want a life that is more than just about work. I want a family and a home. I might even want children.

That thought makes me pause. Does Sophia want kids? She hasn't said anything about them, but to be fair, we didn't spend a lot of time in conversation yesterday. I make a mental note to ask her.

What about me? A threesome makes things complicated, but it doesn't make things impossible. I don't have a burning need to pass down my genes. Cristiano and Magnus are starting a family. They're using an egg donor fertilized with Magnus' sperm. Their surrogate is only three months pregnant, and already, Cristiano is besotted. A family is what you make of it.

If I want this relationship to work, I'm going to have to make a lot of changes in my life. Starting with work. My mother is not going to take it well. Knowing her, she won't bat an eye at the threesome. The Cardenas Group is different. My father gave his life to it. My mother's feelings aren't rational when it comes to the firm. I'm setting up for a confrontation with her, a confrontation I've avoided ever since my father died.

She was grief-stricken then, and I didn't want to upset her. Things are different now. She's happier. Tomas is good for her, calm and even-keeled.

I rub my chest again. Fucking indigestion. When I was twenty, I could have eaten a dozen burgers without any consequences. But I'm getting older, in my late thirties. If I don't take a stand, life will slip away from me.

And I refuse to let that happen.

18

JULIAN

Holy fuck, last night. I find myself grinning like an idiot as I drive back to Kincaid Castle. Not even the condition of the house can get me down today.

Last night was *everything.*

Ten years ago, I should have tried harder to stay in touch with Sophia. Why hadn't I? My mother falling ill had been part of it. But deep down, I didn't think I deserved her.

All my life, I've had things handed to me. My parents treated me like the golden child. When I started making comics, I struggled for a few years. But right before I met Sophia, *Kingdom Night* hit it big.

There's no fairness in publishing, no rhyme or reason why some comics and games make it and others don't. Several of my peers are still searching for their big break. It's all so random. So unpredictable. When *Kingdom Night* exploded, I was overjoyed, of course. But deep down, my success felt undeserved. Unearned.

Ten years ago, I hadn't fought for Sophia. But I'm not the same person I used to be. I don't give a fuck whether I deserve her or not. Lady Luck has smiled on me, and I'm going to grab this second chance with both hands. She wants me, and she wants Damien, and if she's unfazed by being in a polyamorous relationship, then so am I. This time, I'm not going to give her up.

Monday is a shitshow. First thing that morning, Chris Quinn swings by to look at the greenhouse floor. "It should have underfloor heating," I tell him. "But it doesn't seem to be working. Can you figure out what's wrong with it?"

"Hmm," he says. "When was it installed?"

"Twenty-five years ago?" I guess. "Maybe thirty?"

Quinn gets to work. An hour later, he has an answer for me. "There's good news, and there's bad news," he says. "Good news, the coils under the concrete are intact. Bad news, your boilers are busted. Both of them need to be replaced."

The news is not unexpected. "Okay. Let's do that. How long will that take?"

"To replace the boilers? A day. But that's not the issue. A boiler large enough to heat a place this size is a custom job. I can place the order today, but they're not going to show up until the new year."

My mouth falls open. "January? You have got to be kidding."

"I wish I was. The cold showers can't be pleasant, I know."

"Is there anything you can do to speed things up?" I ask, a desperate edge in my voice. "It's not the cold showers. My sister is getting married here at Christmas, and we have to have heat and hot water for the guests."

The electrician looks around at the state of the greenhouse. "Is your contractor going to be done in time?" he asks skeptically.

"I can't find a contractor," I confess. "I'm doing the work myself."

He gives me an even more dubious look. "Well, you certainly will have your hands full." Some of my desperation must be obvious because he relents. "I'll talk to the manufacturers. See if they can put a rush on it."

If that wasn't stressful enough, the day continues to go downhill. Come afternoon, I get an email from Francisco Flores. "I've been thinking about how we're going to work together," he writes. "I talked to Kyle Donovan about it. You know the material the best, so I think it makes the most sense for you to write the first draft. Once you've done that, I can tweak and polish it. And I'm always available as a resource, of course."

What the fuck?

"Given the aggressive timeline, I think we should aim for a finished screenplay in the next five weeks," he finishes.

I read the email again to see if I've missed anything, but no, I haven't. My temper rises. This is complete bullshit. Flores is obviously pissed off at having to share credit with me, so he's retaliated by dumping all the work on my plate. I can't write a screenplay in five weeks—I've never written one before. I have no idea what I'm doing.

And Hannah is coming to look at the greenhouse in five weeks. It was already going to be a challenge to get it ready. There's no way I can do both the screenplay and the construction. Something's got to give.

I start to forward the email to my agent and then hesitate. What is Shaun going to do? Flores says he's cleared this with Kyle Donovan, the producer. If that's the case, I already know what Shaun's going to say. He's going to tell me to be a team player. If I insist he takes it up with the production company, I'm going to sound like I'm complaining. Like I'm afraid of hard work.

This is a big deal for Shaun too. Getting *Revenant* made will be a feather in his cap. It'll be great for his career, not just mine.

He worked hard to make this deal happen, and I don't want to seem ungrateful. If I tell Shaun that I can't do the screenplay because I'm renovating my house, he'll tell me to re-examine my priorities. He's going to remind me that getting a show made is the kind of thing that can send a writer's career to the stratosphere. He'll point out that this is a big, huge, once-in-a-lifetime deal.

And he would be right. If there was ever a time to put my career over my personal life, it's now.

Everything is happening at the same time, and I don't know what to do.

I grit my teeth. I cannot let Hannah down. I cannot scuttle the *Revenant* deal. And I will not give up Sophia. Letting her go ten years ago was one of the biggest mistakes of my life. I will not repeat it.

Things will fall into place. They have to.

19

SOPHIA

I have enough time to do a couple loads of laundry, sign up with a sperm donor site, and browse sample entries before Sunday dinner. It's intimidating. Apart from information about race, blood type, height, and weight, there's also something called the Temperament Report, a donor essay about why they chose to participate in the program, a simulation of what the baby might look like, and more.

Information overload.

My head is spinning after just ten minutes on the site, though in fairness, it could also be because I barely got any sleep last night. Not that I'm complaining about that. Not at all.

Thinking about last night makes me think about Damien and Julian again. Is what we have a relationship? Is it heading in that direction? Or is it an extended fling? I wish I had a crystal ball to peer into the future or a time machine because I sure as hell don't know what I'm going to do. If I'm going to go the sperm donor route, I need to commit to it.

Fertility treatments are frighteningly expensive. So if I'm planning to move forward, I have to be all in.

Does Julian want children? Does Damien? They haven't said. I haven't asked either. If we were in a serious relationship, would they want to be parents? But even if they do, how would it work? I don't want to pick between men. Will they draw straws to determine who has the chance to get me pregnant? It's entirely ridiculous.

I should probably have had these conversations before I jumped into bed with them, but I can't bring myself to regret last night.

Thankfully, before I have a chance to brood too much, it's time to cook dinner. Andre shows up just as I'm chopping onions, mushrooms, and peppers. "What are you making?" he asks, looking around curiously.

"Fajitas."

"Ooh, nice. Want help?"

This is a rare offer, and I'm not about to turn it down. "Yes, please. Can you make the rice?"

He makes a scoffing noise in his throat. "I'm a chef, and you're going to have me make rice?"

I roll my eyes. If I put him to work on the chicken, he'd complain that I made him cook the entire meal. My brother likes to grumble. "Siri, find me a polite way of telling Andre I don't care," I retort unsympathetically.

AT FAMILY DINNER, once we're done with our time-honored tradition of talking about what we're eating, we go around the table, giving everyone an update on our lives. "I did the basic fertility tests," I announce when it's my turn.

"When do you get the results?" Aurora asks.

"Wednesday. I have an appointment with Dr. Hernandez. If everything looks okay, it's on to selecting a sperm donor. If my results aren't great, I'm not sure what happens. I guess I'll find out."

"Are you nervous?" This question is from Papa.

"A little bit." Thankfully, Julian and Damien have been a very effective distraction. I would have been a nervous wreck all week had it not been for them.

Some people would think that this is an astonishingly personal discussion to have with your family, but not me. This is just the way we are. We tell each other everything.

Almost everything.

Once again, I haven't talked about Julian and Damien. This time, the reason I'm keeping them a secret is pretty simple. The moment I mention that I'm seeing someone, my family will ask me the obvious question. If I'm in a relationship, does it make sense to proceed with the fertility treatment?

I'm so torn. I genuinely have no idea what to do. My family wants what's best for me, but I need to work this out on my own before throwing it open for discussion. I value their advice, but right now, all it will do is confuse me further.

"What about you, Simon?" Dad asks. "What's going on with you?"

"Cantor Lane is finally done," my brother says triumphantly. "We finished on Friday. The homeowners loved it."

"Of course they did," Papa says. "You do good work."

"Do you have your next job lined up?" Dad is always concerned with our financial stability. Another leftover from the havoc Denise wrecked on our lives.

"Not yet, no. I'm going to take some time off first." He catches sight of Dad's expression and hastily adds, "Just a couple of days. I'll check my messages on Wednesday, I promise."

Ben looks exasperated. "You still haven't checked your voicemails? You can't do it all yourself, Simon. Hire an office person."

"It's on my list."

Simon mentioning voicemails reminds me of Julian's hothouse. "Hey, did Julian Kincaid call you about a job?"

"Soph, there are thirty-eight unheard messages waiting for me to deal with," Simon responds. "I have no idea. Who's Julian Kincaid?"

Ben is staring at me through the screen, his eyes narrow. I avoid his gaze. "He's a friend of mine," I reply. "He lives in that big house on Hill Street."

"Kincaid," Simon says thoughtfully. "Hang on, are you talking about Kincaid Castle?" He sits up. "That place is beautiful."

"It's also falling apart," I tell him. "Anyway, he's looking for a contractor to help him fix up the place."

My brother's eyes sparkle with interest. "Really? I should give him a call. I'd love to work on a place like that."

Ben calls me after dinner. "Julian's not exactly a common name," he says without preamble. "Any chance this is one of the guys you had a threesome with before they got you fired?"

My head jerks up. "How did you know about that?"

"You told me," he replies. "Papa paid for you to fly home for Christmas that year, remember? The two of us went to a bar. You got very, *very* drunk, and then you told me the entire story. I've tried very hard to block out that conversation. After all, you're my baby sister."

"Don't be such a prude. When it comes to sex, my life looks positively tame in comparison to yours."

Ben laughs uncomfortably. "Let's not talk about our sex lives," he suggests. "So, is it the same guy?"

I'm not going to lie to him. "Yes," I admit. "I'm seeing them again. Both of them."

He's quiet for a long moment. "Okay," he says finally.

"That's it? That's all you're going to say?"

"What do you want me to say?" he counters. "Do you want me to warn you to be careful? I can do that. When you talked about them, it was obvious they were important to you, and you really liked them. Be careful, Soph. Don't get your heart broken again."

Don't get your heart broken again. I don't remember anything about that Christmas. I don't even remember having this conversation with Ben.

"I'm glad you're seeing them," he adds. "I always thought you gave up on them too easily."

"What? They got me fired."

"That's what you've always said, but did they?" His voice is skeptical. "You certainly jumped to that conclusion. You never tried to figure out what really happened. I get it, Soph. I do the same thing. I give up on things too soon. You know it's because of Denise, right? If you don't get attached, then you can't get your heart broken."

I don't know what to say to that.

"We're pretty similar, you and me. We're always waiting for the other shoe to drop." Ben's voice softens. "But it doesn't have to be this way. Whatever happened when we were children, it's over. Denise has no power over us anymore. We're all grown up, and she can't take away our happiness. Only we can do that."

. . .

TUESDAY AFTERNOON, just after lunch, I'm struggling to focus on a spreadsheet when Julian calls me. As soon as I see his number flash across my display, my heart leaps. Stupid heart. "Julian," I say, doing my best to keep my voice casual. "How is the renovation going, or shouldn't I ask?"

He groans. "Don't ask," he says. "Listen, about tomorrow. Any idea what you want to do?"

"I haven't thought about it," I answer honestly. Relive our night together in excruciating detail? Check. Use my new memories as prime spank bank material? Also, check. But I refused to let myself think about the future, and that includes tomorrow night's date.

"You seemed to enjoy being tied up on Saturday," he says. "If you wanted to kick it up a notch, I thought we could go to Club M."

"Club M?" My pulse starts to race. "Is it even open on a Wednesday?"

"No, and we're not members either. But this is where it helps to know Xavier. Occasionally, people use the club when it's officially closed. Politicians, celebrities, and people who can't take the risk of being seen in a sex club. The monitors will still be there, but there won't be any other guests." He hesitates. "After what happened the last time around, Damien wasn't sure if you would be up for it."

"What do you think?"

"We both enjoy domination, and you seem to like stretching your limits. I think that you might be nervous about the idea, but you're also a little turned on." His voice lowers intimately. "Am I wrong, Sophia?"

I squirm in my seat. Is it wrong that I'm getting aroused at work? Yes. Bad Sophia. Thank heavens my office door is closed. "No," I whisper. "You're not wrong. About either of those things."

Do I want to go to the club? *Yes.*

Why am I hesitating then? I don't work for Mrs. Caldwell anymore. I just raised three million dollars for the community health center. Patricia's not going to fire me.

Ben's words from earlier this week echo through my mind. I can't spend my entire life waiting for the other shoe to drop. The worst-case scenario isn't always going to come true. I control my own happiness.

Julian's waiting for me to answer. "Yes," I say before I can change my mind. "I'm in."

"Good girl," he murmurs, his voice a seductive purr. "The club has rules. Things are more formalized now. You'll start by filling out a checklist of your hard and soft limits. That way, a monitor will know to check in on you if they see you do something you've marked as a limit."

BDSM has been in popular culture lately, and Julian's words don't take me by surprise.

"Okay." If I sound breathless and needy and aroused, it's because I am all of those things. The promise of tomorrow sends a shock of anticipation through me.

"I look forward to spending all night learning what turns you on, Sophia," he says. And then, before I can make my sex-addled brain form words, he hangs up.

How am I supposed to focus on work after that conversation? I shake my head dazedly and get up to splash some cold water on my face. Maybe that'll help douse the fire running through my blood.

20

SOPHIA

First thing Wednesday morning, I go to my doctor's appointment.

Dr. Hernandez smiles widely when he sees me. "I've reviewed your results," he says. "There doesn't appear to be any problems with your fertility. Your ovaries look excellent. We can schedule the first procedure once you have a donor selected and determine your ideal ovulation period. In your case, I'm going to recommend intracervical insemination."

I clear my throat. "I have a question. What would happen if I put this process on hold?"

He gives me a puzzled look. "On hold?"

"I met someone," I mutter. A pair of someones, though I don't tell the doctor that. "It's early days. I'm trying to figure out what to do."

"Ah. Well, that's obviously a personal decision that only you can make."

"I know that. Let's say that I wait a year. Would I still be in good shape fertility-wise?"

He purses his lips. "I can't make any definitive promises,

Ms. Thorsen," he replies. "You're thirty-five. If you want to try to get pregnant the natural way, well, that's certainly understandable. Fertility treatments are not easy, and people aren't usually here voluntarily. They are here because they've exhausted other options."

I think back about the support group meeting I went to last week. Any one of those women would be ecstatic to be in my position.

"I will say one thing, though. Your fertility declines exponentially with each passing year. Things look good right now, but there's no guarantee that it will stay that way."

Was I hoping he'd have a yes or no answer for me? I guess I was. But of course, Dr. Hernandez can't tell me what to do. Only I can make that decision.

In three weeks, Damien will be leaving Highfield. Will we have a conversation about the future before then? "In case there's any doubt about it, I want to see you again," Damien said on Sunday. But what does that mean? Are we heading toward a serious relationship? And kids. That's a lifelong commitment. Shouldn't we know each other a lot better before making that decision?

Dr. Hernandez has given me a lot to think about, but unfortunately, I am no closer to an answer.

Time to talk to the family. Well, not all of them. Aurora is the only one of us with a child. Maybe my baby sister can help me make sense of this situation.

"You're in a threesome?" Aurora screeches.

I wince and hold the phone further away from my ear. "Will you keep your voice down?" I demand.

She ignores that in favor of her next question. "And it's

not a one-time thing? You did it once, and you're going to do it again?"

"Tonight." At a sex club, but I skip that part. I've shocked my sister enough for one day.

"Okay, Soph, this isn't going to work. You can't just call me up out of the blue and tell me you're banging two guys. I'm missing several key details here. Start at the beginning, and tell me everything."

I sigh. I was hoping not to get into it, but it's too late for that now. Aurora has a stubborn streak in her, and if she wants to worm something out of me, she will. She's always been able to.

"Okay, it started ten years ago."

She squeals loudly. "You've been dating these guys for ten years? You've kept them a secret for that long? What the hell, Soph?"

Oh, for fuck's sake. "No, of course I haven't been dating Damien and Julian for ten years," I say in exasperation. "Do you want the whole story, or would you rather just jump to conclusions on your own?"

"Fine, don't get huffy. What started ten years ago?"

"Ten years ago, I worked in a hospital in Pennsylvania, remember?"

"The place you hated?" she says. "The one with the horrible boss, the one who made you miserable?"

"Mrs. Caldwell." I don't remember mentioning her to my family, but I obviously did because Aurora remembers.

Back in those days, I was contemplating going to medical school. I believed a stint in the hospital would be a good way to gain some experience and decide if I was cut out to be a doctor. But even before I got fired, Mrs. Caldwell had made me reconsider that career plan. In retrospect, being fired was the jolt I needed. I switched gears, and I'm happier now than I ever was back then. Getting fired was shocking, but it might have been the best thing that ever happened to me.

Huh. I've never seen it that way before.

"Soph?" Aurora prompts.

"Sorry, I just realized something important. Anyway, Damien worked in that hospital too. He was a management consultant. The board brought his team in to figure out why the hospital was performing so poorly." I take a deep breath. "I had a pretty big crush on him."

"You did?"

"You sound like that's weird."

"Not weird. It just wasn't anything you did. I was the one who lost her head regularly over a boy. You were my self-possessed older sister. You and Ben, the two of you were pretty intimidating role models."

I shake my head. "I'm the last thing from intimidating. Anyway, one evening, I finally summoned enough courage to ask him out. He turned me down. He said he had prior plans. A friend of his was opening a nightclub, he said."

It had been obvious I was fishing for an invitation, but Damien hadn't taken the hint. When I got to Xavier Leforte's club and saw the orgy on the main floor, I figured out why he hadn't wanted me there. It wasn't exactly a work-appropriate gathering.

"I followed him to that club," I continue, ignoring Aurora's little squeak of surprise. "There, Damien introduced me to his friend Julian. One thing led to another, and we had a threesome."

"Did they blow you off the next morning?" she asks. "Is that why I've never heard of them?"

"No, I did." It feels so strange to talk about this. I've kept this to myself for ten years. "When I went back to work on

Monday, Mrs. Caldwell called me in. Somehow, she'd found out that I slept with Damien. She fired me."

"The fucking bitch," Aurora says indignantly. "How did she find out?"

"I've always thought it was because Damien let something slip. Now, I'm not so sure. It doesn't matter anymore." I take a deep breath. "They came back into my life, Aurora, and I still want them. And I think they want me too. We slept together Saturday night, and it wasn't just as good as I remembered. It was better."

My sister is no fool. "Your doctor's appointment was today, wasn't it?"

"Yes."

"And?"

"No fertility issues. Nothing stopping me from moving forward. I should be ecstatic, Aurora. But all I can think about is how fucked up the timing is. I've been going on Friday night dates for ages, and the moment I decide I'm done with dating, they reappear in my life."

"Are you serious about them?" my sister cuts in. "Do you want to be in a relationship with these guys, Soph? Would you want children with them?"

Would I? The only time I've thought about it, I've dismissed the idea. Damien is too rich. If I had a child with him and something were to go wrong, he could take my baby away. He could destroy me.

But would he? Is he capable of being that ruthless? Is he capable of breaking my heart?

"I don't know," I whisper. "It's too soon to tell, and it's too soon to talk about. We've only just got together. What am I doing, Aurora? I should break things off with them."

"That doesn't make any sense," my ever-practical sister replies. "Look, you have time, right? I'm assuming you're supposed to monitor your cycle to know when you're ovulating? You have at least a month before you have to make any decisions."

"Is that fair to them?"

"I don't see why not," she replies. "Stop worrying about them, Soph. If the sex is good—"

"It's amazing," I murmur.

"I don't want to know the details. Or maybe I do. I'm still trying to decide if using my sister's sex life as spank bank material is creepy or not."

Even through my turmoil, that makes me laugh.

"You're over-thinking this," she continues. "If the sex is good, why not keep sleeping with them? If you decide you want to try to conceive naturally, you can. If you figure out they're not dad material—"

"What do I do then?" I interrupt again.

"Be a little self-centered for a change," she advises. "The sex is good, right? So, use them. Keep banging them through the treatment. Use a condom, obviously."

My first instinctive reaction is no. *I can't do that.* It's not right, and it's not fair to them.

Besides, I can't be in a friends-with-benefits relationship with Damien and Julian. I know myself. I won't be able to keep it about just sex. My feelings will get involved.

Still, Aurora is right about one thing. There's no reason not to track my cycle. There's no reason not to pick out a sperm donor. I'm not committing to this course of action. I'm just keeping my options open.

21

SOPHIA

The plan for the evening is to eat dinner at a restaurant and then go to Club M. That means that whatever I wear tonight can't be too risqué. Not that I have fetish clothing, anyway.

I wear a black knit dress that hugs my curves. It has spaghetti straps and leaves my arms and much of my cleavage bare, and the hem stops just above my knees. It's not the most adventurous dress in the world, but when Damien and Julian pick me up, heat flares in their eyes.

"You look amazing," Damien says.

"It's a very nice dress," Julian agrees. He gives me a devilish grin. "Pity you won't be wearing it long."

Ha. That's not a pity. *It's part of the plan.*

Damien is driving today. I start to open the back passenger door, but Julian tells me to sit in the front. "For the moment, anyway."

"But you have longer legs," I protest.

A smile flickers across his face. "I insist."

I know that smile. "Are you planning something?"

"Of course I am," he replies calmly. "And no, Sophia, I'm not going to tell you what it is. You'll find out soon enough."

Highfield doesn't have a wide range of restaurant options, so we drive to La Vecchia, the local Italian restaurant. Their lasagna is to die for, but I skip it tonight in favor of a salad. I don't usually turn down pasta—I never met a carb I didn't love—but tonight, I want to eat light. A stomach full of lasagna does not make me feel sexy.

"Would you like a drink?" the waitress asks me.

I'm going to a sex club after this. Drinking is probably not a good idea, right? I look at the two men inquiringly. "Would I like a drink?"

The waitress gives me an odd look. "You can have one drink tonight," Damien answers. "It's your choice about whether you want it now or later."

Something tells me I'm going to need a drink when I get to Club M. "Later, then," I say. I smile at the waitress. "I'll just have a glass of water."

"Me too," Julian says.

"And me." Damien leans back. "Waters all around, please." He waits for her to get out of earshot and then turns to me. "She thinks I'm controlling you."

So he noticed the way the waitress looked at us. "She probably does. Do you care?"

"Do you?" he counters.

I shake my head. "If she's looking out for me, then I appreciate it. But if she's judging me, that's her problem, not mine."

"That's your answer then," he says. "If you don't care, I don't either."

I finish my salad and decline the offer of dessert. Damien gestures for the check and flatly refuses to allow me to chip in. "No," he says. "I invited you to dinner, and I'll pay."

I roll my eyes and don't press the issue, at least not until we're in the parking lot. "What about if I invite you out to dinner?" I ask. "Will you let me pay, then?"

Julian laughs. "No, he won't," he says. He puts his hand on the small of my back and steers me toward the car. "And neither will I."

Damien unlocks the car. I start to move toward the front, but Julian nudges me toward the back seat. "This time," he says, "You're getting in with me."

Julian had something planned. I guess I'm going to find out what that is now.

Dinner was just a prelude. The evening is finally beginning.

My pulse races.

JULIAN WAITS until Damien pulls out of the parking lot and lifts a plastic bag from the floor. "About tonight," he says. "How hard do you want to play?"

"Are we talking about pain?"

"No, domination. Submission. Tonight, at the club, I'll expect you to follow instructions. To obey. I'll punish you if you don't. Within reason, and with safewords, of course, and only if you want it. It's meant to turn you on."

I'm already turned on, Julian. "That sounds good to me."

"What's off the table?"

My eyes are glued to the bag. *What's in it?* "What do you mean?"

"Someone will make you complete a checklist in the club," he says. "But just so we're clear, is sex on the table?"

"Absolutely." I think about his question and add, "As long as it's not on the center stage or anything like that."

Damien chuckles from the front seat. "Nothing public then?"

"Not tonight."

Julian's eyes flare with heat. "Interesting," he murmurs. "What about double penetration?"

Need surges in my blood, and I squirm on the leather seat. They'd asked me this question ten years ago, and then, after what seemed like hours of teasing and foreplay, they'd both fucked me. Hard. It was overwhelming in the best way. "I'm into that, yes."

"Good." His lips curl up in a half-smile. "You know how safewords work?"

I nod. "Red, yellow, green?"

"The club monitors will discuss this too. Safewords exist for a reason. If something we're doing isn't working for you, use them *at any time.*"

A wave of lust sweeps over me. I nod again. "I will."

"Good girl." He pulls a buttplug out of the bag, along with a bottle of lube. The plug is new, still in its packaging. He opens it and squeezes some lube over it.

I watch his fingers work, and my body throbs with desire.

"Pull the dress up to your waist," Julian orders. He leans back against the leather seat and watches me. He might look relaxed, but I see the bulge in his trousers. He's not as unaffected as he's pretending to be.

I unbuckle my seatbelt, half-rise out of my seat, and yank the dress up.

Damien swears under his breath. "You keep that up," he says, "And I'm going to crash." He brings the SUV to a stop at the side of the road. We're on a dark side street. It's mostly businesses here, so there's not much traffic after work hours. "Okay, carry on."

"Someone could see."

"There's no one around," Julian says. "And Damien's windows are tinted. Take off your panties, Sophia."

I have a safeword. I can call this off anytime. *But I don't want to.*

Damien watches me in the rearview mirror, his eyes dark pools of lust.

I wriggle my panties down my hips, my heart pounding in my chest. "You're a voyeur tonight?" I ask Damien. "Not planning on participating?"

"All in good time," he replies.

"Eyes on me," Julian says, his tone steely. "There are only two words I want to hear from you, Sophia, and those are 'Yes, Sir.' Is that clear?"

A dizzying wave of arousal slams through me.

"Plus, your safewords," Damien reminds me. "You can use those at any time."

I'm about to tell him I know that and then remember Julian's instructions. "Yes, Sir."

"Good girl," Julian says again. "Lie on your back. Spread your legs for me."

Order after order, all spoken in a calm, controlled voice. This is so sexy. A molten ache spreads through me. My pussy is hot and slick. On Saturday, Julian tied me up and drizzled wax down my back while I sucked Damien off. He trailed ice down my spine, spanked my ass, and then fucked me.

On Saturday, he'd been improvising, playing with household objects he'd found in Damien's home. Today, we're going to a sex club filled with actual bondage equipment. What does Julian have planned for me? What does Damien?

I can't wait to find out.

I position myself as instructed, my dress hiked up to my waist, my naked pussy splayed open. Julian swipes his finger through my folds. I gasp as he finds my clit. "I think you like this game, Sophia," he says, his voice silky. "You're drenched."

He yanks me closer, lifting my hips on his lap. My right foot is on the floor. My left leg is bent at the knee, the sole on the seat. I'm completely exposed. Spread open.

Julian holds up the plug. "I like glass plugs," he says. He drizzles lube between my ass cheeks. "They have a very satisfying weight. You might be able to forget about a plastic plug, but this one, you'll feel with every step you take." Another smile ghosts over his face. "Or so I've been told."

He slips his fingers between my cheeks. He works the lube into my tight hole, his movements unhurried. Damien continues to watch as Julian's fingers fuck my ass. First one, and then two. When he adds the third, I groan out loud.

"Don't fight it," Julian says. His thumb taps the hard nub of my clitoris, the rhythm maddeningly light. Every time he touches me, my entire body jerks like I've touched a live wire, but he knows just how hard to push. I rock my hips, but he refuses to increase the intensity. He keeps me on the edge as he fucks my ass with three fingers, and then, when I'm a gasping, writhing, twisting, aching mess, he pushes the plug into my ass.

"Good girl," he says again. He wipes his hands clean on a conveniently located roll of paper towels and meets Damien's eyes in the mirror. "Want me to drive the rest of the way?"

"Fuck, yes," Damien says instantly.

The two of them swap places. "What a pretty picture you make," Damien says, a smile creasing his lips. He slides two fingers into my dripping pussy. Holding my gaze, he drags them out and sucks them into his mouth. "I'm addicted to the way you taste," he murmurs. "I can't get enough."

Julian starts the engine, and we're moving again. The car picks up speed as Damien bends his head toward me.

His tongue dances over me. He circles my clit and sucks my lips between his teeth. He thrusts his fingers inside of me, one, then two, and finally three. He brings me to the edge of orgasm, over and over.

But he does not let me come.

My body is on fire, and my heart pounds. I throb around the unyielding plug. I pant and gasp, thrusting my hips into his face, but no matter what I do, Damien doesn't take me over the edge.

The car glides to a stop. "We're here," Julian announces. I'm limp, a sheen of sweat on my skin. If either of them as much as breathes on my clit, I swear I'm going to explode. And they both know it.

I *hate* them.

They drive me *crazy*.

I can't wait to see what else they have planned for me.

Damien pulls his mouth free and wipes it with the back of his hand. He hands me a bottle of water. I take a swig from it, and so does he, and then he smiles cheerfully and offers me his hand. "Shall we?"

22

SOPHIA

We enter the castle and take the elevator down to the club. The plug shifts around with every step I take, heightening my arousal, already at breaking point. "You are evil," I grit out.

Julian grins. "Hey, Damien's the one that didn't let you come. I would never be so cruel."

Damien snorts. "Yeah, sure."

A pretty, curvy woman dressed in black greets us at the club entrance. Damien breaks into a smile when he sees her. "Brooklyn, it's good to see you," he says. "How is school? You're almost done, aren't you?"

"Hello, Mr. Cardenas," she says, smiling back at him. "Yes, less than a year left. I'm looking for internships now."

"In media?"

She nods. He pulls a business card out of his wallet and hands it to her. "Call me if you want help," he says. "I can put you in touch with people."

She nods immediately. "Thank you so much," she says, taking the card. "I would love to take you up on that offer."

"Of course. I should probably let you get on with your spiel. Sophia's new, so she needs to fill out a checklist."

Brooklyn gives me a welcoming smile. "Please follow me." She leads us to a sitting area and hands me a tablet. "It appears that you were here ten years ago, Ms. Thorsen," she says. "Some of our safety features have evolved since then. This is a checklist of various BDSM activities. Please go through it, and mark what you'd be interested in trying or not. If you don't want to try something, please also note if that's a soft limit or a hard limit."

She looks in her mid-twenties. She's pretty and young and doesn't have a ticking biological clock. Plus, she appears to know her way around BDSM. I try not to be jealous. "I'm not really experienced," I mutter. "I won't know if I'm interested in something or not until I try it out."

"Of course. Why don't you start by marking off things that you have absolutely no interest in trying?" she suggests.

"Okay, I can do that." I scroll down the eye-popping list. "Yeah, nothing involving electricity," I say out loud as I mark that as a hard limit. Nobody's bringing a live current near my ladybits, *thankyouverymuch.* "Nothing involving blood, either. I get squeamish around it."

Damien tilts his head to the side. "You do? Is that why you didn't go to medical school?"

"It's one of the reasons," I reply.

Regret flashes on his face. I know he's thinking about me getting fired and living in my car, and I don't want to rehash that tonight. I don't want to dwell on the past. I'm at Club M to have a good time. Tonight, I want to focus entirely on the present.

I don't rule out a lot. Anything to do with watersports is out. I decline to be exhibited on the main floor. The roleplaying section offers me options like kidnapping, interrogation, sleep deprivation, and gang bangs. My eyes go wide, and I hastily decline all of those.

The next item in the role-play section is a schoolroom scene. I hesitate. Julian looks over my shoulder and chuckles. "Do you want to get spanked for not doing your homework, Sophia?"

My cheeks go pink. I shoot a glance at Brooklyn, but her expression gives nothing away. This must be something she's used to, I remind myself. She works at Club M. There is nothing I'm going to say or do that will shock her.

When I'm done, I hand the tablet to Brooklyn. She scans my list and then presses a button. "I'll share this with the monitors," she says. "Will the scene today involve the three of you?"

"Yes," Julian replies. "Can you prep a room for us?"

"Certainly, Mr. Kincaid." She addresses me again. "There are security cameras everywhere in the club, including in the private rooms. The club is officially closed today, but you are still being monitored via the cameras. At any point in time, if the scene looks unsafe, or if it looks like it's going to violate one of your limits, a monitor will stop the scene. Your safety is paramount at the club. Do you consent to this?"

"Yes."

"Perfect. There's only one more thing. You haven't ruled out breath-play, but the Club M rules override your preference. Breath-play scenes are not allowed unless you have prior approval."

"That's not going to be a problem," Damien replies tightly. He takes my arm. "Sophia, why don't we go have a drink while Julian tells Brooklyn what we need?"

The club is supposedly closed today, but there's a bartender on duty, a young Black woman. I ask for a glass of white wine. Damien sticks with water. "Have you slept with her?" I ask Damien as we wait for our drinks. Ugh. I guess I didn't do a very good job throttling my jealousy.

He looks puzzled. "With who?"

"With Brooklyn."

Damien shakes his head immediately. "God, no. She's staff. It's frowned on. Xavier has made an exception to that rule before, but there were extenuating circumstances. But even if it wasn't frowned on, I wouldn't."

"Why not? She's pretty."

He looks amused. "Are you jealous, Sophia?" he teases. He hands me my glass. "This is a new side of you." His expression softens. "I only have eyes for you, sweetheart. Surely that's obvious by now."

It's not obvious at all. "Why wouldn't you sleep with her?"

"Apart from the fact that you're the only woman I want to sleep with? Brooklyn has student loans and needs this job. I'm very rich. Consent gets murky under those circumstances. If I asked her out, she might not feel that she can turn me down."

"You gave her your business card."

"Sure," he says easily. "If she calls, I'll grab coffee with her. It's a basic professional courtesy. Brooklyn wants to work in media, and I have several contacts in the field. I'll connect her with the relevant people." He takes a sip of his water. "People like me, we already have a built-in network. I went to the right school and the right university. I know everyone. Brooklyn doesn't. I do what I can to help."

Oh. I thought Damien was unaware of his privilege, but he really isn't. That'll teach me to form snap judgments.

"You're staring at me, Sophia."

"Sorry." I hunt about for a different topic of conversation. "Why is breath-play against the rules?"

"Ah, that's a long story."

"Julian's still working out the details of the scene. Should I be concerned about that, by the way?"

He laughs. "You said you wouldn't know if you were interested in something or not until you try it out. Knowing Julian, he's preparing a smorgasbord of options for you to try." His expression turns serious. "I was at college with Xavier. So were Julian and some other people. We were very young and very cocky, and we all liked control. We all got into BDSM in a big way."

Julian joins us just then, but he doesn't interrupt.

"My friend Stephan really liked this girl, Lina. He was reckless; they both were. They liked to push limits." His lips twist. "One day, a breath-play scene went wrong. Lina died. When Stephan realized what he'd done, he shot himself."

"How old were you?" I whisper.

"Twenty."

"That's why Xavier founded the club," Julian says soberly. "It affected all of us, but it hit Xavier on a different level. Layla, the girl he was in love with, was Lina's twin. It's his way of asserting control over uncertainty."

"You're not a member of the club. Neither of you."

Damien shrugs. "I like domination. I like control. I enjoy sex when the opportunity presents itself. But I spend all my time working. My life is really not that exciting."

He's not lying; he does spend all his time working. His phone rings constantly. I don't know why I assumed he's a player—more snap judgments, Soph—but he doesn't seem to be. He's just a guy.

A really good-looking one.

"And you?" I ask Julian. "Why aren't you a member?"

"I've thought about it," he replies. "It's a good place to have casual sex with somebody who's on the same wavelength as you. But like Damien, I have other things going on." A slow smile forms on his face. "Of course, when I'm at the club, I'm going to take full advantage of the facilities." He runs his fingers down my arm, and goosebumps erupt on my skin. "Finish your drink, Sophia. Our room is ready for us."

23

SOPHIA

The private room is small, with doors on two sides. There are only four pieces of furniture: a futuristic-looking chair in the center of the room, a dresser and a long padded bench along one wall, and a bed pushed against the other. The walls are covered with mirrors, except the wall directly opposite me. That wall has, apart from the mirrors, a large flat-screen TV.

"Is there a show you want to watch?" I quip.

Julian slants me a look. "What do I want to hear from you, Sophia?" he asks, his voice stern.

A thrum of excitement winds through my core at that tone. "Yes, Sir," I say meekly.

They're both wearing suits tonight. Julian enters the room, takes off his jacket, and rolls up his shirt sleeves. Damien points to the chair. "Take off your clothes, all of them," he says. "And sit down."

I want to ask them if they're planning to take off their clothes too, but since that would be against the rules, I bite my tongue. My body throbs with desire as I obey Damien's instructions.

The seat is metal, and it's cool against my skin. Goosebumps break out on my arms, and my nipples harden.

Julian retrieves a tablet from the dresser. For a long moment, he surveys me with hooded eyes. "Your checklist is. . . interesting."

"Sir?" It's not 'Yes Sir,' but it's close. Right?

"There are so many things I want to do with you, Sophia," he continues, as if I haven't spoken. "And I'm trying to decide if I should keep you in suspense or tell you the details. Hmm."

He looks at me as if he's really trying to decide when I know he's decided already. He's just drawing this out to heighten my anticipation.

"I think I'll tell you," he says after a long moment. He picks up the tablet and holds it toward Damien. "Do you want to pick?"

"Hang on," Damien replies. "Let me get Sophia settled first." He picks up a remote control from the dresser and presses a button. The seat of my chair splits into two and spreads apart in a vee.

My legs spread with it.

I squeak in surprise; I can't help it. My pussy gushes anew. Cool air caresses my folds. I can see my reflection in the mirror. Naked, wet, spread open. My arousal, which had cooled somewhat while Brooklyn was going over the checklist, flares back to life.

"I don't want you going anywhere," Damien says. "So. . ." He kneels and fastens thick leather straps around my ankles, my knees, and my thighs. "Perfect."

He rummages through the dresser until he finds what he's looking for. It's a mint-green rabbit vibrator. It looks harmless. *Until he turns it on.* "Here you go," he says, handing it to me. "Play with yourself while we discuss your scene,

Sophia." He gives me a truly evil smile. "No coming, of course."

"No coming?" I wail. "That's not fair."

Julian's eyes narrow. "Do I have to punish you, Sophia?"

"No, Sir." If I sound sulky, it's because I am. I want to come, damn it. It's not fair.

He bites back a smile. "Get going," he says. "And if you're thinking about disobeying, don't. You won't enjoy your punishment."

"I won't?"

Damien laughs. "He'll edge you all night and won't let you come," he says. "You've been warned, Sophia."

My nipples are hard. My pussy is soaked. I *hate* them for their deliciously wicked imagination, but I *love* everything they do to me.

JULIAN AND DAMIEN pour over the tablet. I turn the vibrator on and slide it into me. I don't dare touch my clit; I'm incredibly close and can't risk it. I do my best to hold back my orgasm. I think of the most boring things I can. I make to-do lists in my head, but they don't really help. My body is poised on a knife's edge. Waves of pleasure run through me. In the background, I can hear snippets of Damien and Julian's conversation, and to distract myself, I listen to what they're saying.

"Yes, that sounds good," Julian says. The TV in front of me powers on, and one by one, words appear on the screen, each line highlighted in red.

Blindfolds. Bondage (light). Gags (phallic). Spanking. Riding crops. Hair pulling. Fellatio/Cunnilingus. Anal sex. Anal plug (public, under clothes). Vibrator on genitals.

Double penetration (anal and vaginal). Orgasm control. Nipple clamps.

These are all the things they're going to do to me tonight. A powerful shiver rolls through my body as I read the list, and I snatch the vibrator away before I tip over.

It's a close thing. For a few minutes, I can't think. I can't breathe. I clench my eyes shut and hang on the tip of the precipice, clinging for dear life.

"Such a good girl," Julian says softly. He kneels in front of me. His hand closes around the vibrator, and he takes it from me. "Good girls should get rewarded, shouldn't they?"

"Yes, Sir," I whisper. We've barely been in the room for ten minutes, and I feel different. Don't get me wrong. Most of the time, I enjoy being in charge of my pleasure. I want to be an active participant. But letting go, surrendering to their desires—it feels heady. My fathers used to take us to the circus when we were young, and I would watch the trapeze artists soar through the air, daring and weightless and free. That's how I feel.

"Do you want to come, Sophia?"

"Yes, Sir," I say again. I look into his eyes. Desire flares in those dark pools.

"Pick a number between one and ten," Damien calls out.

He's surveying the contents of the dresser. Is he going to spank me? I look up at my list on the screen. *Riding crop,* it says there, in forty-eight-point font, highlighted in red.

Is that what he's looking for?

Is he going to crop me?

Will it hurt, or will I love it?

Or both?

"Four."

"You want four orgasms tonight?" Damien moves behind me, his fingers tangling in my hair. "You're a greedy little thing, aren't you?" His lips kiss the side of my neck. "Then again, like Julian said, good girls should be rewarded."

He tugs with his fingers, and a thousand spikes of pain prickle my scalp. "I was surprised by your list," he says. "Hair pulling. A riding crop. A phallic gag." I can see him smile in the mirror. "Does it count if I shove my cock in your mouth, or does it have to be a gag?"

Julian moves closer. His fingers trace my puffy, swollen lips. I catch my breath. If he tells me not to come, I'm going to burst into tears. I just know it.

He kisses the inside of my thigh, his lips soft. "Come any time you like, sweetness."

Then his mouth collides with my pussy.

Oh fuck. *Oh fuck.* I'm already wound tight. The plug in my ass, Damien teasing me on the way over here, and the rabbit... they've all done their job. Julian barely has to put the tip of his tongue on my clit, and I'm *there*. I shudder and writhe, pant and gasp.

Damien's grip on my hair tightens. The pain contrasts sharply with the pleasure. I moan out loud, and he gives me a disapproving look. "Now, now," he says. "If you can't be quiet, I'll have to gag you."

I can't say I didn't ask for it.

Julian keeps his mouth on my pussy. Damien's grip on my hair loosens, and I watch him walk away to the dresser. He returns with a black leather gag, a small red ball, and a riding crop. "Julian, let up for a minute," he says.

Julian stops right before my orgasm hits. I groan in frustration, and Damien bites back his smile. "Sophia, pay attention," he says. "And then, I promise, you can come."

Heat ripples through my body. It's a struggle to make myself focus, but I do. Damien hands me the ball. "You won't be able to use your safewords when you're gagged," he says. "Hence the ball. Drop it, and we'll ungag you and do a check-in. Okay?"

I nod.

"I need you to repeat it back to me, Sophia," he says firmly.

His tone cuts through my fog of lust. His friends died in a BDSM session gone wrong. Damien won't take any chances with safety.

"If I drop the red ball, you'll ungag me and check-in," I repeat, taking the ball from him. I look up at one of the cameras on the ceiling. It's a small room, but I've counted five cameras, and there are probably more. "I understand."

The gag is, as promised, a penis gag. On one side—the side that goes into my mouth—is a short, stubby rubber cock. It's two inches long, tops. Easy-peasy.

A bulb dangles from the flat leather end. I don't pay attention to it until Damien straps the gag in place and squeezes, and the penis inflates in my mouth.

Damien laughs at my expression. "Did you really think it would be that easy?" He brushes my hair away from my face and strokes my cheek. "Sweetheart, you're going to earn your four orgasms tonight."

Julian dives back into my pussy, his tongue caressing my clit. Damien walks around me thoughtfully, and every time I clench my eyes shut, he hits me with the crop. The pain is sharp but not unbearable. I moan into my gag.

Julian's bringing me exquisite pleasure. Damien's offering me glorious pain. The two sensations collide and mingle, and I can't tell one from the other. I throw my head back. I struggle in my bindings as my long-denied orgasm nears.

And then ecstasy takes me. I throb around Julian's

fingers and the plug. My body is bathed in sweat, and I come hard.

Their hands quickly untie me and remove the gag. Only the plug is left. "You good?" Julian asks softly.

"I can't speak," I say pertly. "I can't be expected to form coherent sentences after an orgasm like that."

His lips quirk. "Do you want a break?"

"Just a little one." I get to my feet and stretch lazily. "That was great." I look at Damien with a wide smile. "The riding crop was wicked."

He grins. "Water?"

"Yes, please." I take the bottle he hands me and drink deeply, washing the taste of the rubber gag out of my mouth.

Julian picks up the tablet. "We can cross gags, bondage, riding crops, hair pulling, and cunnilingus off the list," he says. Each of the entries turns green. "Oh, and anal plug under clothes. We've got that taken care of."

"You should also cross orgasm denial off the list," I point out. "We're done with that. Right?" He doesn't reply, not immediately, and my eyes narrow. "Julian?"

He chuckles. "Okay, fine. We're done with that." He perches at the edge of the bench. He's hard. His erection is clearly visible under his trousers, but unlike me, he doesn't seem to have any problems keeping his arousal in check. "What do you think? Anything you want to do again, anything you don't want to repeat?"

I think about it. "I wasn't a fan of the gag," I say at last. "I didn't hate it, but I didn't love it either. I'd much rather swallow a real cock. The rest was amazing." I take another drink of water. "You're both still fully dressed, by the way. Is that going to change any time soon?"

Julian tilts his head to the side. "If you've recovered enough to be a smart ass, we can get going again."

DAMIEN PULLS me in front of a mirror. His fingers trace the faint red marks the riding crop has left on my skin. "Poor Sophia," he murmurs, his breath tickling my ear. "Should I kiss them better? Or should I fuck your pretty little ass?" He spanks me hard, the sound echoing in the quiet room. "Decisions, decisions."

Julian pulls the bench away from the wall, and Damien bends me over it. He strips efficiently, removes my plug, drizzles fresh lube between my cheeks, and then pushes his cock in.

I do my best to relax, but even with the plug loosening me up, there's still resistance. Damien kisses my neck and strokes my back. He moves slowly, giving me time to acclimatize, and pushes his cock steadily forward. I clench my fingers into a fist as I feel my muscles stretch to accommodate his thickness.

Julian's cock is suddenly at my lips. I wrap my fingers around his length and close my mouth over his thickness. I swirl my tongue over his head, licking him and teasing him before I take him deep.

He groans out loud, and I can see him in the mirrors, head thrown back, face etched with desire.

Damien pulls out and applies more lube, then pushes in again. Inch by inch, he fills me, and it is glorious.

It's intense. So intense. And Damien takes it up a notch when he shoves the rabbit into my pussy and turns it on. I suck Julian's cock down my throat as Damien fucks my ass, and it doesn't take me long to get to Orgasm Two. Then Damien comes with a groan, which triggers Orgasm Three.

This time, we cross off anal sex, vibrator on genitals, spanking, and fellatio off the list. Well, Julian does. I lie on the bench, absolutely drained from my three orgasms.

There are only three things on the screen still highlighted in red. Nipple clamps, blindfolds, and double penetration.

I'm feeling the oddest sense of déjà vu. The last time we were here—the only time we were here—Julian had wrapped a blindfold over my eyes, and then they'd taken me at the same time, one cock in my pussy and another in my ass.

And now we're going to do it again.

This time, it's Damien who blindfolds me. Two sets of mouths lick and suck my aching nipples until they're erect, and they place the clamps on my swollen nubs.

I hiss.

"Too much?" Julian asks. He does something, and the sting eases. "How's that?"

Fire blazes through my core. "It's good," I breathe. "Perfect."

Someone—Damien, I think—brushes a kiss over my lips. Someone else—Julian, if I'm guessing correctly—gently strokes the tips of my nipples while squeezing my breasts. I wriggle and squirm, my body desperate for them all over again.

"Come here, Sophia," Damien says. He laces his fingers in mine and tugs me down. I feel the mattress sink under his weight. "Straddle me," he orders. He grips my hips, and I rub my aching pussy against his erect cock before lowering myself on his thick length.

It's the first time all night I've had a cock in my pussy.

Damien pulls me close. My breasts mash into his chest, and I shiver. My clamped nipples are tender, and his thrusts are powerful and demanding. Once again, the slight pain dissolves into searing pleasure. Electric sparks run through my body.

Then Julian's fingers are at my ass, and he's penetrating that tight ring of muscle, lubing me up again for his cock. "Ask me," he says.

An hour ago, I might have protested. Not now. I want this too much. "Please, Julian," I whimper. I'm shaking with need. "Please fuck my ass."

He rubs my asshole with the head of his cock. Damien holds me in place as Julian presses his length inside me. I dig my nails into the sheets as he pulls back and presses in further. He isn't shoving himself in; he's moving with deliberate slowness. His fingers stroke my shoulders. Damien kisses me, his mouth swallowing my moans.

And then Julian is completely buried inside me.

They give me a minute to get used to the overwhelming fullness. I can't see, and every other sensation feels heightened. Sizzling, forbidden heat dances over my skin, but more than lust, what I'm feeling right now is intimacy. Being held like this—sandwiched between the two men—is dangerously intimate.

"You ready to get fucked, Sophia?" Julian asks, his voice strained.

Fucked. Yes. That's exactly what I'm here for. *Nothing else.* "Yes," I breathe. "Yes, Sir."

He laughs softly and thrusts. He wraps my hair around his fingers and tugs, and Damien swallows my whimper. "One more orgasm, Sophia?" His fingers find my clit as his cock drives deep.

They move in unison. Julian bites my shoulder while Damien pinches my clit. I cling to them as wave after wave of relentless pleasure washes over me. I am battered by their cocks, *and I crave it*. My body is aflame, *and I need it*. They fuck my pussy and my ass, *and I love it*.

This time, my orgasm hits me with the force of a tidal wave. Dimly, I hear Julian grunt out his pleasure as he comes. Damien's thrusts turn uneven. His fingers grip my hips, and he explodes. I slump between them, utterly exhausted.

This was everything I wanted it to be. No, it was *more*. And that's a problem. Because getting involved with Damien and Julian isn't really part of my plan.

24

JULIAN

Something miraculous happens on Thursday. A contractor actually calls me back.

"Hi, this is Simon Johnson," the man says. "You left a message for me a while ago looking for somebody to renovate your house?"

"Yes," I blurt out. To be perfectly honest, I don't remember leaving a message for Johnson, but that first weekend, I called over twenty contractors. "Thank you for returning my call."

"Sorry it's taken me a few days," he replies, sounding sheepish. "Are you still looking for somebody?"

"Yes."

"I can come by this afternoon to look at the house, and you can tell me what you want done. A little after lunch? Between one-thirty and two, if that works."

True to his word, Simon Johnson shows up exactly at one-thirty. He's younger than I expected, in his late twenties. Tall and broad-shouldered, with dark wavy hair and warm brown skin, he doesn't look like a contractor. He looks like a male model.

He sticks his hand out. "Hey, I'm Simon."

I shake it. "Julian. Come on in. Let me show you the greenhouse."

He looks around with interest as I lead the way to the back. "I've seen this place dozens of times from the road," he says. "I've always wondered what it looks like on the inside."

"As you can see, it's something of a disaster."

I expect him to tell me to level it and start over, but he doesn't. "Good bones, though," he says. "It would take some work to get it up to date, but it would be worth it. The world is filled with cookie-cutter suburban houses. Homes like this are special." We walk through the kitchen, and he shudders in horror when he takes in the circa mid-seventies sea foam green cabinetry. "This is dated."

"Hey, the stove works, and so does the refrigerator. It might not be the prettiest room in the house, but it's the most functional."

Simon chuckles. "There is that," he agrees. He flicks on the ceiling light. "Better lighting will go a long way."

Huh. He's right.

We arrive at the greenhouse. "This is it," I announce, bracing myself for his reaction. I'd vetted the contractors I called for obvious red flags, but right now, even if half of Simon's reviews are one-star, I'd hire him. I'm desperate. I sent Francisco Flores ten pages of my first draft, and he returned it to me with a terse note saying it wasn't working. No details on what wasn't right or how to fix it. Just a pointed suggestion to start over. I'm trying to stay optimistic about the collaboration, but just less than a week into the process, and it's shaping up to be hell.

The greenhouse renovations have taken a back seat to the *Revenant* screenplay all week. I'm woefully behind schedule. Damien has been helping where he can, but he's got troubles of his own at work.

Hiring a contractor would be such a relief.

Simon doesn't look horrified. He looks like he sees a challenge. "Sophia said it would take some work," he says. "She's not wrong."

I raise an eyebrow. "You know Sophia?"

He must hear the note of jealousy in my voice. He looks up, amused. "Yeah, she's my sister."

And now I feel very stupid. "She is?"

"Is it the skin color that's throwing you? We're both adopted."

"That's partly why, but you also have different last names."

He grins. "Ah, that. Yeah, people always get confused about why that's the case. My fathers didn't care if we kept our last names from birth, but we all wanted to change them. Since Sophia and Ben were already Thorsens, Andre and I decided we wanted Hank's last name. My sister Aurora picked both. She's Aurora Thorsen-Johnson Vallejo. Quite a mouthful."

Simon's far chattier than his sister. I'm not above pumping him for information about Sophia. "She's biologically related to your father, though, she said."

"Yeah. Dad is technically Ben and Sophia's uncle."

"It didn't make a difference?" Neither Hannah nor I were adopted, but my parents still treated us differently.

"To Dad?" He shakes his head. "Nah, man. It never seemed to matter. There was always enough love to go around."

"Your parents sound amazing." And so different from mine. After my childhood, children were never on my radar, but maybe I just needed different role models. Like Sophia's parents, who adopted five children and knit them into a family.

For a split second, I have an image of Sophia holding a baby in her arms, Damien and I looking on proudly. I shake my head and dispel that fantasy. It's too soon—we haven't even gone out on a proper date yet. Sex after a day of hard labor doesn't count, and neither does the hasty dinner we had before Club M. Plus, I don't even know how Sophia feels about the threesome. She's said she wants both of us, and I believe her, but does that translate into a relationship?

Simon kneels on the floor and places his hand on the concrete slab. "You have under-floor heating?"

I drag my attention back to the hothouse. "It's not working. The electrician says the boilers won't be here until January."

He looks up. "Who did you talk to?"

"Chris Quinn."

His expression clears. "Ah, that makes sense. Chris only uses one supplier, and they're often backed up. I'll talk to him and suggest some alternatives. When do you want the job started?"

Does this mean he has capacity? Does this mean he's going to do the work? Hope flickers in my chest. "As soon as possible. My sister wants to get married here on Christmas."

"On Christmas Day? That's romantic."

"It's also four months away."

Simon looks unfazed. "So you're looking to be done about the start of December, more or less? That shouldn't be a problem. We need to special order the glass panes for the roof and the walls, but I have a contact at a manufacturer in upstate New York. Do you need a bathroom renovated as well for the guests? And will they enter through the house or come in through the yard?"

Holy fuck, this is a miracle. If I wake up, if this turns out to be a dream, I'm going to be gutted.

I show him the bathroom closest to the greenhouse. He looks around. "New tiles, new toilet, new fixtures. Not a problem."

A massive weight lifts from my shoulders. "When can you get started?"

"I just finished up a job. I've got nothing going on right now. Kevin and I can be here tomorrow morning if you'd like."

"Fuck, yes."

He bites back his smile. "Okay. I'll go back to the office and work out a more detailed quote, but what you want done will cost anywhere from seventy to a hundred grand. Sorry about the cost. I know that's high, but the glass panes are custom orders, and they can get expensive."

All things considered, his quote is extremely reasonable. I'm desperate and running out of time. Simon could have charged me double, and I wouldn't have cared. I tell him that, and he laughs. "Sophia will kill me if I overcharge her friends. I need a check for ten percent to move forward. Seven thousand sound good to you?"

"It sounds great."

We head back inside, and I write him a check. "I can't thank you enough," I say. "I've been trying to hire a contractor for weeks, but I can't even get someone to come out and look at the place."

"It's a busy time, that's for sure," he agrees. "But it's not me you should be thanking. It's Soph. I had thirty-seven messages on my phone, and the temptation to delete them all without listening to them was really strong." He shakes my hand. "I love old houses. I'm going to enjoy working on this place. See you tomorrow. We'll be here at seven."

Sophia. The renovations have been such a source of stress, and just like that, it's gone. And it's all because of Sophia. She had no reason to help me out, and she did anyway. Because that's who she is. She's kind and warm and truly lovely, and I'm crazy about her.

She said she likes roses. There are not enough flowers in the world to express my gratitude.

25

SOPHIA

Thursday is a little chaotic.

Overnight, Donna's water broke. She was in labor for a few hours and gave birth to a baby boy, Ethan. Ethan is three weeks premature, but he weighs five pounds, which is considered a good weight. The doctors think he'll only have to be in the NICU for a week or two, fingers crossed.

While fantastic for Donna, this leaves us without a receptionist at work. We're a pretty lean operation. Most of our budget goes toward paying the salaries of our nurses and doctors. There's really just Patricia, Donna, and me in the office. And now, Donna is out on maternity leave for a minimum of three months. Of course, we knew we'd have to find a replacement for her, but we've been busy and thought we'd have another month. After we visited Donna in the hospital this morning, Patricia promised to bump the search to the top of her priority list. I believe her, but we're seriously short-staffed until that person comes along.

I'm grabbing a cup of coffee to power through my afternoon slump when the front door buzzer sounds. I walk out to the lobby to see who it is at the same time as my boss.

It's Julian. He's holding a gigantic bouquet in his hands. Deep pink roses jostle with purple hydrangeas and green ferns in a tumult of color. Tiny white orchids are nestled between the larger blooms.

His face lights up when he sees me, and he hands me the flowers.

Crap.

Patricia gives me a sidelong glance. Since I can't exactly pretend I don't know who he is, I take the offered vase, grit my teeth, and introduce the two of them. "Patricia, meet Julian Kincaid. Julian, this is my boss, Patricia Adams."

Julian shakes Patricia's hand. "Good to meet you."

"Likewise," Patricia says. "I've met you before, haven't you? Yes, at the recent fundraiser. Now I remember. You donated several first edition comics."

Yeah, I was afraid that would happen. Technically, Julian isn't a donor of the Health Center. Xavier organized the fundraiser he'd donated comics to, not me. But that's splitting hairs. Nothing forbids me from dating a donor, but it's not exactly smiled upon either.

My boss is looking at the vase in my hands. She's obviously wondering what's going on. "Julian is a friend of mine," I say awkwardly.

"These are lovely flowers," Patricia says with a smile. "Sophia, if you have this under control, I'm going to head back to my emails." Saying that, she vanishes back to her office.

Am I in trouble? "Come on in," I tell Julian, leading him to my office and shutting my door. God knows what my boss is thinking right now. Is she going to interrogate me about the flowers once he leaves? Patricia isn't unreasonable, and the logical part of my brain knows that I have no reason to panic. But I got fired by Mrs. Caldwell, and the scars haven't entirely faded.

Julian picks up on my unease. "I shouldn't have come," he says. "I'm sorry. I wasn't thinking."

He's scarily perceptive. I shake my head, throwing off the shackles of the past. "No, of course not. Thank you for the flowers." I bury my nose in the blooms and allow their fragrance to wash over me. "They're lovely."

"It was the least I could do. Your brother Simon dropped by. You have literally saved my life."

A smile breaks out on my face. "Oh, good. He's going to work on the greenhouse then?" I ask happily. "I wasn't sure. . ."

"Good? It's *amazing*, Sophia. I am so happy I could hug you. If we weren't in your office, I would. I didn't even know your brother was a contractor."

"I didn't tell you," I admit. "Simon's been really busy, and I didn't want to get your hopes up."

"He's going to start tomorrow morning." His expression is warm and appreciative. *Be still, my beating heart.* "Sophia, I don't have words to tell you what this means. My relationship with Hannah has always been a little strained because of how my parents treated her. I tried to counter it the best I could, but I could only do so much, and I didn't always succeed."

He leans forward. "When my sister asked if she could hold her wedding at Kincaid Castle, I felt like I was given an undeserved second chance. And despite how important it was to me, I was still well on my way to fucking it up. You tossed me a lifeline. I can never thank you enough."

My heart warms in the face of his obvious happiness. I

smile back at him. "You're making me blush. All I did was tell Simon to check his messages. It was nothing, really."

"No, do not diminish what you did. It means the world to me. I know we're getting together Saturday, but do you have plans for tonight? Want to come over? I'll cook dinner. It's the least I can do."

"Tonight?" Two nights in a row? My heart speeds up. I want to go; I really do. But is it wise?

He nods. "I'll invite Damien too, obviously. Do you like steak?"

Ugh. What is with guys and raw meat? "Not really. I don't mind red meat in burger form, but there's something about a steak that feels a little too close to the animal for me."

"Okay," he says agreeably. "I'll make something else. Grilled chicken, maybe, if that works?"

Why am I holding back? I push aside my misgivings and nod in agreement. "Sounds good. I can bring dessert if you'd like."

The corner of his mouth tilts up. "Dessert," he murmurs, his voice lowering into a caress. "I do like dessert." I blush, and his smile widens. "I should leave before I'm tempted to do something very inappropriate." He gets to his feet. "Thank you so much," he says again. "See you tonight? Come over any time."

There are two of them. It should be complicated, but it's not. On Saturday, they'd both been concerned I wanted the other one. I had to insist that no, I really did want both of them. And since then, things have been remarkably drama-free. They're dominant in the bedroom—and I love it—but outside of sex, both Julian and Damien are easygoing. I really appreciate that. I'm in my thirties—I don't have the time or the patience for high-maintenance men. When I think about Julian's simple acceptance of my steak preferences compared to Matthew Barnes' high-handed ordering for me...

Oh, come on. The date with Matthew Barnes is hardly the yardstick to measure other men by. Tell me you're not thinking that Julian is a catch because he took your dietary preferences into account? Is the bar really so low?

But of course, it's not just that. It's everything else as well. It's the flowers Julian brought me. His obvious appreciation. It's the fact that he recognized I was uncomfortable with Patricia's reaction. It's Damien admitting he shouldn't have made his donation dependent on me teaching him how to be a better person. Recognizing his privilege and smoothing the way for Brooklyn, the Club M employee. It's the way both Julian and Damien held me during aftercare.

These men *see* me. They both do. That's why I fell for them ten years ago.

And that's why I'm falling for them again.

Crap. This isn't part of the plan. Not at all.

26

DAMIEN

My strategy team comes back with their recommendations. First thing Thursday morning, I meet with Melanie and Colin so they can outline their findings. "We've divided up the work into three categories," Melanie says. She clicks a button to load up her presentation. "There are the changes that can be made immediately, changes that are possible in the next six months, and finally, recommendations that will take longer to implement."

She moves on to the next slide and highlights changes I can make immediately. Colin jumps in with the long-term stuff. I ask questions, and both Mel and Colin answer them. Clearly, they've done their homework.

"This is great stuff, you two," I tell them when they're done. "Seriously impressive. You've done an amazing amount in an extremely short period. Did you get any pushback?"

"Nothing we couldn't handle," Melanie says diplomatically.

"Who wasn't cooperative?" I ask bluntly. I told everyone

on the leadership team to help them out, but there are some old-timers at the Cardenas Group that get very territorial about their fiefdoms.

"Ted Boric at M&A," Colin says. "Arthur Scott." Melanie looks at him, and he says, "What? It's true."

"It was nothing I couldn't handle," Melanie says to me. "Damien, you don't have to ride to my rescue."

"I wasn't planning on it," I tell her dryly. "Not unless you ask for help. I asked because I want to know who's going to cause problems when I set these changes into motion."

After that meeting, I pour myself a glass of water and think through my next steps. My mother will not be happy with the changes I'm planning. There will be tears. Emotional blackmail. She'll tell me I'm wrecking the company that my father built.

I rub my chest. I'm not looking forward to that confrontation.

Of course, my mother is officially retired. Technically, Tomas is the CEO, and he's the only person I need to clear this with.

I call him. He listens to my spiel in silence and then says, "Let's do it."

I blink. Tomas doesn't usually second-guess my decisions, but I didn't expect it to be this easy.

"My mother isn't going to like it," I warn him. "I should probably talk to her about it."

"Let me," he replies.

It's a tempting offer. "Tomas, I don't want her to feel like I'm dismissing her opinions. But the way my parents did things—it's just not sustainable."

"I know that," he replies calmly. "And believe me, so does Maria. She really wants to let go, Damien, I promise you. She just doesn't know how to do it."

"She certainly doesn't act like she wants to let go."

"She does. Last weekend, we went to a yoga retreat in the mountains. There was no technology allowed at the site. No Internet, no cell phones. There was a landline in the main building for emergencies, and that was it."

"And my mom survived?"

He chuckles. "More than that, she thrived. Maria was happy. She was relaxed. Trust me on this, Damien. She knows she should let go of the Cardenas Group."

I wish I had Tomas' faith.

"This needs to be done, Damien. You've held off from making changes for three years. Cristiano has already pulled back from the company's demands. Victoria is struggling. How much longer can you all go on like this? Three years? Five? Then what?"

My parents loved us, I know that. But I can count on one hand the number of times we all sat down for dinner. It just didn't happen. Victoria, Cristiano, and I grew up eating with the maids while my parents went off to various business dinners.

Vicky's being forced to make some hard choices between work and family. Choices that are straining her marriage and her relationship with her children. It's fixable now, but if she waits for five years, her kids will be older, and their mother will be a stranger.

I consider the prospect of living this way for the next five years. Letting everything come second to work. Attending meetings at all hours of the day. Being tethered to a phone that never stops ringing.

I hate admitting failure, but Tomas is right. I can't take much more of this.

"Maria will see that it's necessary," he says. "Trust me. I'll talk to her. Have Luis draft up a memo, and I'll sign it. You'll want the department heads in on this, yes? When?"

I feel a rush of affection for the other man. Tomas has worked for the company all his life. He's not brilliant, not a risk-taker, and he has a tendency to get overwhelmed when he has to juggle between tasks. But Tomas makes up for all that with rock-solid integrity and a genuine sense of right and wrong. His heart is always in the right place.

"I want to move quickly," I tell him. "But people won't like it."

"So what? Since when did you let that bother you? Damien, you are the Chief Operating Officer of the Cardenas Group. This is your job. These men and women are your direct reports. If they don't like the changes you want to make, they are welcome to leave."

That's uncharacteristically harsh. Tomas usually only cares about one thing, and that's keeping my mother happy. Maybe he's right. Maybe this won't blow up in my face.

"How about this afternoon?"

WE GATHER the leadership team together, and I present my plans to shake things up. "Some of these are in effect immediately," I say. "Some others will take a few weeks to implement. My strategy consultants will reach out to each department to ensure the process goes smoothly. Any questions?"

Ted Boric raises his chin in the air. "This is not how we do things here," he says to Tomas, his voice belligerent. "Don't tell me you support this insanity. The Cardenas Group has grown and thrived for forty years because of our policies. Now you're letting Damien throw them all out of the window?"

Tomas gives Ted a long look. "I have full confidence in Damien," he says mildly. "If the Cardenas Group is to survive the next forty years, the changes he's making are absolutely necessary."

Boric's face flushes red. "Does Maria know?" he demands. "Does she approve? I can't see her going along with this, not in a million years."

I count to ten in my head. When I speak, my voice comes out cold as steel. "This isn't optional. If you find yourself unwilling to cooperate with my team, please schedule some time on my calendar to discuss your future with the firm. Have a good evening, everyone."

I'm absolutely drained by the time the meeting is done. On autopilot, I check my phone. There's a text from Julian, sent earlier this afternoon.

Sophia is coming over for dinner tonight. Join us.

My stress melts away, leaving only pure anticipation. This is it. This is the reward. This is what I'm doing it for. This is what makes it all worthwhile.

I'll be there.

27

SOPHIA

Damien's Range Rover is in the driveway when I pull in. I step out of mine and ring the doorbell. Julian throws open the door and smiles at me. "Come on in."

I take a step inside. He wraps his hands around my neck, tugging me closer and kissing me, his lips warm against mine. "I'm glad you could make it."

"Me too." I hand him a grocery bag. "I didn't know what kind of dessert you like, so I brought three kinds of ice cream."

He winks at me. "You already know what kind of dessert I like, Sophia."

Heat creeps up my cheeks. "Stop that," I say severely. "You made me come so many times last night that I cannot possibly have sex today."

He laughs out loud. "Is that so? That sounds like a challenge, baby, and I'm very competitive."

Something's different in the foyer. I look around until I figure out what it is. The chandelier had been dull and dusty the last time I was here, but it's gleaming today, throwing bright, sparkling light around the space.

"This looks really nice."

"Thank you. Damien's in the kitchen. I left him in charge of the spinach."

"Can he cook?" I ask curiously as I follow him.

"I certainly can," Damien responds from the stove. "Better than Julian, I might add." He flashes me a grin. "Hello, Sophia."

"Talk is cheap," Julian responds. "Put up or shut up."

I laugh and go over to give Damien a hug. Purely because I'm being friendly. Not because I want to feel him up. No, not at all. Today, he's wearing a navy-blue shirt with small white anchors printed on the fabric and gray shorts. His hair is damp, looking like he just got out of the shower.

My mouth waters at the idea of showering with the two men.

Sheesh. Down, girl. Eat first before you jump them.

"You look very nautical," I tell Damien. "Should I call you Captain for the rest of the evening?"

His eyes spark to life. "I like the sound of that." His gaze runs over me. "And you look like a strawberry, pretty and pink and luscious."

He called me *luscious*. Once again, I feel myself blushing. I stopped at home on the way here and changed out of my work clothes. I'm wearing a pale pink sleeveless cotton sundress with a fitted bodice and a gently flaring skirt. "Is that a compliment?" I ask, resorting to pertness to cover my pleasure.

"I want to hoist you on the table, drag your ass to the edge, spread your legs wide, and devour you," Damien replies. "So, yes. It's definitely a compliment."

My entire body comes to life. Unfortunately, that

includes my stomach, which chooses that moment to rumble. Julian, who's been watching our exchange with a predatory look on his face, jumps into host mode. "Sophia, what can I get you to drink?"

"Whatever you're drinking." I don't like to drink and drive, and I should stick with water, but who am I kidding? I want to spend the night.

Julian holds up his bottle of beer. "It's an IPA."

"That'll work."

I look around as Julian gets me a beer. The kitchen looks different from the last time I was here. The space feels brighter somehow. Less sterile, more lived-in. Pale pink calla lilies overflow from a cut-glass vase. The windows above the sink are thrown open, and the aroma of cooking fills the air. Whatever Julian's making, it smells delicious.

I look up. "Ah, you changed the light fixture."

"Good eye," he replies, handing me a bottle of beer. "Yeah, your brother suggested it. I stopped at the hardware store on my way back from your office. I was a little concerned that the wiring would be a mess, but it wasn't too bad. Do you want a glass for that?"

"Nah, I'm good."

"There is a formal dining room," he continues. "But it hasn't been used in years. I figured we'd eat here."

The round wooden table is covered with a white tablecloth, a trio of brass candlesticks in the center. Julian pulls out a chair for me. "Sit," he invites, setting a plate of cheese and crackers in front of me. "I'm just finishing up. Dinner will be ready in ten minutes."

JULIAN HAS MADE a roasted chicken with couscous and

wilted spinach. The couscous has roasted pistachios and plump raisins, and it is *delicious*. I turn into a glutton.

"How's your week going?" Damien asks Julian as I inhale the food.

"Hell."

I look up at that. "What's going on?"

Julian sighs. "It's Francisco Flores. This is the first time I'm writing a script, and I thought he would be more helpful. But so far, he isn't being very cooperative."

I frown. Julian mentioned Flores on Saturday. "Hang on. That's the Hollywood screenwriter, isn't it? If he's the expert, why are you writing the script?"

Damien leans forward. "I thought Flores was supposed to write the first draft, not you," he says, his voice sharp.

Julian shrugs. "I thought he was too, but I guess Donovan changed his mind. Flores wanted me to write the first draft, which was okay, and he said he'd be available as a resource." He exhales in frustration. "But he's not. All week, his only feedback is that it's not working. It's annoying."

"Why aren't you doing something about it?" Damien says bluntly.

"What am I supposed to do? Whine to Shaun that the mean Hollywood screenwriter is making me do my homework, and I don't like it?"

Shaun's his agent. "Why wouldn't you complain to your agent?" I ask, staring at the dish of couscous, wondering if I'd appear greedy beyond belief if I eat a fourth helping. "I'm not a writer, but isn't your agent supposed to be your advocate in these matters? If you don't tell him you're having a hard time, how will he know?"

Julian heaps a spoonful of the grain on my plate with a smile. "I don't want to be high maintenance," he says. "Yes, Flores is rubbing me the wrong way, but I don't know if I have a right to be irritated. Maybe this is all about my injured pride."

Damien stares at his friend with exasperation. "Julian, nobody in their right mind would call you a complainer. I'm honestly shocked you're even talking about your problems. You usually do a great job pretending they don't exist."

Julian rolls his eyes. "Please," he scoffs. "As if I'm the only one doing that. How many work calls did you take this week? Or have you lost count?" He turns to me. "Damien's supposed to be on vacation."

"You are?" I blink in confusion. "Wait, haven't you been working the entire time?"

"I didn't work on Saturday," Damien replies.

"Saturday is the *weekend*."

He winces. "I've taken steps to reduce my workload," he says. "Pissing off half the leadership team in the process, but that's to be expected." Unlike the two of us, he's drinking wine. He drains the rest of his glass and pours himself another. "Enough about my problems." He turns to me. The full force of his attention washes over me. "How are things with you, Sophia?"

"You saw me yesterday," I point out.

He laughs softly. "I did, yes. We didn't really get a chance to talk."

How are things with me? Let's see. I've been trying to decide what I'm going to do about my fertility treatment. Trying to sort out what this relationship means and what it could be. I'm supposed to select a sperm donor and be tracking my cycle. I've started doing the latter, but not the former.

It's so tempting to just lay it all out there, but something holds me back. "I don't lead as interesting a life as the two of you," I murmur.

"I beg to differ," Julian replies with an amused smile. "You were at a sex club yesterday. That seems pretty interesting to me."

"True," I say, keeping a straight face. "You'll never guess what happened to me there. Two guys tied me up."

"Tell me more," Damien says silkily. His eyes have gone dark. Suddenly, the couscous isn't the most important thing on my mind.

"They made me beg for my orgasms," I whisper. Underneath my dress, my nipples harden to aching points.

Damien opens his mouth to say something, but his phone rings. He glances down at the display, mutters a curse under his breath, and swipes the call to voicemail. "My mother," he explains in response to my questioning look. "Tomas must have told her about the changes I'm making."

Before the phone rang, he was seconds away from burying his face in my pussy. Now, he's tense. His shoulders are squared, and his jaw is set. I put my hand on his. "Are you okay?" I ask softly. "Do you want to talk about it?"

I expect him to say something light and flippant. Instead, he sighs heavily. "My father and mother founded the Cardenas Group forty years ago," he says. "It's a multi-billion-dollar corporation, yet they ran it like a family company. Every decision was made by either my mother or my father. Only family could be trusted. My father believed that if he wanted something done right, he needed to do it himself."

I listen without interrupting.

"When I joined the company a few years ago, it led to some clashes. My father wanted me to be his successor, but he wouldn't let me make any changes." His expression turns frustrated. "We fought a lot. We'd reached a tentative peace when he died." His mouth twists in a wry smile. "My mother is the controlling shareholder. She didn't make me the CEO. Arthur Scott, our General Counsel, took over on an interim basis, and when she married Tomas, she put him in charge."

"Why didn't you leave?" I ask, even though I already know. Julian told me what motivated Damien the day we had lunch. That was only a week ago. It feels like so much longer. I remember his exact words. *Underneath that flippant, devil-may-care exterior, he has a very strong sense of duty.*

"I can't," he says flatly. "We have thousands of employees. Tomas can't handle the job. I cannot walk away." He stares into his glass as if the wine has answers for him. "Last month, I had a health scare."

Alarm jolts up my spine. It must show on my face because Damien squeezes my hand reassuringly. "It was nothing, just some random chest pains. I wouldn't have paid attention to it, except we have a family history of heart disease. My doctor tested the crap out of me, and nothing showed up. He figured it was probably stress and told me to take some time off."

I bought the lake house the year after my father died. None of us saw it coming. One day he was alive and well; the next day, he'd been felled by a massive heart attack.

I'm taking a break. It was either sailing around the world or sitting on my ass by the lake. I chose the lazier option.

"That's why you're here," I whisper. You think that in the process of becoming an adult, I would have learned not to jump to conclusions, but alas, no.

"Don't look so alarmed, Sophia. There's nothing wrong with me." He flashes me a blinding smile, but I'm too worried about his health to fall for the charm. If he's supposed to be taking it easy, what the hell is he doing working around the clock? "Anyway, with Tomas' support, I made some organizational changes today. My mother probably wants to chew me out."

On cue, his phone rings again. Damien makes a face. "If I don't pick up, she's going to keep calling. And then she'll start worrying herself sick."

"Worrying?"

"My father didn't answer his phone. When she went to check on him, she found his body."

Oh God, that's awful.

He picks up the phone. "Hello, Mama."

I expect him to excuse himself and take the call privately, but he doesn't. "I can't talk now," he continues. "I'm having dinner with my girlfriend."

And then he hangs up.

My heart almost leaps out of my chest. I gape at him. "Girlfriend?"

He holds himself still. "Did I jump the gun?" he asks. "We haven't had a conversation about it, I know, but there it is. My intentions, out in the open. I really like you, and I want to keep seeing you. I want this to be a relationship, Sophia."

"And so do I," Julian says.

Joy explodes inside my chest. They want to be with me. The universe has offered me a second chance, a miracle I don't deserve. "I want that too."

Tell them you want a baby. Tell them you've been exploring the idea of a sperm donor.

"Listen, there's something I need to tell—"

The doorbell rings, a loud clanging that makes us all jump.

28

SOPHIA

"I'm not expecting anyone," Julian says, looking adorably grumpy as he gets up to investigate. "It's dinnertime. If it's the Jehovah's Witnesses people, I'm going to be very annoyed."

His footsteps recede down the passageway. A minute later, I hear a woman's voice yell, "Surprise!"

It's his sister Hannah and her fiancé Samir. Julian looks slightly dazed as he comes back into the kitchen with them. "Sophia, meet Hannah and Samir. Hannah, you already know Damien."

Damien rises to his feet, faultlessly polite as always. He comes around the table and hugs Hannah. He's just told me he wants to be in a relationship with me, so I ignore my twinge of jealousy.

"Damien Cardenas," he says, holding out his hand to Hannah's fiancé.

"Samir Shah. Sorry to barge in like this, Julian."

"Yeah," Hannah chirps, looking completely unrepentant. "We didn't mean to interrupt your evening. We were in the neighborhood, so we thought we'd drop by."

Julian rolls his eyes. "Liar," he says amiably. "You weren't in the neighborhood. You live in Manhattan, and it's a four-hour drive. Admit it. Jamila told you the house was a wreck, and you couldn't stay away. You had to investigate."

Hannah turns pink. "That's not the only reason," she says. "Jamila's mother is making my dress, and I came down to do a fitting."

He chuckles. "Sit down," he invites. "Have you guys eaten dinner? There's plenty of food."

His sister glances at the table. She takes in the candles and the flowers, and it's obvious when she realizes she might be interrupting something. She gives Damien and me a curious look and nods her head slowly. "Sure," she says. She glances at her fiancé. "If you don't mind, honey?"

"I never say no to a meal," Samir replies cheerfully. "You know that."

We make polite conversation as they eat. Samir is a commodities trader on Wall Street. Damien's eyes brighten with interest, and the two of them start talking shop. Hannah shakes her head indulgently. "Well, at least it isn't me," she says, linking her fingers with his. "I love him to bits, but I can only fake being interested in copper prices for so long."

Samir clutches his heart exaggeratedly. "And here you are, destroying all my illusions," he says with a laugh. "Julian, this is fantastic. Hannah told me you were a good cook, and she was not wrong."

"Right?" She looks at Damien and me. "Julian used to cook for me all the time when we were growing up."

"He did?" I shoot Julian a curious look. "He never mentioned that."

"Yeah, it was our secret thing. We'd wake up early, sneak downstairs to watch cartoons, and Julian would make me mac and cheese for breakfast." She looks around the kitchen. "I don't miss this place. Is it weird for you to be back here?"

"I'm slowly getting used to it," Julian says. He gives his sister a concerned glance. "It's been a while for you, hasn't it?"

"Fifteen years, give or take," Hannah says. Samir squeezes her hand, and she gives him a warm smile. "I'm fine, honey. The cabinets look exactly the same. Still hideous, after all these years."

Julian chuckles. "Sophia's brother is a contractor. He came to look at the place today. He promised me he liked old houses, but when he got to the kitchen, he was ready to set it on fire."

That's Simon for you. Always diplomatic. "He does like old houses," I assure Julian. "Really."

He gives me a warm smile. "I'm not concerned," he says. "You recommended him. That's enough for me."

Something squeezes my heart at his easy confidence. He trusts me, and so far, I've done *nothing* to earn that trust.

It all feels very surreal. Damien called me his girlfriend. Julian didn't plan on introducing me to his family, but he's not treating me like a dirty little secret, either. They said they wanted a relationship, and their actions back it up.

And mine aren't. I'm the one with secrets. I'm the one putting up barriers between us.

This needs to stop. First thing tomorrow, I'm going to call the fertility clinic and call the whole thing off.

AFTER DINNER, Julian shows Hannah the hothouse. "It doesn't look in great shape, I know," he says. "But Sophia's brother is starting work on it tomorrow, and he's promised me he'll get it done in time."

"I'm not worried about that," Hannah says. "But look at how much work you have to do, Julian. I shouldn't have railroaded you into holding my wedding here." She smiles ruefully. "Julian feels terrible about the way my parents treated me and takes it upon himself to compensate for their shortcomings. He's never said no to me, no matter what I asked him for. I'm afraid I took advantage of that."

I exchange a glance with Damien. From the way Julian tells it, his sister hates him, but that's obviously not the case. They might have grown apart, but she seems fond of her brother.

He's so hard on himself, and he doesn't need to be. He's a really good guy.

"Bullshit," Julian says firmly. "You did no such thing. I'm happy to do this for you."

Hannah and Samir are staying at a B&B on the outskirts of town and leave shortly after midnight. "I should go too," I say. It's been an eventful evening, and I feel both drained and adrift. I still need to tell them about the fertility clinic. "I have to be at work in the morning."

"Or you could stay," Julian suggests, his eyes holding mine.

"Or I could stay," I whisper in agreement.

This time, there are no candles. No ice. No crops and no spanking. I'm still sore after last night, and I crave gentleness. They give me what I need. This time, there's kissing and caressing, slow strokes and unhurried thrusts. And when I come, my body writhing and twisting against theirs, I realize something terrifying.

I've fallen in love with them.

29

SOPHIA

A week goes by, and then another. For some strange reason, I continue to track my ovulation. I buy a kit from the Internet, and every day, first thing in the morning, I pee on a wand. It's a little complicated when I stay over at Damien's or Julian's, but I manage.

The three of us spend a lot of time with each other. By now, all my siblings know something is going on. My oldest brother Ben has always known, I've asked Aurora for advice, and Simon's working on Julian's house. I haven't discussed Julian and Damien with Andre, but he's not completely oblivious. He's bound to notice something when I'm not sleeping in my bed more than three nights a week.

But two weeks in, and I still haven't discussed children with them.

"What is wrong with me?" I ask Ben one Sunday afternoon as I drive back from Damien's place. "Why am I not telling them? What the hell is holding me back, Ben?"

My brother doesn't reply right away.

"It's a real relationship; I know it is," I continue. "So why am I not telling them that I'm thirty-five, I'm on a timeline, and I want children? Why am I avoiding having this conversation with them?"

"Well, it's only been a few weeks," my ever-practical brother points out. "It's quite soon."

"They told me they wanted to be in a relationship with me. *They* didn't have any trouble expressing their feelings. Why am I struggling with this?"

"They didn't have our childhood. When things get intense, I run, and so do you." He hesitates for a moment. "Don't tell Papa and Dad because I don't want to hurt their feelings. But I've been seeing a therapist. About never feeling safe because Denise could take us away at any moment. Talking it out helps; it really does."

"Ben, I can't afford a therapist, not with the fertility treatments."

His voice sharpens. "You aren't still thinking about going the sperm donor route, are you? Shouldn't you at least have a conversation with the men you're dating first?"

He's absolutely right. I don't know why I spent three hours on the sperm donor site last week. I don't know why I've narrowed it down to two candidates. I don't know why I'm peeing on a wand every morning. It's as if I'm stuck on a path I can't deviate from, which makes no sense whatsoever. I don't understand my brain.

My silence speaks volumes. "You don't trust them," Ben says.

"No, that's not it. I do trust them." We went to Club M again last night. Julian and Damien found out about my trapeze fantasies, so they suspended me from the ceiling in a sex swing-like contraption in a private room. They blindfolded me and spun me between them. Unable to see, I couldn't tell if I was going to swallow cock, get fucked in my pussy, or in my ass. (Spoiler alert: I did all three.) It was the hottest thing I've ever done, and I could only do it because I trusted them completely.

Right?

"Is it still about them getting you fired?"

"No," I reply instantly. *Is it?* "Damien told me he had nothing to do with it, and I believe him."

But I've never found out how Mrs. Caldwell knew that we'd slept together.

"It was ten years ago, Ben."

"I know that. The real question is, do you? Because something's bothering you, whether you want to admit it or not. If you tell me they haven't done anything to erode your trust in the present, then it has to be about the past. You still have unresolved issues."

Could he be right? But that's insane. Yes, getting fired changed my life, but it turned out to be a good thing in the end. I have a job I truly enjoy, working in a field where I can make a difference. Our community health center does so much good. Patricia is someone I can look up to. I have a beautiful home, good relationships with my family, and now, an amazing sex life. Surely I can't still be hung up about something that happened *ten years ago*.

I'm never going to learn how Mrs. Caldwell found out about us. I haven't kept in touch with anyone from the hospital; I'm never going to get closure on this. I'm never going to learn the answers.

And it doesn't matter.

I can't let the past stand in the way of my future.

On Monday, Patricia corners me in the kitchen. "Sophia," she says as she heats her lunch in the microwave. "I want to talk to you about two things."

My heart beats faster. After Julian brought me flowers, I expected Patricia to ask me about it, but she hasn't. Maybe she's just been biding her time.

"Of course." My grip tightens on my coffee mug. "Shall we head to your office?"

She looks puzzled. "If you want, but these are quick things. First, dinner with Damien Cardenas. You were supposed to schedule that?"

Oh, right. Patricia wanted to take Damien out to dinner to thank him for his million-dollar donation. "I completely forgot about it," I tell her honestly. "I'll set it up."

"Perfect. You have access to my calendar." The microwave beeps, and she takes out her bowl of soup. "The second thing. Finding Donna's replacement. It's been challenging, but I think I've finally found someone who might work. She has a lot of relevant experience, and she's coming in this afternoon. If you have time, I'd like you to interview her."

I cannot keep the surprise off my face. Historically, Patricia conducts all our interviews. "Me?"

She smiles. "Yes, you. I turn fifty-two in February. As much as I'd like to pretend I'm still as young as I was ten or twenty years ago, it's made me realize I need to think about succession plans. A lot of nonprofits are held together by the founder, and when she retires, the organization falls apart. I don't want that to be the case with us, which means I need to train my successor." She takes in my dazed expression. "That's you."

"Yeah," I murmur. For a second, I really thought she was going to fire me. "I'm beginning to understand that."

"So, can you do it?"

She's talking about the interview. "Yes, of course."

. . .

The candidate Patricia has chosen is Arlene Webb. I didn't have time to look at her resume before the interview, so it's not until she's in the lobby that I realize with a start that she looks extremely familiar. I am trying to figure out where I know her from when her face breaks out into a smile. "Sophia," she exclaims. "What a delightful surprise. We worked together at Harrisburg General Hospital, remember? I was Florence Caldwell's administrative assistant."

My body goes cold. "Of course," I choke out. "Please come in."

I conduct the interview on autopilot. "I retired last year," Mrs. Webb tells me. "For the first few months, I was delighted. I spent time gardening, baking, and making clothes for my grandchildren." She smiles ruefully. "And now I'm bored. This job is temporary, but it will keep me busy, and it'll keep my mind active." She looks up at me. "Is that going to be a problem?"

"Will what be a problem?"

"Well, I'm sixty-seven, dear."

It's not as if we have hundreds of candidates beating down our door. Even if we did, it wouldn't matter. I remember Mrs. Webb. The hospital was a miserable place to work in, and Mrs. Caldwell had been a terrible administrator. But Arlene Webb was always calm, always composed. She was an oasis.

Patricia told me I was in charge of this decision. "No, it's definitely not a problem. If you want the job, it's yours."

Pleasure fills her face. "Thank you," she says. "When would you like me to start?"

"Tomorrow?" I ask hopefully. "I can get you the paperwork right away. I'm not going to lie; we're more than a little desperate."

She laughs. "How about Wednesday?"

I print out an offer letter, and she signs it. She gets up to leave, and she hesitates at my door. "I might be out of line," she says. "But I'm so happy to see you thriving, Sophia. What George and Florence did to you was so very unfair."

"George?"

"You wouldn't know, would you? Well, it's been ten years, so there's no harm in telling you. George Turner came into the office to talk to Florence, and I overheard their conversation." Her expression turns disapproving. "He made some disgusting insinuations about you, and Florence believed him."

George Turner, the guy on my team? "What did he say?"

"I don't feel right repeating it," she replies primly. "It wasn't decent."

My heart is beating faster. "Please, Mrs. Webb. It's important to me."

"He said that you were with more than one man." She shakes her head. "It was obvious that he was out to cause trouble. Florence should have sent him away at once, but instead, she fired you. She was always ready to believe the worst of you."

"Because I have two fathers," I reply on autopilot. My brain is working overtime. George Turner didn't accuse me of sleeping with Damien; it was more specific than that. He evidently told Mrs. Caldwell I had a threesome.

But how did he know? We'd been at Club M. Xavier Leforte prides himself on discretion. How did George Turner find out?

"Even so, it was a vicious lie and—"

I could let her believe that, but something inside me

rebels at the idea. I'm not going to hide who I am anymore. I'm not going to hide Damien and Julian. "It wasn't a lie," I interrupt. "It was true." I hold her gaze. "If that changes your mind about working here, then I understand."

Her mouth falls open. She blinks. For a long moment, she struggles for words but seems to reach a decision. "Your personal life is your business, my dear. I cannot judge you. Let he who is without sin cast the first stone." She gets up and holds out her hand to me with a small smile. "I'm looking forward to working here, Sophia. I'll see you on Wednesday."

AFTER MRS. WEBB LEAVES, I text Damien about Patricia's dinner invitation, and we pick a date in two weeks. He said he was only here in Highfield for four weeks, but the dinner date we pick is past when he's supposed to leave. I want to ask him about it, but I don't.

I try to focus on my work, but concentration is impossible. Over and over, I keep circling around the same thing. How did George Turner find out about my night at Club M? Was he there? I can't see it. Club M's members have always been part of the billionaire class. George was like me: neither of us belonged to that world.

I barely remember him. He was on my team, he wasn't too bright, and Karina, my boss, didn't like him. He had a bad habit of taking credit for other people's work. Especially the work of the women on his team.

But there is a vast difference between being a somewhat slimy coworker and getting me fired.

I tell myself to let it go, but I can't. Ten years ago, getting fired was the most awful thing that ever happened to me. It made me believe the worst of Damien, and it killed the prospect of a relationship between the three of us. Even now, I find myself hesitating to trust them completely. Yes, I let them tie me up, but I can't put my future in their hands.

Something is holding me back. Maybe it's this? Maybe George Turner is at the root of it all?

I have to talk to him. I have to find out what really happened.

But how? I turn to my computer and search for him. It doesn't take me long to find his profile on a professional networking site. He's currently looking for a job. The site lists his phone number and his email address.

I could get in contact with him. He has his address listed, and the town he lives in is eighty-five miles away. I could be there in an hour and a half.

Before I can talk myself out of it, I make myself dial his number.

30

DAMIEN

For a few days after the leadership meeting, matters simmer along. Some people are discontented—Ted Boric, Arther Scott, Lina Aquino—but nobody wants to come out and oppose me directly. That's fine with me. I'm done playing nice. As long as my changes are implemented, I don't care if they're refusing to link arms and sing "Kumbaya."

But on a Monday morning a couple of weeks after the shake-up, matters come to a head.

Jack Rutherford, the president of the Australian division, calls me at eight in the morning. He gets right to the point. "I wanted to let you know that I'm quitting."

Fuck.

I pour myself a cup of coffee and struggle to wake up. "Where are you going?" I ask him, running down the list of potential options. If Jack wants to stay in Australia, which I assume he does—he has three children, two of them still in school—then he's being recruited by either Laverton, Neale Minerals, Elliot Chemicals, or Wells Petrochemicals. Laverton would be my best guess. Their last earnings report was disappointing, and their board would be looking for new leadership. "I'd appreciate a chance to counter."

"Laverton."

I wish I felt better about being right.

"And I don't think you can counter, Damien," he continues. "It's not about the money. I've been in the industry for twenty years. When I joined Cardenas, I thought it was a good place to grow. But I can't work with my hands tied behind my back. I have to have the freedom to make decisions. When your father died, I thought things might improve, but they didn't. And now, the Bonnie Rock thing is the last straw."

"What Bonnie Rock thing?" I open my laptop and send Luis a note, asking him to get me details on Bonnie Rock and Laverton ASAP.

He doesn't appear to hear my question. "The M&A team doesn't know a damn thing about Australia," he grits out. "Ted Boric is an idiot. My team did the due diligence. An opportunity like Bonnie Rock doesn't come along every single day. It would have set us up for another five years of double-digit growth. Instead of moving quickly, Ted Boric put it at the back of his queue, and now it's too late. They're going to sell to Neale."

Luis is on it, as usual. He replies to my email in seconds. I read the details. Bonnie Rock is a samarium mine. The rare earth mineral is mined mostly in China and used in control rods of nuclear reactors.

Fuck. Fuck, fuck, and more fuck. Jack is right; this is an opportunity we should have jumped on. But anything to do with nuclear technology would be a new market for us, and Boric doesn't think big. And now we've lost out to Neale Minerals.

No wonder he's ready to quit.

"I'm either in charge of the Australian division or not," he finishes. "And it's obvious to me I'm not. I don't want to work in this environment, Damien. I don't need the aggravation."

I close my eyes, take a deep breath, and fight to keep him. "Laverton is headquartered in Perth," I point out. "That's a long way from Sydney. Your daughter is in high school. It's a hard time to move your family across the country."

"I've thought about it," he says. "Evelyn will adjust."

I feel terrible about this. I've been avoiding the problem. I knew Boric wasn't on board with my changes; I should have kept a closer eye on him. But for the first time in a long time, I prioritized my personal life. Dating Sophia, hanging out by the lake. I even took the canoe out.

It came at a cost.

"I'm making changes," I tell him. "My team has a list of items to tackle. In six months, I promise you that the Cardenas Group will be a very different place to work for."

"I saw your proposal," he acknowledges.

He did? "Then you know what I want to do. I have Tomas' buy-in. Things are going to get better."

"And do you have your mother's buy-in?" he asks shrewdly.

Damn it.

"Give me two weeks, Jack." My team routinely analyzes our competitors, and Luis has forwarded me Melanie's Laverton assessment from last year. "Laverton isn't perfect either. They've been showing declining earnings for three years straight, and their board isn't noted for their patience. There will be a lot of pressure on you to deliver results immediately, but there's not a lot you can do in the short-term."

His silence tells me he knows the problems he's inheriting. Thank you, Luis and Melanie.

"I promise I'll make it worth your while."

"I don't know, Damien." He's quiet for a long time. Then he says, "Okay, fine. Two weeks."

It's time to talk to my mother. I hang up and pour myself another cup of coffee, ignoring the dull ache in my chest. I'm going to need all the caffeine in the world for this conversation.

I'VE TALKED to my mother in the last two weeks, but we've both tiptoed around the changes I'm making. I know she doesn't approve, but she hasn't come out in opposition, and I've been happy enough to avoid this confrontation. No matter what she might think, I don't want to stress her out.

But it's time.

I dial her number. She picks up. "Damien," she says, sounding pleased to hear from me. "You're up early."

"I just got a call from Jack Rutherford," I tell her. "Why did Ted Boric turn down the Bonnie Rock acquisition?"

"Ted didn't think it fit our strategic priorities."

She knows exactly what I'm talking about. Retired, my ass. She's more informed than me. Or maybe Gisele's pulling up the information for her, the way Luis did for me. Or, the most likely scenario, Ted bypassed me and told her directly.

"Ted wouldn't know a strategic priority if it slapped him in the face," I retort. "He's the most risk-averse person on the planet." I take a sip of my coffee and attempt to calm down. "At our leadership meeting a couple of weeks ago, I made it clear that our divisions were to have more flexibility. Ted went against my wishes."

"He's watching out for the company."

"I want him out." My frustration boils over. "Mama, I'm trying to make changes, and Boric has been resistant at every turn. He's not the only one. They come to you, and they cry about my decisions, and you back them up. This isn't the first time. You told Vicky to attend the Arca negotiations even though I put Rafal Loyola in charge."

"He's only been with the company for three years."

Suddenly, I'm weary. I can't keep pushing uphill. *I don't want to.*

"You overruled my decision," I reply. "You've done it ever since I joined the company." A sense of peace washes over me. "I don't want to start a war with you, Mama. I love you. But you're not leaving me any choice."

"Your father sacrificed—"

"Stop. This isn't about what Papa did or didn't do. The Cardenas Group is a multibillion-dollar company. We cannot run it like it's a small family firm." I'm done holding my tongue. "You don't trust me. It was always understood that I would get some experience and come back and run the family firm. If you've changed your mind about that, that's okay. Let me know, and I'll go elsewhere. But if you want me here, then you have to let me lead."

"Ted Boric—"

I don't give a fuck what Boric thinks. "When Papa died, I didn't push it. You were grieving, and so was I. It wasn't the right time for this conversation. But it's been three years, and nothing has changed with how we run the company. Here's my ultimatum, Mama. Either I get a free hand, or I'm out. You have two weeks to make up your mind."

And then I hang up.

31

SOPHIA

Three hours after making that phone call, I sit down for coffee with George Turner.

The years haven't been kind to Turner. His eyes are bloodshot, his hair is thinning, and there's a mustard stain on his shirt I'm trying very hard not to stare at.

"Did you get me fired from the hospital?" I ask bluntly. I'd debated the best way to approach this topic on the drive over, but I couldn't decide what to do. Evidently, I left subtlety fifty miles down the road.

Turner doesn't give me a direct answer. At least, not immediately. "For ten years, I thought you might ask me about it," he says. "How did you figure out that it was me?"

I won't tell him what Mrs. Webb told me. "Did you do it?"

"Oh, what the hell? Yeah, fine. I did. I told Mrs. Caldwell that you were in a threesome. I knew she would fire you, that uptight bitch."

She was a bitch, but it still makes me angry when he calls her that. "How did you find out?"

"I overheard Cardenas talk about it." He sneers. "The pretty boy with his bespoke suits and his handmade shoes."

Damien wouldn't have been indiscreet. I need more details. "Where? At work?"

"At the IHOP. I went for my usual Sunday morning breakfast, and Cardenas came in with another man. He didn't even realize I was there. Can you believe it? People like me are nothing to him."

You're nothing to me too, George, you fucking slime.

"What did they say?" I probe.

"I can't remember. Cardenas said something like he didn't expect that to happen. And the other man said that he wanted to see you again. He asked Cardenas how he felt about sharing, and he said, 'If Sophia is fine with it, then so am I.'" He leers at me. "That's when I knew who they were talking about. You."

I ignore his expression. "And you told Mrs. Caldwell. Why? What the hell did it matter what I did outside of work?"

"Karina was looking for another job," he replies. "When she left, she was going to recommend you as her replacement. I wanted the job, so I did what I had to do."

I don't know why I'm shocked. I shouldn't be. Turner always took credit for our work. This is only a short step away. "You got me fired so you could get promoted?"

"Don't pretend that you wouldn't do it," he snaps. "Don't pretend to be saintly. I would do anything to get ahead, and so would you. It's a dog-eat-dog world. You have to watch out for yourself because nobody else will watch out for you."

They'd been overheard at an IHOP. It's so ridiculous I want to laugh. All the while, I thought it was a grand betrayal, but it was just bad luck that Turner was at the same diner as Damien and Julian. If I wanted, I could be angry that they discussed me at all, but that would be completely irrational.

Damien and Julian didn't get me fired. George Turner did.

"You're wrong," I say, getting to my feet. "People don't have to screw people over to get ahead. I'm sorry you never learned that lesson."

I always pictured Damien telling Mrs. Caldwell that he slept with me, but even in my deepest rage, it hadn't rung true. I clung to it anyway, clung to my anger. It was easier to believe they got me fired than to face the alternative. Which is that after just one night, *I was well on my way to falling in love with them.*

I glance at the dashboard. It's eight. Damien and Julian were going to paint Julian's foyer. They invited me, but I've barely been at home and have laundry to do, so I declined.

They're going to be at Julian's house. I need to talk to them. It's time to put it all out in the open.

32

JULIAN

I'm having a particularly shitty day, so when Damien comes over an hour earlier than he was supposed to, I'm pretty happy about the interruption.

Then I look at his face. "What happened?"

"I gave my mother an ultimatum," he replies wearily. "Either she stops interfering in the way I run the company, or I'm out."

I stare at my friend. This is long overdue, but I didn't think Damien would ever rebel. "How did she react?"

"I'm not sure. I turned off my phone." He shakes his head. "Enough about me. What's going on with you?"

He looks like he could use a break from his problems, so I tell him mine. "I sent Francisco Flores a completed screenplay, and he wrote back saying that the work wasn't good enough, and I needed to start over."

"What the hell?" Damien demands. "What did Shaun say?"

"I haven't talked to him yet."

Damien gives me an exasperated look. He opens his mouth to yell at me, and I hold up my hand. "I'm going to," I tell him. "I'm done. Flores hasn't been helpful. We're supposed to be working on this thing together, and he hasn't done a damn thing. This is his script too. I'm not going to rewrite it."

"So, what's the hold-up? If you're out of fucks, why haven't you talked to Shaun? Be like me, Julian. Blow up your life with one well-placed phone call."

He's more bothered about his ultimatum than he's letting on. Not surprising. Damien's too responsible to take this lightly. He won't be able to walk away that easily. "I know I should. But it's hard to sweat the small stuff when you're happy."

A smile breaks out on his face. "There is that," he agrees. "Once upon a time, the thought of walking away from the company would have wrecked me. But now, I just feel peaceful. Don't get me wrong, I didn't want to make this move. But if my mother accepts my resignation, life will move on." He opens my refrigerator door, grabs a couple of beers, and hands me one. "My doctor sent me here to take time off, and I've failed miserably at that. But one thing I did figure out is what I wanted from my life."

I feel exactly the same way. The last few weeks have really crystallized what's important. It's not my career. It's not whether this pilot gets made. It's not whether Francisco Florez cooperates with me.

No, what truly matters is the people in my life. Hannah having her wedding at Kincaid Castle. Finding Sophia again, rekindling a relationship with her. Being happier than I've been in a long time.

"Things are good."

"They really are," Damien agrees. He fiddles with the beer label, worrying it with his fingers. "I'm in love with her."

"Welcome to the club."

He flashes me a grin in response. "I've been thinking," he says. "If I'm still working at the Cardenas Group next month, I can work out of the Manhattan office. I'll probably need to be there two days a week, but I can work remotely the other three. I don't know where we're going to live, but—"

I hold up my hand, laughing. "Aren't you getting a little ahead of yourself?"

"It's an occupational hazard," he replies wryly.

Just then, my phone rings. I pick it up, and it's Damien's brother, Cristiano. "Julian, Damien's phone is turned off, and I need to reach him in a hurry. If you hear from him, can you ask him to call me back?"

Yeah, Damien's family won't let him walk away. "Sure thing," I tell Cristiano. "I'll pass on the message." I hang up. "That was for you. Cristiano wants you to call him back."

"Oh, for fuck's sake," Damien swears. "I would have expected a call from Tomas or Vicky, but I thought Cristiano would stay out of it." He grimaces. "There will be yelling. I better step outside for this. Wish me luck."

"Good luck," I tell him. He doesn't need it, though. For the first time in a long time, things are really going to be okay. Everything is going to be amazing. I just know it.

33

DAMIEN

I head into the garden and take a seat by the greenhouse. It's well into September. The days are getting shorter, and the sun has already set. I sit on a bench under a dusk sky, turn my phone on, and call my brother back.

Cristiano picks up on the first ring. "Listen," I tell him. "If it's about the company and my ultimatum to Mama, I don't really want to—"

"No," he interrupts. "It's not about that. I heard what happened, and I fully support you. So does Vicky. It's about time you put your foot down. No, this is about something else." He sucks in a breath. "Liz called. She wants to reevaluate our agreement."

I sit up. Lizbeth Bernal is Cristiano and Magnus' surrogate. She's three months pregnant. "What does she want?" I ask. "Does she want to keep the baby?"

Technically, Lizbeth doesn't have any parental rights. It was Magnus' sperm and a donor egg. Cristiano and Magnus went through an agency. The agreement they signed with Liz specified that they were responsible for her medical costs, in addition to a mid-six-figure compensation. But the law is one thing, and feelings are another. The woman is carrying a child. She's doing one of the most generous things I can think of for someone else. Cristiano might be frustrated, but he needs to be gentle.

"No," he replies grimly. "That's not it, Damien. She found out who I was. She wants fifteen million dollars, and she wants to change the agreement to have parental rights. *Or else.*" He sighs. "It's extortion, of course. I'd pay it, but I don't think it's a one-time thing."

No. Sophia went through something similar with her birth mother. Even now, there's so much pain in her voice when she talks about how afraid she was that she'd be torn from her home.

I see red. I've had a long, frustrating day, and this is the last straw. I'm done playing nice. Liz is trying to blackmail Magnus and my brother, and I won't stand for it. "We have lawyers," I grit out through clenched teeth. "We have money. Lizbeth made an agreement with you, and she needs to honor it. If she doesn't, she'll find out what we're made of. Our detectives will dig through her life. We will talk to everyone from her past. If she continues down this path, we will destroy her."

34

SOPHIA

I pull into Julian's driveway. Rather than knock on the door, I decide to walk around the back. It's been a week since I was here, and I want to see what Simon's done with the greenhouse.

Then I overhear Damien.

"... Lizbeth made an agreement with you, and she needs to honor it. If she doesn't, she'll find out what we're made of."

Alarm dashes down my spine. I've never heard Damien sound like this. Icily furious. Cold. *Ruthless.*

Lizbeth is his brother's surrogate. I know this because it was her birthday last week, and Damien sent her flowers. "It's the least I can do," he'd said. "She's voluntarily choosing to be pregnant for nine months so Cristiano and Magnus can have a baby. The woman's a saint."

She was a saint, and now she's the enemy.

"Our detectives will dig through her life. We will talk to everyone from her past. If she continues down this path, we will destroy her."

I tiptoe away, shocked tears rolling down my cheeks and realization dawning in my heart.

I get it now.

This is what I'd been afraid of.

My fear hadn't been about the past, after all. It wasn't about getting fired. Ten years ago, that might have bothered me, but time healed that wound.

No, I'm afraid about the future. If I were to get pregnant with Damien's child, and we split up, this is how he would react. He will threaten me the way he's threatening his brother's surrogate. He can take my child away, the way Denise threatened to take Ben and me away. It will break my heart.

I even remember thinking that. After my first appointment with Dr. Hernandez, Ben asked me if there was anyone in my life, and I said no. I thought then that I could never have a baby with Damien. He was too wealthy, I told myself. In a custody dispute, he'd be able to out-lawyer me. As much as I'd like to pretend otherwise, the legal system favors the rich. It always has.

How could I let myself forget? Good sex is its own kind of amnesia, but now, hearing Damien ruthlessly promise to destroy Lizbeth, it all comes rushing back.

Our detectives will dig through her life. We will talk to everyone from her past.

They won't have to dig too much in my case. All they'd have to do is point out that I was in a threesome. If there's a dispute between us, Damien's lawyers can paint me as a slut because that's how society works. Women are shamed, and guys walk away, untouched by scandal.

I can't be in a poly relationship and have a baby. The power imbalance between us is too great, and I can't take the risk. I made myself a promise that I would never put my child in a situation where someone could take her away from me.

I'm going to keep that promise.

I want a child. I really do. My heart yearns for a baby. And if that's going to happen, I need to end things with Damien and Julian.

I CRY MYSELF TO SLEEP. All night my dreams are fragmented and filled with a sense of dread. I wake up feeling sick to my stomach, and when I pee on the wand, it shows that my hormone levels are elevated.

I'm ovulating.

I can wait a few months. But how long will it take my heart to recover? Years. *Decades.* And I don't have that much time.

My heart is broken, but I have to be practical.

I make myself call the fertility clinic. "I know this is last minute, but according to my tracker, I'm ovulating," I tell Laura at the front desk. I grope in my purse for a coin and toss it in the air. Heads, it's Donor Sperm #181. Tails, Mr. 155. 155 wins. "I've picked a donor from the registry. Is there any way to rush this thing?"

Laura probably thinks I'm crazy. Who orders vials of sperm for next-day delivery? This isn't Amazon.

"Which registry?" she asks.

I give her the details, and she looks them up. "Yes, that should be possible."

"It is?"

"They're in Pittsburgh. They can FedEx it, and it'll be here tomorrow morning."

"They can?"

Her voice softens. "You sound like you're having second thoughts. If you're not sure you're ready for this, wait."

I shove thoughts of Damien and Julian out of my mind. I want a baby. "I'm ready."

Tuesday evening, with fresh tears pouring down my cheeks, I send Julian and Damien a text breaking things off. *I don't want to talk about it,* I write. *Please don't try to contact me. I've made up my mind.*

Then, for good measure, I block their phone numbers.

Wednesday afternoon, Dr. Hernandez injects a vial of sperm from Donor 155 into my cervix. I stay immobile for fifteen minutes after the procedure, and then I walk out of there.

I tell myself it's better this way. *Safer.* I tell myself I'm doing what I need to do to protect myself.

But my heart feels like it's been scoured with bleach. It's raw and bruised and bleeding.

35

JULIAN

At first, I don't believe it. It's a prank. *It has to be.* We saw Sophia on Saturday, and everything was good. We went to Club M. We got a private room and did the hottest scene in my life. We ate dinner afterward, soaked in Damien's hot tub, and talked about everything under the sun. She spent the night, ate breakfast with us the next day, and kissed us goodbye.

Everything seemed perfect.

What happened?

I tell myself frantically it's got to be some kind of joke. But my heart is racing, and my palms are clammy. A sense of déjà vu washes over me. This is exactly what happened ten years ago. We went to the club, everything seemed fine, and then she stopped talking to us.

Worry grips me. Did something happen at her work? Did she get fired? Was it because of the stupid flowers I took her?

I dial her number, still convinced this has to be a mistake. Still convinced whatever happened, we can work it out.

The call doesn't connect.

She's blocked my number.

Bile rises in my mouth. I stumble around my house, dazed, shocked, not knowing what hit me. The next thing I'm aware of is Damien coming over. "I just got a text from Sophia breaking things off," he says dully.

"Me too." I want to throw something. I want to scream. Shout. And more than anything, I want to *understand*.

"I thought she got into trouble at work, so I tried to call her." Pain stabs through me. "She blocked my phone number."

"She blocked mine too." Damien looks the way I feel. Lost. "I had Xavier call her boss. She's still there. This isn't about her work."

"Xavier asked her boss if she fired Sophia?"

"I assume he was more subtle than that," he replies. "What the hell happened, Julian?"

I don't know. Just yesterday, I thought everything I ever wanted was within my grasp. The greenhouse was going to be ready for Hannah's wedding. My sister wanted me to give her away. We're closer now than we've been in a long time.

And I was in a relationship with Sophia.

Just yesterday, I thought I had everything.

"We have to do something," I tell Damien.

"What do you suggest we do?" my friend snaps. "Because her message is pretty fucking clear. She says she doesn't want to see us. She blocked our phone numbers. There's no ambiguity here, none at all."

"We could go see her," I reply mulishly.

"And then what?" he asks. "We ignore her wishes and force ourselves into her life, and then what? Should I dangle another million dollars in front of her so she'll talk to me again? Should I buy the health center and become her boss so she can't avoid me?"

Pain flashes over his face. "She either wants to be with us, or she doesn't. I hate this, but she has the right to make these choices. I won't turn into a stalker, Julian."

Damn it. I hate when he's right. I sink into a chair and cradle my head in my hands. "What are we going to do?"

"I don't know," he says bleakly. "I guess we survive."

Damien gave his mother an ultimatum yesterday. He needed to make space in his life for Sophia, and he was prepared to renounce the family firm for it. Twenty-four hours later, he has neither the firm nor the girl. "Have you heard from your mother?"

He shakes his head. "That's the least of my problems right now." He gets to his feet abruptly. "I'll see you around, Julian."

He's lying. He won't be around, and I won't go looking for him. It's too painful.

What do you do when your world ends? Over the days that follow, I ask myself that question, but the answer eludes me.

I write a note to Flores telling him I'm done working on the screenplay. He doesn't respond. I might have blown up the *Revenant* deal, but I can't bring myself to care.

In the past, when I've been overwhelmed, I always reached for my sketchpad. I buried myself in a concept and ignored everything else.

Not this time. My brain is blank. I'm entombed in a world of pain. It hurts to breathe. This time, when I pick up a pencil, all I can sketch is her. When I draw, my fingers remember her face.

And so I fill page after page with drawings of Sophia. That's all I can do.

36

SOPHIA

I cry. I cry a lot.

I regret going to the fertility clinic and going through with the sperm donation. I miss Damien and Julian. My life narrows to the essentials. I hold it together at work. When I return home, I head straight to my room, shut the door, and cry my eyes out. I skip the gym; I skip my cooking turn. I hide.

By Friday, my entire family has figured out something is wrong. Ben calls, but I swipe it to voicemail. Same with Aurora. Papa calls, and I have never not picked up his call, but this time, I can't face him. I can't face anybody.

I swing from one extreme to another. One minute, I'm convinced I made a mistake breaking up with them; the next minute, I'm telling myself it was the right thing to do.

It was smart to end things before I got in too deep, I think. But even as that thought forms, my heart knows it's a lie. It's too late.

This is for the best, but it doesn't feel like it. I feel like I've been hollowed out from the inside. The only emotion left is misery.

I drive by the turnoff to Damien's lake house, and I cry. I pass Julian's house on Hill Street, and I cry again. I keep thinking about them. I keep poking at the wound.

On Sunday, I do the unthinkable. I skip family dinner and go for a long drive instead. I head to Taco Gus, get tacos to go, and then drive to the park where Julian and I had lunch. I sit on the same picnic bench. Here, less than a month ago, he spilled marinara sauce on his T-shirt, took it off, and I ogled him shamelessly.

It seems so long ago, and it feels like yesterday.

What are they thinking right now? They've got to be feeling hurt. Bewildered. Or maybe they're angry with me for taking off without an explanation. *Again.* Maybe they realize they're better off without me.

Because I've done it again. Ten years ago, when Mrs. Caldwell fired me, I ran from Damien and Julian.

But this time, it's justified. You heard Damien. You heard him with your own ears.

Or is it?

You didn't bother to ask them for an explanation. You didn't hear Damien's side.

Ben's words echo in my mind. *When things get intense, I run, and so do you.*

I can't keep blaming my biological mother for how fucked up I am. I need to take responsibility. Denise didn't wreck my life. Mrs. Caldwell didn't wreck my life either. I did this to myself.

Maybe I should talk to them.

No. Stop. And then what? What are you going to say? That you're sorry, and that you won't do it again? Words are cheap. The next time something happens, you'll run again. Stop fucking up their lives. They deserve so much better than you. They have given you unconditional love, and again and again, you've thrown it in their faces. You don't deserve them. Let them move on.

I feel thin and fragile, hollowed out and hopeless.

Ben told me to find a therapist. I told him I couldn't afford it, and I still can't. I've put the fertility clinic on my credit card. There have been multiple charges, each of them thousands of dollars. I don't want to total it up.

But I have to do something to change the situation.

A donor, Hunter Driesse, is a therapist at the local hospital. I can't ask him to be my therapist; that would be completely inappropriate. But I don't think Patricia would object if I ask him for a recommendation.

I pick up my phone and dial.

Simon and Andre are waiting up for me when I finally come back home. "You want a beer?" Simon asks.

"No, thank you."

"You missed dinner," Andre says carefully. "We can hear you cry. Do you want to talk about what's going on with you?"

He looks so worried. Fresh tears well in my eyes. "I was dating Damien and Julian, and I'm not anymore."

"What happened?"

I shake my head mutely. "I don't want to discuss it," I mumble. Because if I do, I will cry again. Then I flee.

37

DAMIEN

What do you do when your life crashes around you?

Some people drink. Me, I drown myself in work.

I haven't heard from my mother, but that doesn't mean I don't have things to do. The day-to-day demands of my job never go away. Meetings, emails, phone calls—everyone needs something from me.

It's relentless, but I'm done fighting for balance. I don't want to hear from my strategy team about the changes I'm pushing through—I can't seem to bring myself to care. I tell Luis to stop protecting my calendar. "Schedule me in for every meeting you can."

I try to keep my voice matter-of-fact, but Luis has known me for a very long time. "Are you okay, Damien?"

One way or the other, no matter what happens to my future at the Cardenas Group, I'm going to make sure Luis is taken care of. If he wants to stay, I'll make sure he's protected. If he wants out, I'll arrange it. Loyalty is a rare thing, and Luis has it in spades.

"Yeah," I lie. "I'm fine."

I sit through the most mind-numbingly boring meetings imaginable. Anything to while away the hours. Anything to keep my mind off *her*. Anything to stop thinking about Sophia.

It doesn't work. For two weeks, I was given a glimpse of a future filled with possibilities. For two weeks, I cooked and ate good food. I swam in the lake every morning. I soaked in the hot tub. I didn't rush from one meeting to another; I stopped to smell the roses.

It was because of Sophia.

For two weeks, I had everything.

And it's been snatched away from me.

I should keep up the good habits, but it all feels meaningless. So I drink too much coffee, I work too hard, and I avoid Julian. He's in pain too, and I can't bear it. It's too much of a reminder of my own heartache.

I tried to fight, and I failed. I tried to push for something better, and everything fell apart around me.

Xavier calls me one day. Is it a Monday? Wednesday? I've lost track of time. "I've been meaning to ask," he says. "You've gone to the club a couple of times as my guest. You seem to be spending quite a lot of time in Highfield. Do you want to buy a membership?"

Xavier is worth billions. He doesn't give a fuck whether I buy a membership or not. I asked him to check if Sophia had been fired, and Xavier is as curious as a cat. This is his way of finding out what's going on with me.

"No," I reply. "I don't foresee any more trips to Club M in my future."

"What happened with Sophia?"

"I don't know, Xavier," I grit out. My frustration boils over, and I snap at my friend. "I don't know what happened, and I don't know why, but it's off. And there's nothing you can do about it. Please let it be."

I clench my eyes shut as a fresh wave of grief washes over me. It'll be okay, I tell myself. Time heals all wounds. This, too, will fade.

I wish I could believe it.

38

JULIAN

Simon shows up to work on Wednesday and Thursday, but there's no sign of him on Friday. Maybe he's found out that Sophia has broken up with us, and maybe that means he's done with this job. I can't bring myself to care.

I'm surprised when he knocks on my door on Monday. I let him in. He looks like he's trying not to punch me. "Did you break up with my sister, you asshole?" he demands.

My expression must be answer enough because he deflates. "You didn't?"

"No."

"Did the other guy break up with her? Damien?"

"No," I repeat. Short, one-word answers are all I have energy for. Anything else seems impossible.

"What the hell happened, man? You guys seemed happy. Was it the threesome? Did one of you get jealous?"

I shake my head. "No," I say for the third time. "I don't know what happened. Sophia sent us a text ending things."

Simon looks sympathetic. "She doesn't do relationships," he says. "She doesn't put herself in situations where she can be hurt. She's always been this way. When you guys came along, I hoped..."

His voice trails off, and then he shrugs awkwardly. "Anyway, your boilers will be in next week."

"Oh."

"Months ahead of schedule," he points out.

Hannah will be delighted. A sudden hope strikes me. Simon is Sophia's brother. "Will you pass on a message to her?"

He takes a step back and holds up his hands. "I don't know, Julian. I don't want to get in the middle of things. Sophia is my sister. I'm always going to take her side."

"Please." I'm practically begging. "Just tell her I love her. Tell her that Damien loves her. Whatever we did, we'll fix."

Simon doesn't meet my gaze. He looks deeply uncomfortable. "I'll think about it," he murmurs.

I've never fallen in love. Never had a relationship that lasted longer than a few months. Neither has Damien. This is why. It's always been Sophia. It will always be Sophia.

39

SOPHIA

Hunter Driesse recommends a colleague of his, Dr. Annette Reeves. "She's excellent," he says. "She might be booked up, though. I'm having lunch with her tomorrow. I'll tell her you'll be reaching out."

Dr. Reeves agrees to see me on Friday. I show up at her office feeling nervous and heartsick. By the time I leave, I'm cried out and drained, but also a tiny bit hopeful. Ben was right. I should have seen a therapist years ago.

Simon corners me in the kitchen when I get back home. I didn't expect to see him there. It's Friday night, and my brother is still in the 'must-go-out-every-Friday-night' stage of his life. "Did your plans fall through?"

"No, I thought I'd hang out with you."

"What if I hadn't been at home?"

He makes a scoffing noise in his throat. "Please. You've been moping all week." He grabs a beer out of the refrigerator and offers me one. I decline it. *Just in case.* He cracks open the bottle and takes a long swig from it. "I talked to Julian on Monday," he says carefully.

My heart does a funny leap in my chest. "Oh." I have so

many questions. How is he doing? Did he mention me? Was Damien there? Are they angry? Do they hate me?

"Does it bother you that I'm working on his greenhouse? Should I stop?"

"What?" I stare up at my brother. "No, of course not. I'm not asking you to take sides. You agreed to work on his place. His sister is getting married there in December. You can't walk off the job."

He gives me a quizzical look. "Why do you care, Sophia?"

I swallow the lump in my throat. My eyes are prickling again. I'm ridiculously emotional nowadays. I'm so fragile from breaking things off with Julian and Damien that everything makes me cry. Last night, a stupid insurance commercial made me tear up.

I dig my nails into my palm and do my best to keep my voice steady. "I don't hate him," I whisper. "I don't hate either of them."

"Why did you break up with them, then?"

Annette asked me that too. I'd poured the whole thing out, and she frowned at me, puzzled. "What did Damien say when you asked him about the conversation?"

"I didn't ask him," I confessed, shamefaced. I've always thought of myself as a responsible adult. I've been working since I was eighteen. I get along with most people, pay my bills on time, and don't read or respond to the comments section of the Internet.

But I ran out on them. Didn't ask for an explanation. Didn't listen to what they had to say. I assumed the worst of them.

I was so impulsive. So thoughtless. So stupid.

I don't deserve them.

I'm drained from telling Annette everything, and I don't

have the energy to talk about this with my brother. "It's complicated."

"Do you regret it?"

"Yes." With every fiber of my being. If I could roll back the clock, I would. But I can't. There are no time machines in real life.

"Why don't you call them?"

Because they deserve better. They deserve someone who isn't this fucked up. They deserve someone who will stick around when times get hard.

"It's complicated," I say again.

"Do you want to?"

I nod wordlessly, my eyes filling with tears.

He gives me a long look. "Julian asked me to pass on a message to you," he says. "He said, 'Whatever we did, we'll fix.'"

Hope sprouts in my heart, but I trample it. It's not them that need fixing. *It's me.*

SATURDAY MORNING, I finally rouse myself out of my stupor and head to the community garden where I volunteer. Rosemary Travis, the founder, is there, weeding a bed of lettuce. "Sophia," she exclaims. "I've been meaning to call you."

I blink in confusion. I've seen Rosemary around, of course, but I didn't realize she knew my name. I'm just one of many volunteers.

She gets up, brushes mud off her knees, and gives me a hug. "I can't thank you enough, my dear."

"Umm, for what?"

"For connecting Julian Kincaid and Damien Cardenas with us," she replies.

"I didn't—"

"The two of them have been so helpful," she gushes. "And the timing! We'd lost our grant. Without money, we would have been forced to shut down next year, but—"

"I didn't know you were going to shut down," I interrupt.

"Yes, well. I try not to alarm our volunteers. I'm sure you can relate. Things were looking really bleak, and then Damien and Julian showed up. Damien said you mentioned that we were always looking for volunteers."

I did?

"And they donated some money?" They would. They both have generous hearts. Julian donated his signed comics to the health center's fundraiser, and they both bid generously at the auction. And, of course, Damien followed up with another million-dollar donation.

"Money, yes, but they did so much more," she says. "For a couple of years, I've been meaning to set up a CSA box to generate some revenue, but I don't have a technical background. Damien built us a website, and Julian designed our packaging. Can you imagine that? Then he mentioned us on his social media, which led to a flood of donations, which led to articles in the press. . ." She shakes her head. "Our CSA box hasn't even launched yet, and it's already sold out. I'm still pinching myself."

I don't know what to say. What to think. "When did they do this?"

"They've been volunteering for weeks," Rosemary replies. "I think they showed up in mid-September? Damien was here yesterday."

My heart gives another leap. He's still here? I thought he'd go back to Manhattan or Lima or wherever else he had a house. Why hasn't he left? Why is he still in Highfield?

. . .

I dream about a baby that night. I'm in the hospital, giving birth. Damien and Julian are there, beaming with pride. My family is there too. My fathers, brothers, and Aurora all crowd into the hospital room where I'm holding my baby girl.

The dream is so vivid it takes me a few minutes to realize it isn't real. But I can't shake the images. They stick with me all morning. A voice inside me whispers that it isn't a dream. Not anymore. *It's coming true.*

That same voice drives me to the drugstore, where I buy a pregnancy test. It's been eleven days since the procedure at the fertility clinic. It's too soon to know.

Yet I lock myself in our upstairs bathroom and pee on the stick.

And it comes back positive.

I'm pregnant.

My heart overflows with joy. My heart tears in two. I'll have the baby I've wanted. What I won't have are Damien and Julian.

I've kept secrets from them. I'm having a baby via a sperm donor.

This is not a betrayal that I can undo.

I'm still in the bathroom when my phone rings. It's Patricia. "Sophia, I wanted to give you a heads-up. My car won't start." She sounds resigned. "Ron's going to give me a ride to dinner, but he has a prior commitment, so there's a chance I'm going to be a few minutes late."

Dinner? Oh fuck. I've forgotten all about it, but the dinner that Patricia insisted I set up to thank Damien—it's tonight.

40

DAMIEN

The only good thing that happens in the next two weeks is that I'm able to straighten things out with Lizbeth. We talk, her and I, for a very long time one evening.

She's openly regretful about her demands. "I started seeing someone new," she says. "Alex is the one who found out that Cristiano was wealthy. He kept going on about how unfair it was that I was getting so little out of this deal. I told him that your family had been very generous, but he insisted I could get more. He said this could set us up for life."

Fifteen million definitely would have done that.

She sounds really sad. "What happened?"

"I told him I had second thoughts, and he hit me."

I sit up. I hate—loathe—men who hit women. "Are you safe?" I demand. "Do you need protection? What can I do?"

"You didn't ask if the baby was safe."

My heart lurches. "That was going to be my second question. Is it?" Magnus thinks they're having a girl, and

Cristiano thinks it'll be a boy. I'm not taking any sides in this ridiculous discussion, so 'it' will suffice.

"You're a good guy, Damien. You asked about me first. The baby is fine." She takes a deep breath. "I broke up with Alex after that. I'm too ashamed to talk to Magnus and Cristiano. Can you tell them I'm sorry about everything?"

"I'll take care of it." Lizbeth is a decent person. It wouldn't have struck her to blackmail Cristiano. "I'm going to arrange some protection for you for the next couple of months, okay?"

"Alex wouldn't hurt me again," she says.

Gods, she's so naïve. Or is this what hope looks like? "Let's not take any chances," I say grimly.

I hang up with her and call Brody, who I went to college with. He runs a private security company with Adrian Lockhart, another good friend. I outline the situation and ask him if they can keep an eye on Lizbeth for the foreseeable future. "No worries," Brody says.

"Send the bill to me," I tell him. "Oh, and can one of your people find this boyfriend of hers? She said his name was Alex. Warn him to stay away from her, if you would. And don't be gentle."

"I wasn't planning on it," he replies grimly. "I don't like men who hit women. I'll take care of it."

"Thanks, Brody."

At least Cristiano and Magnus will be happy.

EVER SINCE SOPHIA broke up with me, I've been waiting for her to cancel the dinner with her boss. After all, she clearly doesn't want to see or hear from me again. I don't know if she's going to be at La Vecchia or if it's just going to be

Patricia Adams and me. If Sophia's there, I don't know what I'll say to her. I don't know how I'll react.

But I don't hear from her.

So, on Sunday night, I set out to have an excruciatingly awkward meal with a woman I'm head-over-heels in love with.

Tomorrow, it'll be two weeks since I last talked to Sophia. I thought the pain would lessen, but it shows no sign of abating. Maybe it's too soon.

Or maybe this wound will never heal.

It's also been two weeks since I gave my mother an ultimatum, one she hasn't responded to. I've talked to her, yes, but she hasn't brought it up again, and neither have I.

Am I going to go through with it? Am I really going to leave the Cardenas Group? *Yes. I think I am.* Nothing feels right anymore, and nothing seems very important either. My heart feels shredded, battered, bruised, and broken. Nothing brings me pleasure anymore. Everything is empty and flat and colorless. When I see the lake from my window, I can only remember the meals we ate outside. When I cook in my kitchen, that first memorable evening plays in an endless loop in my head. Sophia sat on Julian's lap, looked at me with laughter in her eyes, and asked if I was planning to join them.

And I'm thinking of Sophia again.

I force my thoughts back to the Cardenas Group. Deep down in my heart, I know I need to push this. I need to act without my mother second-guessing my every move, and if she can't commit to doing that, it's time to leave. No matter how broken I feel about that decision, it's the right one to make.

What a miserable thirteen days it's been.

I glance at my phone. For a change, it's silent. The Italian restaurant we're meeting at is thirty minutes away. If I leave now, I'm going to be a little early, but I'll cope. Maybe I'll drink too much at the bar and make a fool of myself. That'll be special.

I get into the car and start driving. I'm turning a corner when there's a pain in my chest. It's been hurting for a few weeks now, but this is worse. It's an uncomfortable pressure, as if someone was squeezing me tight. Bile fills my throat, and I reach for the bottle of water at my side.

It isn't there.

I break out into a cold sweat. My head is swimming, and my pulse is racing. This feels like a heart attack. I take my eyes off the road for a second to find my phone, and when I look up again, I'm on a bend, hurtling full speed toward a tree.

I grab the steering wheel and pump my brakes, but it's too late.

Everything goes dark.

41

SOPHIA

My siblings are great, but sometimes I need my fathers. This is one of those times.

Dad and Papa listen in silence as I let it all out. I tell them everything. The stuff that happened ten years ago, and the stuff that's happened this month. Jumping to conclusions ten years ago and running away, then repeating the same behavior two weeks ago. Then, finally, I tell them the thing I'm dreading. "I went ahead with the sperm donation," I whisper. "I thought it was the right thing to do. I found out today that I'm pregnant."

"You're going to have a baby?" My dad's voice is saturated with joy. "Sophia, this is wonderful. I'm *delighted*."

"It's early," I warn them. "Anything can happen. I can miscarry. According to the Internet, it's a real risk at my age."

Papa cuts to the heart. "Are you happy?"

Tears well in my eyes again at his tone of concern. "About the baby, yes. But I've killed any chance of getting them back. Even if they wanted to be with me, they're going to change their mind after this."

"They might," Papa says. "Or they might not. You don't know how they'll react, not unless you talk to them."

Dad sighs. "We thought we protected you from Denise," he says. "I didn't realize how much damage we caused."

"You did protect me," I say fiercely. "Don't you dare blame yourself. You gave me a home. You gave me a family. And you didn't cause damage; Denise did. This is not your fault." I take a deep breath. "This is mine."

"You know what you need to do, don't you?" he asks softly.

Annette asked me the same question on Friday.

And I do.

I've spent my life being afraid. I ran from love because love made me vulnerable. If I was in love—if I was happy—it could be ripped away from me.

I've learned the wrong lesson from my childhood. No matter how ridiculous Denise's demands were, my fathers always met them. No matter how broke they were, they always found the money to pay her off. From the moment Denise dropped Ben and me off at her brother's door and took off, Dad and Papa have been my family. I might have spent my entire childhood dreading being taken away from my home, but they never let it happen.

Somehow, I held onto the fear and not to the faith.

It's over with Damien and Julian. Our relationship can't survive my betrayal. Even so, I need to face them. I need to tell them the truth.

It's finally time to stop running.

I PULL up in front of La Vecchia. Damien's SUV isn't in the parking lot. Neither is Patricia's, but that's to be expected if her husband is dropping her off.

I go inside. The hostess shows me to my table. "Can I get you a drink while you wait for the rest of your party?" my waiter asks.

"Just water, please."

Patricia arrives ten minutes later. We talk about work while we wait for Damien. Ten minutes pass, and then fifteen. I glance at my phone and frown. He's always on time. Is he standing us up? But he wouldn't. No matter what, Damien Cardenas is faultlessly polite.

Patricia's phone rings. She answers and holds it out to me. "It's for you."

It's Julian. "Sophia?" he says, sounding tenser than I've ever heard him. "Damien's been in a car accident. He's at the hospital."

My heart stops. The room swims around me. This can't be happening. It just can't. This has to be some kind of sick, twisted joke.

I make my mouth form words. "I'm on my way."

42

JULIAN

They whisk Damien into surgery. I don't remember the next few hours at the hospital. Sophia gets there not long after I do. I hold her hands, and she holds mine, and all I register is that her skin is cold. So icy cold. We don't talk. We just wait.

I had no idea I was Damien's emergency contact.

As soon as I got a call from the hospital, I called Damien's brother, Cristiano. Cristiano and Magnus live in Manhattan, and I didn't think they would get to Highfield until well after midnight, but they arrive at the hospital two hours later. "Helicopter," Cristiano says tersely. "Xavier has a landing pad. Mama and Victoria are already in the air, but it'll take them seven hours to get here." He sits down in one of the plastic chairs and gets up immediately, as if he can't bring himself to relax. "Have the doctors said anything?"

I shake my head. "Just what I already told you. He hit a tree. He has several broken bones, and they're concerned he has a concussion." I take a deep breath. "They think he might have had a heart attack, and that's why he crashed."

Cristiano's face turns gray. His father died only three

years ago of an unexpected heart attack. Magnus is at his side immediately, pulling him into his embrace. "It will be okay," he says soothingly. "Damien is young, and he's in good shape."

Damien's father had been in good shape, too.

Sophia is huddled in a chair off to one side. I introduce them. "Ah," Cristiano says, a small smile on his face. "You're the girlfriend. Damien's announcement caused quite a stir."

She sent us a text out of the blue saying she wanted nothing to do with us. She blocked our numbers. I didn't really expect her to be here. I still don't know where things are at with us.

I wait for her to contradict Cristiano. To say, "No, I'm not dating Damien."

But she doesn't. She doesn't say anything at all.

She looks ill.

And that stirs up my protective instincts. I can't do anything for Damien right now, but I can for Sophia. The hospital cafeteria is closed, so I get her a bottle of water and a candy bar from the vending machine and crouch in front of her. "When was the last time you ate?"

"It doesn't matter," she mutters, not meeting my eyes.

"Sophia."

"Breakfast," she says.

She's not eating. She's lost weight since I last saw her. There's a pallor on her face that's new.

The hospital cafeteria might shut at six, but it's not too late for delivery. "Have either of you eaten?" I ask Cristiano and Magnus.

Cristiano shakes his head as if he can't bear the idea of eating—something I agree with—but Magnus responds firmly. "We haven't, no," he says. "You're ordering food? Thank you, Julian."

I pick up my phone to call the nearest restaurant—a Thai place Hunter likes—but before I can dial, I see there's an email waiting for me from Francisco Flores.

Oh, for fuck's sake. He's ignored me for the last week, but now, of all the times, he writes back.

I read the email. It's a snotty, pissy note, accusing me of not bringing my best work to the table and jeopardizing the series. He condemns me for being a big-name, egotistical author who isn't pulling his weight.

I snap. I've been patient with Flores, and I tried hard to work collaboratively, but I can no longer deal with his bullshit. My best friend is in surgery. I don't know if he's okay or not, and this is the last thing I need right now.

So I do something I've been avoiding doing for weeks. I call Shaun and explain the situation to him. All of it.

Shaun listens to me in silence. When I finish, he only asks me one question. "Why didn't you bring this to me earlier?"

"You told me to play nice. And I didn't want to do anything to sink the deal."

He sighs. "There's playing nice, and then there's this." His voice turns grim. "Forward me all the emails Flores has sent you, Julian. And leave this to me. After all, this is what you pay me for."

I thank him, hang up, and order some Thai. When it arrives, I make sure Sophia eats. After that, there's nothing to do except pace up and down, fear pulsing through me. There's nothing to do except wait.

43

SOPHIA

The minutes tick by, and then the hours. It's a long, terrifying night. The four of us huddle in the cold hospital waiting room, under too-bright lights, and we wait, hearts in our mouths.

Sometime during that wait, Julian brings me food and insists I eat it. His expression makes it clear that this isn't up for debate. I shouldn't skip meals—it's probably not good for the baby—so I drink some soup and choke down some vegetables.

Around midnight, I find myself alone with Magnus. Cristiano has left to take a phone call, and Julian is nowhere to be seen either. He probably doesn't want to be alone with me, I think with a stab. Well, I can't say I don't deserve it. But even that pain is buried under a thick layer of shock. Everything seems unreal. This isn't right; it isn't fair. I can't lose Damien. I'm not ready.

"Can I ask you something?" I find myself saying to Magnus. Cristiano's partner is tall and blond and looks like a Nordic god. Not Odin. One of the kind ones.

Magnus looks up. "Of course."

"I overheard Damien talk." I flush. It all seems so unimportant now. "About your surrogate. You were having some problems?"

"Ah, that." He gives me a small smile. "A momentary scare. Lizbeth wanted fifteen million dollars and a new contract granting her parental rights."

She wanted what? "But that's not possible, is it?"

"She implied she'd harm the baby." He grimaces. "She caught us at a bad moment. Damien just had a huge argument with his mother. He was going to quit. Cristiano was stressed about that, as was Victoria. Damien insulates them from a lot of the bullshit that comes with running the Cardenas Group. Then Lizbeth called us, and I'm afraid none of us dealt with it well. For a few days, we all collectively lost it." He shakes his head. "Damien sorted it out."

"Damien was going to quit?"

He frowns. "You didn't know? It shouldn't really have taken any of us by surprise. After all, Cristiano and I almost broke up over his work. Damien wouldn't have wanted that to happen with you."

I don't know what to say. Damien was prepared to leave his family company to spend more time with me? A weight presses down on my chest. "You said he sorted it out, the surrogate situation."

Magnus nods. "I mean, you know how Damien is," he says. "He's good with people. He listens. He remembers shit about them."

"He told me he's bad at dates."

"Terrible," Magnus agrees with a laugh. "He almost forgot his mother's birthday last year. That would have been a disaster—Maria can be quite dramatic. His assistant Luis runs that part of his life. But Damien is empathetic. He makes people feel important. And it's not an act; he's genuinely interested in them."

The health center. Brooklyn. The community garden. I have so many examples of that.

"Anyway, he talked to Lizbeth. He found out there was a greedy boyfriend involved. The blackmail was the boyfriend's idea, evidently. I'm still furious with Lizbeth, don't get me wrong. But we're slowly getting back to normal."

She'd wanted fifteen million dollars, and he'd had a really bad day. So he'd vented.

And I'd heard him, jumped to conclusions, and run away. And now, I'm pregnant.

I feel sick. How could I have made so many mistakes? How could I have been so wrong about everything?

AT THREE IN THE MORNING, the doctor comes out. She looks at our group with tired eyes. "Are you all family?" she asks.

I grab Julian's hand and squeeze it tight. Oh God, I'm not ready for this.

"Yes," Cristiano replies, standing up. "I'm his brother. Sophia's his girlfriend. How is Damien? Is he going to be okay?"

The doctor nods. Relief shudders through me. I sway, and Julian grabs me tight and wraps his arm around my waist. He presses a kiss on my forehead before he realizes what he does and stiffens.

"He's in recovery right now," the doctor says. "He had a broken femur, a broken wrist, and a couple of broken ribs. A punctured lung too."

That doesn't sound good.

"The nurse said something about a concussion?" Magnus asks.

"We're keeping him under observation," she says. "But his vitals are good."

Cristiano swallows. "Did he have a heart attack?"

"His tropin levels are normal," she says. "So it wasn't a heart attack. We'll test him more thoroughly in the coming days, but I don't think it's something to be concerned about."

"He's had a scare before," I murmur. "His doctor was concerned about his stress levels. He told him to take a vacation."

Cristiano snaps his head up. "I didn't know that."

"He didn't want to worry you," Julian says. "Is Damien awake? When can we see him? How long will he be in the hospital?"

She blinks at the barrage of questions. "He's coming out of anesthesia now," she says. "He'll head to the recovery room. He won't be ready to see anyone tonight. You should go home and get some rest."

Home. But home isn't a place. It's people. And right now, there are only two people I want to be with. Damien and Julian.

Be brave, Soph.

I swallow hard and look up. "Can I come home with you?"

For a long moment, he stares down at me. Then his eyes soften. "Of course, Sophia."

44

DAMIEN

I wake up not knowing where I am. It takes me a few minutes to realize I'm in a hospital. I try to sit up and realize it's a terrible idea as pain washes over me.

A nurse bustles in almost immediately. "Ah, good, you're awake," she says. "How do you feel?"

"Like an elephant sat on me."

She chuckles. "That might have caused less damage. You broke your leg, your wrist, a couple of ribs, and you punctured your lungs. We're monitoring you for a concussion."

I blink. "It doesn't hurt."

"You're pumped full of painkillers," she says. "Trust me, you're not going to enjoy it when they wear off." She opens a bottle of water, puts a straw in it, and holds it to my lips. "Drink."

Ugh. I hate being sick. I take a sip and make a face. "It tastes weird."

"Those are the drugs in your system. Now, do you feel up to visitors? Your family is in the waiting room."

Sophia? My heart leaps, and then reality sets in. No, she

wouldn't be here. But if I were in a crash and they called Julian, he would have let my mom and my siblings know.

"Yeah, sure."

MY MOTHER IS A BEAUTIFUL WOMAN, always impeccably dressed, never a hair out of place. Not today. Her face is white with worry. "Damien," she exclaims, hurrying over to my side. She bends down and kisses my cheek, her eyes swimming with tears. "I thought you died."

"Still here," I tell her with a smile. "You're not getting rid of me that easily. How long have I been out?"

"It's Monday afternoon," she replies.

Ouch. The last thing I remember is driving to La Vecchia. That was Sunday evening. No wonder she's freaking out. She worries over me, and I promise her I'm going to be alright.

Then it's Cristiano and Victoria, both looking pale and anxious. "I'm fine," I tell them bracingly. "I'll be up and about in no time. Going to run a marathon in December."

Cristiano makes himself smile. "The painkillers have made you delusional, I see," he says. "Are you up for more visitors?"

"Sure."

I'm expecting Tomas, but it's not my stepfather who steps into the room. It's Julian, and a half-step behind him is Sophia.

I can't quite believe it.

She comes over to me. "Hey," she whispers. "You gave us a scare." She laces her fingers in mine. The unbroken hand, that is. The other one is in a cast.

She's here. She's holding my hand. If this is a dream, I don't want to wake up.

"Sorry. Didn't mean to."

Her eyes fill with tears. "Don't apologize. I should be—"

I want to talk to her; I really do. But the room swims around me, and I need to close my eyes. The nurse can see that. "Everyone out," she says firmly. "He needs rest."

There's just one thing I need to know before I can fall asleep. I make my eyes focus on Sophia. "When I wake up," I whisper. "Will you be here?"

"I promise."

A wave of relief washes over me. "Good." Then I close my eyes and let darkness claim me.

A WEEK LATER, I finally have a long-overdue heart-to-heart with my mother. "When you told me you were quitting, I was angry," she says softly. "You told me I was wrong, and nobody enjoys hearing that. Me more than most."

"Mm-hmm."

"Cristiano told me that Dr. Zambrano had advised you to take a month off. Then Victoria said you thought I asked Tomas to run the company because I didn't trust you."

"Umm, yes?"

"No," she says fiercely. "I thought Tomas would take some of the strain off you. I thought he could run the company until you were ready."

"You were wrong."

"I realize that now." Her lips twist. "Tomas is unhappy. You're unhappy. And all I want is for my family to be happy. The company, it is nothing."

"It's a multi-billion-dollar corporation that employs thousands of people, but okay."

She makes a dismissive sound. "What does the company matter compared to your health?" she demands. "Your father died, and I thought. . ." Her voice trails off. "Never mind what I thought. When Cristiano called me, I realized I could lose you, too. And I'm not going to do that." She squeezes my shoulder. "What do you want, Damien?"

"I want a free hand."

"It's yours. Tomas is stepping down next year. The CEO job is yours if you want it."

"I want it, on one condition. No more protecting people like Ted Boric."

"Done." A smile flickers on her face. "Did I tell you Tomas took me to a yoga retreat?"

"You didn't, but he did. I asked him how many people you strangled when you realized you didn't have Internet access, but he promised you enjoyed it."

"Strangely, I did." She's quiet for a long time. "We're going to take an around-the-world cruise, Tomas and I. The one your father and I never got a chance to take."

"Good," I tell her sincerely.

"It's a six-month cruise," she continues. "The ship sails just after Christmas. Six months at sea, with very limited access to my email. I will either become a changed woman, or I will go crazy. If you hear about a homicide at sea, that's probably me." She gives me a wry smile. "That'll give you time to implement the changes you want without me getting in the way."

She bends down and kisses my cheek. "Cristiano tells me that you, Julian, and Sophia are what he called a throuple."

I search her face. "Is that what they're calling it these days?"

"So it appears." Her lips curve up into a smile. "Both Julian and Sophia have spent every spare moment this last week at the hospital. I look forward to getting to know them better. Bring them home for Christmas."

"Yeah, that's not going to happen. Julian's sister is getting married here on Christmas Day. He's not going to miss the wedding."

"A Christmas wedding?" She sniffs disapprovingly. "What a ridiculous idea. Still, what can you do? Bring them home for New Year."

45

SOPHIA

After ten days in the hospital, Damien is finally discharged. He needs a walker thanks to the broken femur, and he can't really use it well thanks to the broken wrist, but he looks delighted to be home.

Me? I'm happy he's home, too. I'm thrilled that he's on the mend. But it also means that it's time to have a real conversation. One that will shatter us.

I let Damien get settled first. Dr. Aziz wanted to make sure that Damien wasn't alone for the first week or two, so both Julian and I offered to move in to take care of him. Julian makes lunch, and we eat, and then, after the meal, I broach the subject.

"I need to tell you why I broke up with you," I mutter, not looking at them. "And I want you to know I'm not making excuses. I'm just trying to tell you what happened."

"Okay," Julian says softly.

"The day I did what I did, I found out who got me fired. It was a guy I used to work with. George Turner. He'd overheard the two of you talk about me at IHOP." My lips twist. "On the drive back, I berated myself for jumping to conclusions. I wanted to tell you about it, so I went to Julian's. I knew you were both going to be there. I was going to tell you everything."

Damien looks up. "Everything?"

I swallow hard. "I'm getting there. But when I got to Julian's, I overheard Damien on the phone." I glance up at him. "You were talking to Cristiano about Lizbeth. You said you'd ruin her life if she went up against you."

Something flashes in his eyes.

"The thing is, Denise did that throughout my childhood. She would threaten to wreck our lives if she didn't get what she wanted. And if she got lawyers involved, my fathers wouldn't be able to do a damn thing. They were a same-sex couple, and Denise was my biological mother. In the eyes of the law, her rights would trump theirs, every single time."

They're both watching me now. Damien is frowning slightly, as if he's trying to figure out a puzzle. Julian looks intent. Focused.

"I panicked," I whisper. "If the three of us got together, and I had a child, if something were to go wrong, you could take my baby away from me. You're rich. You're powerful. You have good lawyers."

"I wouldn't..."

"I *know*. I could have talked to you about it. I could have asked you why you were so angry. But I didn't. I jumped instantly to the worst possible conclusion. That's what I do. When things get serious, I look for an excuse to run. I did it ten years ago, and even though I knew you better this time around, I ran again."

I take a deep, shuddering breath. "I regretted it almost

immediately. I wanted to beg you to take me back. But I couldn't do that, not right away. Not until I could trust myself not to run again."

I still can't look up at their faces. "I've been seeing a therapist. She's helping me work through my past."

"That's good, right?" Julian asks me, his voice cautious. "Sophia, if you're asking if we can be together again, I thought the last week would have been answer enough."

If only it were that easy.

I shake my head. "I still haven't told you everything. I'm thirty-five and want a baby. I wasn't meeting the right guy, probably because I left before I could give them a chance, so I decided I was going to find a sperm donor. I should have told you about it, but it was a very new relationship. I didn't want to spook you."

A small smile flickers over Julian's face. "That's understandable. I'm not saying I would have been spooked, but I'm also not sure how I would have reacted. Things were great between us, but you're right. It was new."

Things *were* great between us. In the past tense, not the present. Does this mean. . .? No. I stop myself before I can go there. I made myself a promise. I would tell them everything. Every damning bit of it.

I think I'm going to be sick. This is the hardest thing I've ever done. "After I broke it off with you, I went ahead with the sperm donor," I whisper. I stare at my palms. "I took a test last week. I'm pregnant."

Silence greets my statement. For a long time, nobody says anything. I look up finally, only to see Damien and Julian exchange a glance. "Let me see if I understand," Julian says slowly. "You're going to have a baby via sperm donor."

"Yes."

"And you want to keep the baby?" Damien asks. "You're happy about the pregnancy?"

"Yes," I say again.

Julian slants a look at me. "Do you still want to be with us, Sophia? Or does this baby change things?"

Why are they so calm? Why aren't they losing their shit? "Doesn't it?"

"Not for me," Damien replies. "It doesn't change a damn thing. I love you, Sophia. I think I've loved you for a very long time. There's nothing in the world that's going to change that. Certainly not a baby." He grins. "I would pay good money to see Julian change a diaper."

"You should talk," Julian scoffs. "Have you ever changed a diaper before?"

"Many times," Damien says smugly. "You forget Vicky has two kids. I've lost count of how many times I've changed Felipe and Johan."

Damien said he loves me. I'm still absorbing that. "Why are you acting like this isn't a big deal?" I blurt out.

Julian looks at me. "Because it isn't," he says. "So you're going to have a baby via sperm donation. So what? You of all people should know that blood isn't the only thing that makes a family." He takes my hands between his. "Sophia, I love you. Why would you being pregnant change anything? You're the woman I want."

Tears roll down my cheeks. I look at Julian and then at Damien. "Really?"

"Always," Damien replies.

Julian kisses me, long, hard, deep. "Are we in a relationship again?" he asks when he pulls away. "Is it official? Because Hannah sent me a wedding invitation yesterday.

She addressed it to Julian Kincaid plus one." He flashes me a grin. "I need to call her up and get her to make it Julian Kincaid plus two."

I hug them tightly. Every time I've run from them, it's always been a mistake. No more. This time, I'm never letting go.

EPILOGUE
SOPHIA

I've learned a lot about Julian and Damien in the last nine months.

Damien is a terrible patient. Seriously terrible. He wouldn't stay in bed, he badgered the physical therapist into speeding up his rehab, and he refused to keep his weight off his leg. When he was finally pronounced healed, we all breathed a massive sigh of relief.

He can also charm the living daylights out of anyone. He flew all of us—Simon, Andre, Julian, and me—out to California for Papa's birthday on a private plane, stopping in Santa Fe on the way to pick up Aurora, JP, and Dawn. He arranged for Papa to play a round at an exclusive golf course where he's always wanted to play. After that, my fathers think he walks on water.

Ben likes Damien, but Julian's his favorite. I asked him about it, and he said that his girlfriend had been the recipient of a scholarship Julian had set up for promising artists. The girlfriend thing is new, but I think Ben really likes Maya. Of course, when I asked Julian about the scholarship program, he'd shrugged, embarrassed, and changed the topic.

I've learned that Julian cries at weddings. Well, Hannah's wedding anyway. My Dom, the one who pulls my hair during a session, spanks my ass and tells me to shut up and take it all like a good girl, teared up as he walked his sister down the makeshift aisle. It was lovely. I cried too, but that's excusable; I'm pregnant and hormonal.

We've been back to the club. I insisted. The guys were hesitant. Mostly because of my pregnancy, but I also think they were a little spooked that I'd run away again.

I didn't run. I'm *never* making that mistake again.

Shaun Zhao, Julian's agent, talked to Kyle Donovan, the producer at Levine Entertainment making *Revenant*. I don't know exactly what he said, but the result was that Flores became much easier to work with. The pilot got filmed, it was shopped around, and the series was picked up by a very well-known streaming company. (Netflix. It's Netflix. It airs next fall, and I cannot wait to binge-watch it.)

Damien's mother kept her word. Tomas announced his upcoming retirement, and she named Damien as CEO. To celebrate, we did a boss-assistant roleplay. We made the four-hour drive to Manhattan one afternoon and went to the Cardenas Group's offices. By the time we got there, it was after hours, and there was no one there. Damien bent me over his desk and spanked me. Then I got on my knees under the table (it's a massive table, I had plenty of room) and sucked his cock while he pretended to have a meeting with a prospective investor played by Julian. It was *extremely* memorable.

Jack Rutherford is still with the Cardenas Group, but Ted Boric isn't. Damien is pretty happy about both of those things.

Double penetration got harder (ha!) as I advanced in my pregnancy. My belly kept getting in the way. But we found plenty of other things to do and plenty of positions to do it in.

Patricia found out about the three of us—how could she not? But she hasn't let it bother her. "I don't understand it, my dear," she said to me. "But it's really none of my business, is it? Now tell me, do you know whether you're having a girl or a boy?"

I don't. We decided we didn't want to know.

THE LESS SAID ABOUT LABOR, the better. I'm a tired, exhausted, cranky mess when it's all done. But when the doctor places our baby boy in my arms, it makes it all worthwhile.

It's exactly like the dream I had nine months ago. My fathers are in my hospital room. And most importantly, Damien and Julian are here with me.

I stare at the baby, this tiny little thing that came out of me, and I look up at Julian and Damien. "Hey," I say to them softly. "Meet your son."

Julian tears up. He totally does. And so does Damien. Okay, I'm crying a little too. I can't help it. My baby is just so small and tiny and perfect.

"Do you have a name?"

"Yeah." I smile up at my fathers. "I'm taking a leaf out of Aurora's book. Meet Leonard Henry Johnson Thorsen."

The nurse in the room writes this down. "We need to fill in some information for the baby's birth certificate," she says. Damien swears under his breath about letting me rest, but she's unmoved. "Mother's name?"

"Sophia Thorsen."

"Father's name?"

While there are states where you can have more than two parents listed on the birth certificate, Maryland is not one of them. I looked it up. I can leave the name of the father blank, or I can fill it in with one name, but I cannot name both Julian and Damien as fathers of my child. Not in the eyes of the law.

Then again, the law isn't really that great about understanding what a family truly is.

About a month ago, Julian and I had a long conversation about this.

I glance at him now, and he nods with a smile.

The thing is, I can tell Damien a thousand times that I trust that he would never do anything to hurt me. That I *know* he wouldn't take my child away from me.

Or I can show him.

And there's a really easy way to do that.

The nurse clears her throat. "Father's name?" she repeats.

There's no doubt in my heart that I want to do this. "Damien Cardenas."

Damien's head snaps up. Shock shows on his face when he realizes what I've done. His expression changes into something so raw and yet so tender that I choke up all over again.

I will cherish the look in his eyes for the rest of my life.

An impatient knock sounds at the door, and Ben sticks his head inside. "Can we come in?" he asks. "Because we really want to see the baby."

I laugh. "Come on in," I invite them. "Come meet your nephew."

They crowd inside, one big, happy family. "Cristiano is

texting me constantly," Andre complains with a smile. "As is Victoria. Here, hold up Lenny Hank Junior."

He snaps a photo with his camera. "There, that'll keep them for a bit."

"Lenny Hank Junior is a ridiculous name," Aurora says, breaking out into a wide smile. "Julian, your sister called me. She said that if you don't call her back with news, she will drive down here. She says she's hormonal and cranky, and you won't enjoy her visit."

The nurse looks appalled at the number of people in the room. I exchange a grin with Damien and Julian. Damien politely sends her on her way before she can raise a fuss and then comes back into the room.

They're all here. My family. Lenny Hank Junior—Aurora is right about finding him a better nickname—has three parents who adore him and more uncles, aunts, cousins, and grandparents than a kid could ever want.

Everything's going to be all right. We're going to live happily ever after.

∼

Thank you for reading Theirs to Covet!

Not ready to say goodbye to Sophia, Damien & Julian? Get the bonus scene! Sophia, Damien & Julian play at Club M for the first time after the baby. Want to know how that goes? Sign up to read it by scanning the QR code below or by going to http://www.taracrescent.com/bonus-theirstocovet

If you enjoy MFM romances, may I suggest my Dirty series? The series is set in the small town of New Summit. Each book is a standalone romance, and features a smart and sassy heroine, and a pair of men who fall in love with her.

Flip the page for an extended preview of Dirty Therapy, the first book of the Dirty series.

DIRTY THERAPY

My O is missing. Two therapists are going to help me find it.

Two hours after Dennis proposes, I find my fiancé with his d*ck buried in Tiffany Slater's hoohah, and he has the nerve to suggest it's my fault.

Because I'm frigid.

Sure, I've never had an orgasm with him, or with anyone for that matter, but relationships are about more than good nookie. (Not that it was ever good. Adequate is more like it. Okay, who am I kidding? *Dennis couldn't find his way down there with a flashlight and a map.*)

Now I'm determined to find my missing O with the help of two of the hottest men I've ever set eyes on. Therapists Benjamin Long and Landon West. If these two men can't make me come, then no one can.

I shouldn't sleep with them. I shouldn't **succumb** to their sexy smiles. I shouldn't listen when their firm voices **promise** me all the pleasure I can handle.

I can't get enough. But when a bitter rival finds out about our forbidden relationship, *everything will come crashing down.*

A PREVIEW OF DIRTY THERAPY

CHAPTER 1

Mia:

I'm going to sum up the suckitude of my life with a three-point list.

1. Though I haven't had sex with my boyfriend for over a month, he proposed last night in an extremely crowded restaurant, and I said yes. Because everyone was looking at me and I didn't want to be the girl that broke his heart in a public setting. Even though I wasn't really sure I wanted to marry Dennis.
2. Once I got back home, I started thinking about whether we were doing the right thing. So, I went over to his place to talk to him, and I found him plowing his dick in Tiffany Slater's willing pussy. That wasn't good.

3. I started yelling. Instead of groveling, he yelled back. "You're frigid," he accused me. "I've never been able to make you come." Right. As if it's *my* fault that I have to draw him a map to my clitoris.
4. (Okay, I lied. This is a four-point list.) Worst of all, when I threw his stupid engagement ring at his pasty-white butt, I missed. Big dramatic moment—ruined.

"So there you have it," I finish reciting last night's humiliating events to my best friend, Cassie, while unpacking a new shipment of cocktail dresses. "Can my life get any worse?"

It's eleven in the morning, or as I like to think of it, 'Treat Time.' Usually, this is my favorite part of the day. The store is quiet, and I can arrange the clothing neatly on hangers, organizing them by color and function. I can fiddle with the display cases of costume jewelry and make sure that everything is perfect.

Cassie, who runs the coffee shop next door, is my supplier of treats. She's watching me now, her eyes wide. "Dennis never made you come?" she asks, honing in unerringly to the most embarrassing part – the lack of orgasms. "Mia, the two of you dated for a year."

"I know."

She takes a bite of her muffin. Chocolate chip, if I know my friend. "Why on Earth did you keep going out with him?" she demands. Crumbs fall on my ornately tufted vintage velvet loveseat. Normally, I'd shoo her out of the way and bust out my hand-vac, but today's not a normal day. "The guy's not a looker, and he has the personality of a wet towel."

I feel strangely compelled to defend my ex-boyfriend,

but then I remember Tiffany, and I clamp my mouth shut. "I tried to tell him what turned me on," I mutter, my cheeks flushed with humiliation. "At the start. He called me a pervert."

Cassie's eyebrow rises, and she gives me her 'what-the-fuck' look. "He called you a pervert?" Her voice is dangerous. "And you still dated him after that?"

Worse, I almost married him.

I avoid Cassie's gaze. This situation would never happen to my friend. She's bold and uninhibited, and she has every guy in our small town wrapped around her finger. Me? I'm the boring one in the corner, grateful for any scrap of attention that comes my way.

"Anyway." Cassie dismisses Dennis with a shrug of her shoulder. "Forget Dennis. You dodged a bullet there. Let's get you back on the horse. Friday night happy hour at The Merry Cockatoo?"

Normally, even the mention of The Merry Cockatoo would get a giggle out of me. The newly opened bar is on the same block as my clothing boutique and Cassie's coffee shop. My landlord, George Bollington, has been waging a low-grade war with the woman who owns the bar, trying to get Nina Templeton to change the name.

"We're a family-friendly town," he grouses every time he sees me. "What kind of woman calls her bar that name?" Mr. Bollington is so uptight he can't even say Cockatoo out loud. Because I'm the town's resident good girl, he thinks he's got a sympathetic audience in me. I get to hear him grumble about Nina, about the sex therapists who've just opened a practice in town, about people who chew gum and listen to loud music, about people who litter... you name it, and my landlord probably disapproves of it.

I agree with him on the litter, but the rest of it is Mr.

Bollington being a grouchy old man. Except for the sex therapists. That's professional jealousy. Mr. Bollington is a psychiatrist, and he's grown accustomed to being the only option in town. He now has competition, and he doesn't like it.

Speaking of Mr. Bollington, the door bells chime, and my landlord walks in. When he sees Cassie sitting in my store, he frowns. Cassie is another person Mr. Bollington doesn't approve of. "Mia," he says, ignoring my friend, "I just saw your window display." His forehead creases with disapproval. "It's very unsuitable. This is a family-friendly town."

Last week, I'd received some incredible hand-made silk lingerie from a small French manufacturer. Each piece was so gorgeous that it should have been in a museum. I'd spent most of Saturday setting up a window display for the bras, panties, and slips. I should have known Mr. Bollington would get his knickers in a knot about it. (Ha ha. See what I did there?)

"Mr. Bollington, I run a clothing store." I try and keep my voice firm. "Window displays are an important part of my marketing strategy."

He's unmoved. "Need I remind you about the morality clause in your lease, young lady?" he demands. The threat is unmistakable. Take the offending display down, or my landlord will make trouble.

Cassie snorts into her muffin once he leaves. "One day," she gripes, "I wish you'd stand up to him and tell him his stupid morality clause isn't legally enforceable. You're going to take the lingerie down, aren't you?"

"Probably." I'm a people-pleaser. I want everyone to like me. And it seems easier to give in to Mr. Bollington's demands than fight him. It's just a window display, after all.

Cassie lets it go. "Back to more important things," she

says. "Friday night. We'll get drinks, get tipsy, and go home with unsuitable men." She winks in my direction. "The kind that will have you screaming with pleasure. The sooner you forget about limp dick, the better."

I feel my cheeks heat. "Yeah, about that," I mumble. "Dennis might be right."

She frowns. "Right about what?"

Oh God. It's mortifying telling Cassie the truth. "I've never had an orgasm with a guy in my life."

Her mouth falls open. Thankfully, she's finished chewing her muffin. "With any guy?" she asks, her voice astonished.

I think back to the three men I've slept with. Brett, my high-school boyfriend, who I went out with for two weeks before he dumped me to date Gayla, a big-breasted blonde cheerleader. Tony, my college crush, who slept with me *once* before confessing that he preferred men. And of course, Dennis, who buried his cock in Tiffany's twat less than two hours after proposing to me. "Nope." I lower my voice. "There's something wrong with me, isn't there?"

"Apart from your horrible tastes in men, no." She gets to her feet and muffin crumbs cascade to the floor. "Friday. Meet me at six. Prepare to party your brains out."

Once she leaves, I stare blankly at the rack of beaded and glittering dresses and think about my ex-fiancé. Even at the beginning of our relationship, I'd never felt the kind of passion for him I read about in books. Maybe he's right. Maybe I am frigid.

Cassie isn't going to tell me the truth. The best-friend rules clearly state that she's supposed to say supportive things.

But there's another way to get the truth. As I vacuum up chocolate chip muffin residue, I make a decision. I'm not the kind of girl who sleeps with a guy she picked up at the bar. Even if I wanted to have sex with a stranger, they never tended to notice me. That kind of attention is reserved for Cass.

No, I'm going to solve my orgasm problem the responsible, adult way. I'm going to see a therapist. Not just any therapist. I'm going to see the sex therapists that Mr. Bollington hates. Benjamin Long and Landon West. Maybe they can figure out what's wrong with me.

CHAPTER 2

Benjamin:

It's been two months since Landon and I opened our practice in this small town, and I can't say that I'm enjoying it so far. While the pace of life is a lot more peaceful than Manhattan, I'm used to the anonymity of the big city. In New Summit, everyone has their noses in our business all the time. Given what we do, that's a problem.

Landon, my partner and best friend, comes into my office at ten in the morning. "I need to talk to you about Amy," he says without preamble, taking a seat opposite me and propping his legs up on my desk.

I give him a pointed look, one that just makes him laugh. Landon knows I like my office tidy and organized, and he takes delight in messing with me. "Make yourself at home," I say dryly. I look him over. His hair is tousled, he hasn't shaved, and his eyes are red. "You look like hell by the way. Late night?"

He grins. "Samantha came over," he says. "She's a tiger, that one. She kept me up all night."

It's far too hard to keep up with Landon's dating habits, but I could have sworn he was seeing someone else. "Weren't you sleeping with Claire?" I ask him.

"Not anymore," he replies with a shake of his head. "She was getting clingy. Talking about clingy, how's Becky?"

I gave him a puzzled look. "We broke up. Didn't I tell you?"

A faintly hurt expression flashes across his face. "No," he says. "You forgot to mention it. When did this happen?"

I do the math in my head. "Three weeks ago."

"Why did you break up with her? The two of you seem to get along well enough."

Landon knows me pretty well, so he's guessed, correctly, that I initiated the break-up. I think about the lawyer I dated for six months. Landon's right—Becky and I got along just fine. We never fought, we never argued, and we never even bickered. It had been an amicable, adult relationship, and it had bored me to tears.

"She wanted to move in," I explain.

Landon raises an eyebrow. "Let me guess," he says, his voice amused. "That suggestion filled you with horror. You thought about Becky's stuff all over your place, her toothbrush next to yours, her pretty lingerie in your closet, and you ran for your life."

"You don't need to psychoanalyze me," I tell him. Landon and I have been friends since college. He knows my flaws, and I know his. After a childhood filled with chaos, I'm almost pathological in my desire for calm. Landon's father cheated on his mother and slept around like a randy tomcat, and as a result, Landon avoids relationships, convinced he wouldn't be able to stay faithful. "I'm quite aware that I'm a little stuck in my ways."

"That's not what I was going to say," he replies, his expression serious. "I was going to tell you that you only pick women that you aren't truly attracted to, so it's easier to walk away from them when you're done."

I glare at my friend. That assessment is a little too close to the truth for comfort. "Didn't you say you wanted to talk about Amy? What has she done this time?"

Amy Cooke is our receptionist. She's new; the receptionist we had in Manhattan hadn't wanted to leave the city. She's still on probation, and at the rate she's going, she's not going to last very long.

"She outed Natalie to her sister-in-law." Landon's voice is angry. "Nat called me in tears this morning. It seems that Amy ran into Doris in church, and proceeded to ask her if Nat's husband knew what she did in our office."

I see red. Our practice specializes in sex therapy, and Natalie is one of our best surrogates. We use her to help clients who are having issues with their sex lives.

Unfortunately, surrogacy is still considered similar to sex work, and while Natalie's husband knows what she does for a living, the couple would prefer that no one else does.

Now Amy has outed Natalie to her family.

"We should fire her," I say flatly. "Amy knows how important confidentiality is. If she can't respect the most basic rules of our profession…"

Landon winces. He's kinder than I am. "Give her a warning," he says. "Tell her that she's out of second chances."

I frown. "You do it then," I tell him. "I'm too angry."

"Not a chance," he says promptly. "She has a crush on me. She'd be more terrified if you yell at her."

"Fine." Amy has to realize how important discretion is in

our profession. Otherwise, she is going to get herself fired. Already George Bollington, the psychotherapist in town, is gunning for us. We don't need any more hassle.

My intercom buzzes just then. "Dr. Long? Dr. West?" Amy's voice sounds in my office. "Your ten thirty appointment is here. Mia Gardner."

"Thanks Amy." I put the phone on mute and grin at Landon. "I hope you're ready to put your thinking cap on."

"New patient?" he asks. Landon and I see new patients together, at least until we have a treatment plan in place. " Let's go."

∽

Landon:

There's only one word I can use to describe the woman who waits in my office. *Hot.*

She's in her mid-twenties. Her eyes glitter like green emeralds. Her hair is dark and lustrous, cascading in long, loose waves down her shoulders. Her body is the kind that a man dreams of, curvy and lush.

Except she's a prospective client, for fuck's sake. And though Ben jokes that I'll screw everything in a skirt, I have some boundaries. Clients are always off-limits.

"Ms. Gardner," I greet her with my most professional smile. "I'm Dr. West. This is Dr. Long. Please, sit down."

I wave toward the deep burgundy couch, and she perches on the very edge of it. Her fingers are clenched into fists, and she's yet to say a word.

"What brought you in today, Ms. Gardner?" Ben asks encouragingly.

She bites her lower lip. My cock takes note of the way

her teeth indent the flesh, and I stir in my armchair, trying discreetly to adjust myself. God, this is embarrassing. I'm a sex therapist. I've watched people get fucked in this office, and I've never yet had to fight off an erection.

Fuck me. My dick hardens even further at the thought of seeing Mia Gardner naked.

Okay. Focus, Landon. She's here for help.

"Ms. Gardner." I lean forward. "It's okay. You can tell us what the matter is. Everything you say in this office is confidential. We're here to help."

She nods. "I have a problem," she says, her face flushed. Her voice is barely a whisper. "I don't think I enjoy sex."

"Why do you think that?" Ben asks her.

Her eyes drop to her lap. "I never orgasm," she mumbles. "My fiancé thought I was frigid."

She has a fiancé? I don't know why that bothers me as much as it does.

Ben is more helpful than I am. "It's pretty common not to orgasm with a partner."

"It's not just Dennis," she confesses, her hands worrying the fabric of her skirt. "I've never been able to come with any partner."

"Couples sometimes fall into a rut," I suggest. "They find it helpful to tell each other about their fantasies. Role play, kink. Whatever jolts you out of your rhythm."

Her face turns fiery. "Have you tried telling him what turns you on?" I continue.

"What turns you on, Ms. Gardner?" Ben's voice drops an octave, and his eyes glitter with heat. Whoa. Benjamin Long is interested in this girl too. Well, well.

"It's too embarrassing." She can't look at us.

"If you don't tell us, we can't help you."

"I just can't," she wails.

I have a brainwave, which is a miracle, given that most of my blood has pooled in my dick. "Sometimes, when our clients are having trouble relaxing, we use hypnosis."

"Good idea, Dr. West," Ben says, giving me a sidelong look. He turns back to Mia. "Would you like to try that?"

She bites her lower lip again. I can see her debate it in her head.

"We record the session," I assure her. "So you don't have to worry about what you say."

She appears to reach a conclusion. "Yes," she nods. "I really want to solve this problem of mine, and if that's what it takes, let's do it."

Ben's the hypnotist. "Lie back on the couch," he instructs Mia, while I set up the recorder.

She gulps, but obeys. She stretches out on the red burgundy velvet, her skirt riding up to mid-thigh. Her skin looks creamy and soft and very touchable.

"You have nothing to worry about," Ben assures her. "Despite what you hear, we can't make you do anything during hypnosis that you won't do otherwise. It's just to get you to calm down."

He looks deep in her eyes, the lucky dog. "Relax," he says, his voice low and soothing. "Let your muscles sink into the couch." He draws out his sentences, the syllables slow and smooth. "Breathe in. Fill your chest and lungs with air."

She complies, and her breasts strain against her shirt. I want to adjust myself but can't. Until Mia goes under, sudden movements will startle her and pull her out of her trance.

"Good," Ben continues. "Now breathe out slowly. Empty your lungs."

After several steadying breaths, Ben proceeds to the next

step. Despite what you see in pop culture, you don't need a swinging watch to hypnotize someone. Just a focal object.

Unfortunately, Ben picks me. "I want you to look at Dr. West's face," he instructs. "Focus on him. Don't move your eyes away from Landon, Mia."

Her pretty green eyes meet mine. There's a hint of nervousness there, but as Ben goes through each step, it disappears. After five minutes of slow, patient encouragement, her eyes grow heavy, and her breathing evens out.

Ben nods at me. She's good to go.

"We were talking about sex, Mia," I say. "Tell us what you want."

"Dennis was tentative," she murmurs, her voice soft. "Sometimes, I wanted him to take charge."

"Take charge how?"

She hesitates. "I wanted him to push me against a wall," she whispers. "Pull my hands above my head and hold them in place. I wanted him to be forceful. I wanted to be taken."

Stay calm, Landon.

"What else?" My voice is strained. "What do you fantasize about?"

"I want to be spanked," she replies. "I want to be dragged over a man's lap." Her expression turns dreamy. "He'll pull my panties down, and he'll order me to take my punishment like a good girl. And if I don't obey, he'll tie my wrists up so I can't move."

Oh my fucking God.

Even hypnotized, her cheeks go pink. "Then, once the spanking is over, he'll push me down on my knees, and he'll thrust his cock into my mouth."

Ben makes a strangled noise in his throat. Thankfully, it doesn't stop Mia Gardner, because she keeps talking.

"Sometimes," she whispers, "I even dream about more than one cock. One in my pussy, one in my ass. Taking me hard."

This girl will be the death of us. Her fantasies are dirty and kinky, and I want to fulfill them.

She's a prospective client, asswipe. Keep your dick in your pants.

Ben's heard enough. He pulls Mia Gardner out of her hypnotic trance. When she's sitting on the couch again, her back straight, her hands clenched in her lap, he continues gently. "Do you remember what you told us you want?" he asks her.

She shakes her head.

I swallow. Mia is an irresistible combination of good-girl on the outside, and hot kinky vixen when her inhibitions are down. Following procedure, I copy the recording on a flash drive and give it to her. "If you want to listen to it later," I say in explanation.

Ben takes a deep breath to steady himself. "It sounds like you want to spice up your sex life," he says. "Perhaps your orgasm problems are tied to that. Have you tried talking to your fiancé?"

Her fiancé. What a douchebag that guy must be. If I had a woman like Mia in my bed, I'd make damn sure I please her.

Ben says *tied*, and I think of Mia stretched out on the couch, her arms above her head, bound together with a tie. Not mine; I never wear one. Ben's tie would work nicely, though.

"I can't. We broke up."

An unexpected surge of triumph runs through my blood. Yes. She's single. *Tell me more about your fantasies,* I want to urge. Ben and I have shared women in the past. We haven't done something like that in a long time, but for this woman, I'll be happy to make an exception.

"We have some other options," Ben says. "If you'd like, we can explore using sexual surrogates to help you climax during sex."

She sits up. "A surrogate? You mean someone will have sex with me while you watch?"

"We're trained professionals," I reply. "I know it sounds awkward, but it isn't as bad as it sounds."

She jumps to her feet, her palms pressed against her cheeks. "I can't," she says, her eyes wild. "What was I thinking? Oh my God, I need to get out of here."

She rushes out of my office. I stare after her retreating back. "Well, that went well," Ben mutters. "Now I get to go and yell at Amy. What a fucking day."

ABOUT TARA CRESCENT

Get a free story from Tara when you sign up to Tara's mailing list.

Tara Crescent writes steamy contemporary romances for readers who like hot, dominant heroes and strong, sassy heroines.

When she's not writing, she can be found curled up on a couch with a good book, often with a cat on her lap.

She lives in Toronto.

Tara also writes sci-fi romance as Lili Zander. Check her books out at http://www.lilizander.com

Find Tara on:
www.taracrescent.com
tara@taracrescent.com

ALSO BY TARA CRESCENT

MFM/WHY CHOOSE ROMANCE

Club M

Menage in Manhattan

The Dirty series

The Cocky series

Dirty X6

∽

CONTEMPORARY ROMANCE

Venice Mafia

The Thief

The Broker

The Fixer

The Fighter

Hard Wood

Hard Wood

Not You Again

The Drake Family Series

Temporary Wife

Fake Fiance

Spicy Holiday Treats

Running Into You

Waiting For You

Standalone Books

MAX: A Friends to Lovers Romance

Made in the USA
Monee, IL
10 April 2025